WHO KILLED PATRICK?

A GUINEA PIG COZY CRIME INVESTIGATION

SYL WATERS

ELEFTHERIA

ISBN: 9781916424531

CONTENTS

PROLOGUE

'Tarah, Tarah... Is that you? Can you hear me?'

I wiped the sleep out of my eyes and tried to mumble a reply that it was me.

'Tarah, you must come now,' the voice urged. 'You must come quickly.' The voice softened and melted into a low, sad sob.

I listened hard as I realised it was Pauline.

'Tarah,' she repeated, 'I don't know what to do... Patrick's dead.'

1

THE END AND THE NEW BEGINNING

'So, did you send that document?'

Burton's eyes bore down into me, his breath hot and sweaty on my face. I nodded in response. I wanted to raise my head higher to meet his eyes, to show him I wasn't afraid, I wasn't a fool, I knew how to attach documents to an email and press the send button. But I daren't. I didn't trust myself. I didn't know what might come out of my mouth.

'And can you prove you did that then?'

I nodded again. Inside I was dying, crying, screaming and being sick. The guy was such a moron. Didn't he know how to save sent emails and retrieve them?

I looked up at him and smiled, smiled through the sickness and the shame and the hatred.

'Yes,' I replied, my voice all light and efficient. 'Yes, I can prove I sent the email with the document attached.'

I switched between screens and dabbed quickly at the keyboard, fingers flying so fast I could hear his eyeballs rotate in their sockets. What a dick, I thought to myself. I jabbed the screen highlighting the dated email, opened the message and pointed to the attached document. I smiled sweetly as I looked up at Burton – didn't want him to think I was being smug – but inside I was twisting his face on a juice squeezer.

'I can open it as well if you want?' I asked in my most pleasant would-you-like-me-to-suck-your-cock-while-doing-the-splits personal assistant voice.

'No, that's fine, thanks. I'll chase them and find out what's going on. As long as I know everything's been done our end, don't want to be caught out...' Burton heaved off to his office at the other end of the building and closed the door. My cheeks stung. I felt so hot and livid with rage. How much longer did I have to put up with this prat? How much longer did I have to go on showing to the minutest detail how I am perfectly capable of doing the job I was employed to do?

I looked about the office and wondered for the millionth time that day, what I was doing here. My gaze took in the gawking faces at their screens, the personal scraps of lives scattered about the desks: the holiday mementos, the reminders of home, the kids' scrawls, the tattered post-it notes, reminders and remainders of a life not being lived. A life existing inside this box. Inside this building. Inside this office. Behind this screen.

I got up and walked to the window on the far side of the office and looked at the lurid purple sofas installed to make staff feel more 'creative'. I picked up one of the gaudy orange cushions – expensively curated to purposely clash with the lurid purple. Why? I think to myself. Why the hell would any office furniture designer think clashing lurid, gaudy colours would inspire overworked, underpaid members of staff? I place the cushion back down in a very slow and measured fashion. I actually want to throw it. I actually want to pick up all of the orange cushions and throw them across the office. I want to slam these pillows into every screen and face and start a crazy pillow fight. And then I want to rip the cushion stuffing out of their ridiculous orange covers and dance about like it's an indoor fluffy snow party. And then when I've had my fun I want to shove it down Burton's throat and watch him die. Watch him choke on the pillow stuffing while I smile.

I carefully sit on the purple sofa. I purposefully put my hands under my thighs ensuring they have no liberty to do any damage with their dexterous cushion-grabbing ways. I try and capture my thoughts and put some sort of logical frame onto them. This isn't Burton's fault. He's just doing his job. What he's asking isn't the most demanding of things. And to be honest it's a simple query. I'm getting myself overly aroused over nothing. It's nothing. It's just one of those days. I readjust my seat and realise, not for the first time, how this sofa is one of the most uncomfortable seats ever designed. The foam is thin and hard and gives no bounce or squashiness to your bum. I take a deep breath trying to ram air into my diaphragm. My colon wheezes in disgust. I can feel my tummy inflate and a fart wanting to escape. I clench my cheeks together. A little pop escapes and I can smell the air around me turning sour. I jump up from the sofa and head to the kitchen – I don't want anybody realising that inhumane smell was me.

Errant instant coffee granules are scattered about the woodblock effect worktop surface. I wipe them away with a damp cloth and empty them into the silver flip bin in the corner. How hard was that really? How hard was it to just try and keep things nice? To keep things clean? I peek out of the kitchen door and ponder on the culprit, my eyes all screwed up and annoyed.

Annoyed. That's it. That's how I spend most of my days and nights feeling. Annoyed about this and annoyed about that. And what have I got to feel so annoyed about? I stand and stare and try to breathe in pithy inspirational quotes. I'm not feeling it. I hurl out a load of abuse under my breath. God, when did things get so bad? How have I stooped so low in my pettiness? I look again at the office, at the activity, at the people, at the way I spend my time, my life. My life.

Really? Is this it?

A sudden movement in my legs surprises me as I find myself gallivanting to my computer. Without thinking, I open up Skyscanner, the flight search engine, and my eyes flick over the possibilities – Malaga, Palma, Malta, Nice, Fuerteventura. I don't know what I'm doing. I want to get away. I want to escape. I want a different life. I don't want to be here, stuck in this office for another year slaving away for a wage that barely covers the cost of minimal living. I don't want this anymore. I want something else. I want a life. I want to feel like I'm alive.

Five minutes later and I've booked a one-way ticket to Fuerteventura. I think I might have lost my mind. My hands are trembling. I don't really know what I'm doing but some force is carrying me along, a voice telling me I should do this. A voice that somehow comes out of me and tells Burton I'm quitting. That I'm leaving this job and going onto pastures new. And for a second I pause as I watch the confusion cross his face, his small beseeching that 'Tarah, you're having a bad day'. I find myself nodding in agreement that yes I'm probably having a bad day, but I can't go on like this. There has to be more to life. And I find myself telling him I can't cope with thinking this is it – that this is all there is to life.

'Do you not wonder if there is anything more than what we do here?' I find myself asking him.

He looks at me, a muddled face.

'Do you not find yourself wondering about a life beyond screens? About a life somewhere else? About a life not trapped in this office?' I can hear myself pleading with him to see the light, like I feel I have found.

And he nods at me with a weary face and says, 'I think the break will do you good.' Like he's placating some sick, crazed woman who's gone off on one due to her menstrual bleed.

'So next week is fine with you for my last day?' I say again, confirming the details of my departure.

He nods, like I'm coming back, like I've just asked for some time off. But I won't be coming back. I'm not going to work in this office again, behind these screens. I'm not going to spend my life tippity-tapping at a keyboard and jumping every time the phone bleeps.

The sky is an iridescent pale blue as we touch down in Fuerteventura. I know it's one of those glib things to say, but the sky is somehow bigger here. It's a blueness that stretches and yawns and seems to engulf all the land around. Not that the land resembles much – it's a pretty barren place. I'd read people said it looked like the moon, but I think the moon would be more white; this is brown. Brown and mountainous and rocky and cratered with dried mud or lava. Arid, the place is arid. I don't see any greenness. There are no fields with cows or trees with leaves, just blue skies and brown lands.

I collect my luggage and make my way across the airfield, the warm wind whipping through my hair, making strands stick in my mouth. The blueness envelopes me. I can feel it seeping into me. The bigness, the vastness, the possibility of a life I have yet to lead. I'm excited and scared. Am I really doing this? Is this really me?

I look about at the other people making their way to the airport building, clutching their belongings, smiling and chattering. There is an air of expectation. A desire to release. A demand for a break from the norm. These people don't want 'everyday', they don't want the life they're leading. They want escape. They want to feel alive. They want to experience. They want to breathe. They want to live. I think they're *my* people. I smile. I need to remember this feeling.

The taxi cruises along with the driver yabbering in my ear. I make pleasant enough conversation but really I would rather sit quietly and take in my new surroundings. My eyes soak up the sea which rims all along the route. Blue, glistening, vast, disappearing into the blueness of the sky. Blue, everything is so blue and bright and natural. There's no filters needed here. Fuerteventura is a speck of rock and sand in the middle of the Atlantic Ocean located 60 miles off the coast of Africa. I've read up on it. Fuerteventura is the oldest Canary Island dating back some 20 million years to a volcanic eruption. Politically part of Spain, but autonomous, the island offers 3000 sunshine hours a year. I sigh as I survey my view. How different is this? How *not* the office is this! I slowly blink again, allowing myself to really take it in. This is life beyond the screen. This is the world not seen through pictures. I feel myself inwardly squeak.

The town of Corralejo to the north of the island and the largest resort, is a thin, long strip of bars, restaurants, shops and hotels encircled by a natural sandy bay. I watch as holidaymakers parade the pavements checking out the wares on offer and vendors smile and wave menus enticingly. A lone singer strums his guitar and sings of love and loss while a gaggle of brightly-coloured black women braid hair in the shade. Children run down the street carrying cheap yellow plastic buckets ready to build sandcastles in the sky. The whole street scene is surreal like some sort of circus crossed with an outside sunny shopping mall.

The taxi turns into a side street and suddenly stops. The white-washed buildings blaze in the afternoon sun.

'OK?' says the taxi driver to me, signalling we have arrived at the random place I've booked online.

'OK' I reply and give him a fistful of euros. I exit the cab. A weathered and beaten wooden sign, hand-painted in tomato-red lettering proclaims 'Jorge's Place'. The building is not the whitest on the street, in fact, it's perhaps the shabbiest, as I finger the crumbling plasterwork and it disintegrates into a powder. Second row back from the sea, the salt and wind have played havoc with the exterior. A palm tree whistles and wheezes in the breeze. I reach up and stroke its hard green leaf. So this is me, this is my new life. This is Tarah's New Life.

2

SETTING UP HOME

'Ah! You are Tarah?' A portly, olive-skinned man enthusiastically opens the white painted gate and smiles at me broadly revealing a set of red-wine stained teeth.

'And you are Jorge?' I reply, smiling back. I want to hug him. I want his portly life-tastes-good belly to brush against me, but I hesitate. He's my new landlord. What are the rules when you're abroad?

He grabs me and crushes a kiss either side of my cheek and I laugh. 'Welcome to Fuerteventura – the land of eternal spring... and hope!'

'Oh thank you, thank you.' I gush. 'I'm so pleased to be here and thank you so much for agreeing to rent me your place, Jorge, it looks wonderful.'

'It's not much, you understand?' He nods at me and I nod back, despite not understanding, but I feel like I should.

He stares at me waiting for me to say something and so I say, 'I know, you've already warned me. Wasn't it the worst one you've got, you said?'

He smiles at me, an awkward, honest smile. 'The

problem is the tourists; I make more money when it's for shorter time than longer time. Don't take me badly, but I have family to feed, bills to pay. I try and make you a fair price.'

'It's OK, I understand and your price was fair,' I reply. 'I'm really happy to be here, and so close to downtown. This is amazing!'

Jorge picks up my small suitcase and looks about for any other luggage.

'This is it?' he asks, pointing to my navy blue carry-on.

I nod and motion to the rucksack on my back. 'Well, you said the place was small and so I didn't see the point in bringing much with me – and the sun is always shining so I don't need many clothes!'

'But you're coming here to live?' He checks.

'Yes.'

'Ah!' He spreads his arms wide and his face lights up. 'With less luggage you have less baggage, you don't bring too many stuff from before... it gives you more space to live.'

I like him. I like him already. I could get used to that sort of attitude.

I follow him down the cobbled path through the palms and up a set of stairs on the side of the white building. He pulls out a bunch of keys bigger than my head from his pocket. I look down again at his pocket, was he really stashing all those in there? I ponder what else may be in his magical pockets as he turns the key to the mahogany-stained door. The brass handle lurches and the door opens inwards to reveal a murky studio room, sun-faded curtains pulled closed.

'Not much, not much, but clean and good price,' he declares as he walks into the studio room and spreads his arms in a half-yielding shrug which seems to communicate – I really did tell you it wasn't much.

'It's super, super,' I say and tug at the curtains to get in some light. 'Ooh I can see the sea,' I squeal as I crane my neck sideways.

'Yes, from the side,' Jorge agrees, and walks me to a tall, thin wooden shutter which he wrenches open. I almost wet my pants. There in all its glory is a tiny terrace with enough room for one chair and a teensy table to reside.

'Oh, can I see...?' I say, trying to squeeze past Jorge onto the terrace which is clearly not big enough for his roundedness and me. He moves aside to let me pass. The terrace – although calling it that is a stretch, it's more like a small box sized balcony – fronts the street and to its side the sea.

'You didn't mention about the terrace with the sea view!' I swoon, my eyes lighting up.

'Ah, I sent you photos, no? Maybe I forgot to take this.'

'This really is wonderful, thank you Jorge, better than I thought!'

'Maybe you want more furniture...?' his words peter out as he looks about the almost empty room. 'I put bed and drawers here to help you, they're from my garage, is OK? If not, I take?'

'Totally OK, that's really kind, thank you. It'll be a start and I can get some more things together over the next few days before I really settle in. It'll be a good way for me to learn more about the island.'

'Ah! As you say, we are an island, everything come here, must come here by boat, it's bit hard, but OK.'

'So what would you advise?' I ask, keen to gen up on island life.

'Here on the island is different to where you come from.

We are not like UK, we keep many things and find new life from many old things. We not like to throw things away; we can make good out of bad or old.'

I nod as I toy with the corner of a frayed fabric border. I feel like Jorge is giving me advice not just about consumerism but about life and I don't want to get too deep right now. I'm still too unsteady, too sensitive, too raw. I need something real, something now, something concrete to clutch onto.

'And you're OK with me decorating – with making it more homely here?' I ask.

'Yes, is good. I had a schedule to make a renovation here,' he looks about and shrugs, 'but you want a long rent for low price and I make you this offer, and now I not make the schedule for renovation.'

'Well, I'm really very thankful, so thank you again.' I clasp his hands tightly, I'm so grateful to him for this chance, this chance to make a new life in the sun and I feel overwhelmed with emotion.

Perhaps sensing my over emotional state, Jorge says, 'OK good. Now, I leave and you make your home. If you need me, I live at the house next door.' He points to the closed door and indicates the space behind it while simultaneously edging a key off the bunch and handing it to me.

'That's super, thank you again Jorge. I'm going to be really happy here, I can feel it.'

Jorge smiles at me and lets himself out, the door banging noisily as it gets caught with a blust of wind.

The studio room is grotty. There are no two ways about it. No matter what angle you look at it from: it's grim. The walls, although white (really-gone-off-white), are dirty with smear marks and stained with old blood from squashed mosquitoes. The curtains, faded yellow and tinged brown at the edges, are thin and ragged with a pale cream paisley pattern embossed from a bygone age. The bathroom is a throwback to I don't know when because I don't know when mint green bathrooms were ever a thing. And to have matching but clashing peppermint coloured tiles – I mean really? Whoever comes up with that colour combination?

The kitchen, if you could laughably call it that, comprises two beige coloured wall units, a base cabinet with a missing door and a broken off piece of wood-effect laminate shoved on top. There's space, or rather a hole, for one appliance and a two-ring plug-in hob thing. This is what would be deemed my 'cooking facilities'.

I sit on the bed, the mattress is springy and spongy and something I'd rather not delve too far into for fear of what I may discover. I pick up my rucksack and get a paper and pen. I need to start making a list. I need to write down all the things to make this place more homely. Because this is it. This is my new home. This is the place where I'm going to start my new life.

'You sure you can manage all that?' Penny enquires lightly while pushing another plastic bag into my hand, obviously keen to offload on me.

'Of course,' I reply gallantly, balancing the pots of paint in my hands and the jut of my elbow. 'If needs be, I can pop back if that's OK? I'm only down the road.'

'Sure thing, I can leave it by the door if you want?'

I nod enthusiastically while grappling precariously with the handles and cans. My hands are pinched tight, the straps of the paint pots piercing my tender flesh. Slowly, I inch down the strip, clattering and battering. I couldn't resist the post I'd seen on Facebook and I'd been the first to respond. Someone local, an English ex-pat, was having a clear out with lots of half-empty and unused pots of paint of varying quantity and unknown shelf life.

'I'm not sure if some of it's dried up or whether it's any good…' Penny had said apologetically.

'It's fine, I can add water to it,' I'd replied, as though I was some sort of ninja-warrior-decorator who knew what they were doing, my gung-ho attitude covering for the fact I was trying to do up the place on the cheap.

I dumped the pots outside my door and returned to Penny's villa to collect the rest.

'If you're after some other bits, my friend Kaitlyn is having her place refurbished, I could call her and check if she's getting rid of anything that may be of use?' Penny enquires, as I heft the last pot into my sweaty, hurting hand.

'That would be great!'

'Stay there – let me call her now.'

I wait patiently by the door as she makes the call. Inwardly I feel ashamed. I feel like some sort of pauper who's begging on the streets and checking for crumbs. Who am I that I need to be dragging half-empty, dried-up paint pots around town to try and freshen up my squalid place? I squirm in embarrassment as I look around at the obvious riches on display. Penny doesn't look like the sort of person who needs to be bagging free paint. In fact, Penny doesn't look like the sort of person who would go without *most* things. And if I'm really honest, Penny doesn't look like the sort of person who needs to be making this phone call for me. Even if it is out of pity, she doesn't *need* to be doing it. So I stay and wait and smile, grateful for the chance of other people's castoffs.

'It must be your lucky day!' Penny opens the door again to me, her face aglow. 'They were meant to be collecting a load of stuff from Kaitlyn's villa today, but something or other happened, and it didn't happen – which means you can hotfoot it over there and take your pick!'

'Wow, that's awesome! Thank you so much,' I reply, unsure what stuff I would be collecting or even how I would get it back to mine. 'Where is Kaitlyn's place? I'll go there after I drop this off,' I say, pointing to the collection of paint pots clustered around my feet.

'It's just over there,' Penny says, pointing an elegantly-manicured burgundy nail in the direction of the sea. 'Grandes Avenue Playa, 7. Hers is the one with the blue gate, 'Casa K' it says on the door. Ring the doorbell and she'll let you in.'

I garble a million thank yous and after dumping my latest paint acquisitions head off for Casa K. Casa K is not hard to find. The blue gate is the *least* distinguishing thing you would say about this property. The big fake castle turret with the big (I'm talking six-foot big) blue metal 'Casa K' sign is the giveaway. Understated, I don't think so.

Before I can even press the buzzer, Kaitlyn opens the secure entry garden gate to me.

'You must be Tarah?' She says, extending her smooth tanned hand to mine.

I proffer my sweaty, pallid hand in response and apologise for my appearance and lack of tan. I've only just arrived and I'm trying to get my place together, I explain weedily.

She brushes off my excuses with a flippant shrug.

'Darling, who cares? If you're here to stay, you have all the time in the world!'

God, I must be going soft. For the second time in as many days I want to hug somebody. What is it with these people and their big philosophical attitudes to life?

'To be honest, I'm not really sure what's here,' says Kaitlyn, casting her eyes over the mountain of stuff heaped in the corner of the perfectly terracotta-patioed terrace, 'but take whatever you want.'

'That's very kind of you,' I say, before I realise she's gone to the words of: 'I'll fix us a drink.'

Fifteen minutes later and having amassed a pile of Kaitlyn's discarded belongings, I'm being educated on the ways of the island.

'Things don't happen like you'd expect,' she says with a hint of a slur, making me think she likes a drink at any time of the day and night – the more often the better. 'But, at the same time, things also happen that you don't expect. Do you get me?'

I nod, eager to please, even though I don't get her or her explanation of things not turning out or perhaps turning out like you'd expect. I chuckle internally, I guess that was to be expected.

'The thing about life here is that it's slow, so slow,' she reaches her jaw downwards so that it's almost touching her chest. 'It's not what you're used to in the UK and that's OK. Things happen here at their own pace. There's no point rushing it or trying to fight against it, it is what it is – and that's the beauty of it. Accept that and you'll be fine.'

I smile and I mean it, I know she's right. I've only been here just over a day, but already I can sense it. I can feel a slowness but an openness on the island, something different to anything I've ever experienced before.

I find myself opening up. 'It's funny, here I feel so different.' I swirl my drink in its glass and try and articulate my thoughts. 'Back in the UK I would never be going round random strangers' houses and picking up stuff. But here, here it's like it's a normal thing. It's like there's different rules for life, like I mean, I don't know if this sounds crazy, but I want to say how it feels normal to be here with you and taking these things. Here, I feel like I can ask and receive, like I can *actually* ask for what I want and be in with a chance of getting it.' I pause, I don't know if I make any sense and wonder why I'm baring my heart to a complete stranger.

'Exactly,' she sloshes and wags her manicured nail at me. 'That's my point, people don't often ask for what they want and so they don't receive! Take you, for example, you asked for some free stuff to do up your place and make it nice. You were focussed on what you were trying to achieve. You knew what you were after and the universe responded... and here you are.' She spreads her arms wide as though I have arrived.

I smile at Kaitlyn. Sozzled as she may be, she makes sense and I like her. I gulp down the warm fizzy cava and say my thank yous again ready to head off with her stuff.

'No, don't be silly,' she tugs at my t-shirt. 'You won't be able to carry all that, let me get Don to help you.'

Before I can reply, she's on the phone and a man has appeared in the front garden.

'Don has a car; it will be much easier,' Kaitlyn says, as she points over to the pile of things I'm taking.

Don smiles warmly at me and starts picking up the items to be loaded. Within minutes the pile has gone and I'm left standing around awkwardly.

'It's OK, get in the car with Don, he's safe, he'll give you a lift and help you carry the stuff in. I'll stay here and wait for him to return.' She rolls her tongue around her top teeth giving me a meaningful look. I glance again at Don, he's at least fifteen years her junior, she's definitely a cougar on the prowl.

The drive to Jorge's place is quick and less than five minutes later we're unloading.

'If you're looking for things for the home, you could also try the market at Campanario,' Don says as he grapples with an overstuffed bin bag of textiles. 'And also the Chinese shops have loads of cheap things. They're not the best quality, but they stock literally *everything* you could ever think of or need!'

'That sounds brilliant,' I reply.

'And if you need any help with things about the house, I'm pretty *handy*,' he says, with what I could only make out was a cheeky wink, unless I was mistaken.

I wave him off and stand amidst the piles of things collected in the last few hours. This is insane – I've only been on the island a short while and already I've met so many friendly people who've helped me so much!

Picking up the little radio Kaitlyn no longer wanted, I plug it in and fill the room with pop music. Time to get on, I say to myself and pull on the scruffiest clothes I own. Three hours and four glasses of wine later and the main studio room is now awash with a pale cream tone. Outside the sun has set and the night is black. I stand on the terrace and look up at the sky which offers up the blackest background to the sparkliest of stars. I take in a deep lungful of the cool night breeze. Tonight I'll sleep well.

The morning sun burns my eyelids. I stretch across and look at my phone: 7:31am. Phew, that's the best night's sleep I've had in ages. My eyes blanch as the sun streams further, its rays reaching into my room and lighting my day. Wow, what an awakening, this never used to happen back in London. I quickly rise and put on the stainless steel kettle, another cast off from Kaitlyn, and shower while it boils. Today I'll head to the market and the Chinese shops to get the last few bits so I can properly finish and get the place in order. I want to have a few days to be able to explore, but the pressure's on to find a job. I may've paid Jorge the first month's rent, but how I'm going to find next month's is anybody's guess.

Having drunk my tea on my side sea view terrace (who can believe!) I head off to the Campanario centre. The market, if you can really call it that, is a straggling affair. In the middle of the shopping centre a few stalls are lined up with various crafts and tourist tat – none of which is really for me. Feeling a bit disheartened I make my way back into the main town, but en route see a large array of tarpaulin sheets. My flip-flopped feet speed up to discover a flea market in a car park. Browsing the stalls, I pick up various pictures and knick-knacks to adorn my freshly painted studio. I don't really have any more arms to carry much else, but I can't resist a look in the Chinese shop (yes, they really do sell everything!) and any other shop that looks like it sells homewares. Stuffed to the gills, yet again, I fall into my studio which is now starting to look rather cramped with all my bits and buys.

After a simple lunch of fresh bread, Majorero goat's cheese and Iberian ham, I roll my sleeves up and set to work.

Fortunately, the cream paint has good coverage and I don't need a second coat. It also looks like the cheat I did to touch up the white ceilings has done the job. But I can no longer resist the aquamarine cabinet paint I've found in amongst my bits. Eyeing up the beige kitchen cupboards I load my brush and begin: I'm going full-on sea theme. Having decided I'm a pretty dab hand, I tackle the bathroom tiles next with a white tile paint, toning down the mint on mint action and giving a fresh whiter, brighter look for my ablutions. I stand back and admire my handiwork – the basics are there, now for some tarting with the textiles and other accoutrements. Just as I'm finishing hanging the last turquoise curtain, which matches perfectly with the underside cream voile (to give the window dressing volume and texture), there's a knock on the door.

'Hello, how is your new home? Is OK?' Jorge's stout frame fills the newly-painted doorway.

'Come in, come and take a look for yourself!' I'm so excited to already have a visitor and can't wait to show off my work.

Jorge tiptoes in, careful of the newly-painted walls. He looks about silently. I stand anxiously. Is he about to explode with what I've done? He did say it was OK for me to decorate and make my own mark – but have I gone too far? Slowly, he looks about and turns to me, his face wide with surprise.

'You did this...? All this? In two days? You?'

'Do you like it? I thought the place looked a lot brighter now?'

'Like it? My eyes cannot believe it! It's like new place... in two days? You spend much money?'

'Not really, less than 50 euros maybe, most of the stuff is second hand or things people were going to throw away.'

He whistles a whoosh of air through his lips and claps his hands. 'Is like a new place, so good, so very, very good, you have skill!'

'Don't you go putting up my rent now!' I laugh awkwardly, but fearfully in case I'd shot myself in the foot with my improvements.

'No, no. Your works are very good, you're a very good worker. What work you do here?'

'I, I, I'm, well, I'm...' I hesitate big time. I don't want to admit I have no employment and no idea how I'm going to make the next month's rent. These things will work themselves out. That's what I figured, hoped, told myself.

'You have job? No? Now you do, you help me at the apartments at Jorge's Place, for the guests and their holidays. You speak English, guests speak English. You make bookings, make some adverts, do some cleaning here and there, give people keys, is OK?'

'Is OK,' I smile and extend my hand to shake on the job offer. I have absolutely no experience or idea what's involved, but it's OK. Everything will be OK.

3

IN AT THE DEEP END

The Facebook notification jolts my joy. Eve, an old school-friend who I haven't spoken to in years (apart from on Facebook), is getting married. She's invited me to go. I know that should be a source of happiness, and it is for her, but for me, it's a reminder of how old I'm getting when most of my friends are getting married, having kids and settling down.

I've still yet to meet anyone. I've had a few dates over the years, but at thirty-five years old, my longest relationship has been about four months and even that was a stretch – I didn't actually see the guy for the last month, but I don't like to think about that. To be honest, I don't really like to think much about the relationships I *haven't* had, because what's the point? I can't magic a man out of nowhere and while everyone raves about Tinder, I just can't get on board with this swiping left and right. I don't want to be swiped. I just want to be loved.

Finding love, even looking for it, is really bloody hard though. I don't understand how people have managed to find the people they do – I mean, I don't know what's wrong with me and why I haven't met anyone yet, but I just haven't. I don't think I'm overly ugly (on a good day) and I don't think I'm overly fat (when I've not feasted out) and I don't think I'm not overly unfunny (I do like to laugh). I mean, I guess by all accounts I'm pretty average. Perhaps that's the problem? Perhaps it's because I'm too average - I'm Miss Mediocre. The thought springs tears to my eyes. I don't want to be an average Annie; I want to be somebody's special someone.

I look at the invite again. It would be churlish to decline it when the wedding's not for another nine months. I mean, a lot can happen in nine months – that's over 6500 hours away! I ponder over pencilling the date in my calendar (as requested in her save the date instructions), and then pause – it's such a long way away – who knows what may happen between now and then.

The insistent rapping on the door tells me Jorge's arrived for my first day of training. I haven't yet had the balls to tell him I'm absolutely clueless about what it is he wants me to do, but I figure I'll go along with it and copy what he says to do. Anyhow, I've been on holiday before and I've been a guest before, so how hard can it be on the other side of the desk?

Four hours later and my head's spinning. We've been sat in Jorge's office while he's been showing me all the lettings pages, how to manage the calendars, reply to reviews, answer emails, make payments to contractors, file bills and so on. There's so much more to running a holiday lettings business than what I'd realised. Nowadays it's not so easy to just list and let like the 'old days' as Jorge tells me, because so many people are fixated on reviews – and one bad review can destroy a business in minutes.

'Before, in the old day, I got more joy from this business,' Jorge says, wistfully looking over the sea view facing complex of nine apartments he built from scratch twenty-five years ago. 'But now, today, everybody wants everything now, nobody waits, no patience, never. And no mistakes, no, never can there be a mistake because the people they get crazy. They demand perfection, everything must never have a problem. But it's a problem, problems happen, no? Life is not perfect and I cannot give this. Bad days happen, problems happen, but this internet,' he points accusingly at the computer screen, 'these reviews, the mistakes – they stay there and are like a nightmare that doesn't stop. You do something good, but you cannot undo the bad, the problems... it's hard, the business has got very hard.'

'But isn't it easier to find more tourists now with the internet?' I ask, wanting to put some positivity into the conversation.

'Ah yes! The guests now they come from all over, all over the world. For this, the internet is good. People like you, people who never heard of the island, they see the internet and us and they come here, they stay at Jorge's Place and is good for this. This is a good thing, a good new thing, I can tell people, many people for what is like here, that never happened before.'

'And so there are opportunities... it's just things have changed a bit. I bet you've managed to put your prices up now?'

Jorge nods a little, conceding to my point. 'Maybe I getting, how you say... 'long in the tooth'. Now, I have a family I want to see. The children they grow so fast and many years I run after the tourists. Many years and things I run to do what they want, to make their holidays, their lives to be without problems, to be perfect.'

'When people come on holiday I think they want to dream their life is perfect,' I reply, thinking back to my own times of being away. 'I don't think it's a bad thing, people want to have a break. They want to think life could be easier, better – they want to forget about their work problems, relationship problems – *any* sort of problems. They want to forget them all and enjoy their holiday.'

Jorge snaps the notebook he was holding shut. 'You are right. You are the right person to do this job. You understand the tourists; you know how the guests think. They don't want problems – you are the problem solver. With you, no problems!'

I puff myself up. 'Problem Solver', I like the sound of that job title. 'Oh, Jorge,' I start awkwardly, 'we haven't spoken about what pay I will be getting?'

'How much you want?' he asks.

'Well,' I stutter, unsure what to say, I hadn't been thinking I was the one to choose my own salary. 'How about we say I get free rent with bills included and then 1000 euros per month?' I've plucked the number out of my head with no idea what pay the role would normally attract, but I reckon if I get that much after housing and bills I'll be set for a good life on the island. Life is cheaper here and 1000 is a good round number that I can make go a long way.

Jorge pauses while he mulls over my offer. 'Fine, is OK price for you to solve problems.'

I reach out to shake Jorge's hand. 'It's a deal,' I smile. He smiles back, finishes the hand shake and hands me the notebook he's been consulting and holding for most of the morning.

'What's this?' I ask, taking the tattered notebook.

'Ah, is my notebook. In here you have numbers for people you need.' He opens the black leather-look cover to reveal handwritten scrawls on the lined paper inside and points to various entries. 'This is number of Diego, he fixes water, is plumber... and here Pedro, electrician, for lights and electricity.' He turns the pages and drags his finger down various illegible lines. 'Here is German builder, his name Hans, is very efficient, can do little jobs and big jobs, very German.' He presses the notebook into my hands. 'This book very important, you call people here with problems and tell Jorge told you.' He takes the notebook back from me momentarily and flicks through some pages murmuring as he reads. 'Here, there, key codes for properties. There is master key, here are passwords, many things... my life, how you run things.' He passes me the notebook back again and smiles proudly. 'This book, it has everything to do with Jorge's Place, now you boss, you problem person.' He stands up to leave.

'And where are you going?' I ask.

'Me? I go home now. You the new boss. Me, I go with my family, maybe I go surfing? You, you run Jorge's Place. You are lettings manager.' He turns to leave. 'Ah, before I forget.' He fishes an old mobile phone out of his pocket, 'you also take this, is phone for business, people call you now.'

'The lettings manager? But I've only just started a few hours ago!' I can feel the panic descending into my tone as my hands sweatily grasp the mobile and notebook.

'Ah, you a fast learner, you use computer quicker, you see when guests come and go. With notebook you have people for problems, is OK. I only next door if you need help, or maybe at beach if I not at home.' He turns to me with a massive cheesy grin that wipes years off his face and waves at me as he exits the building. I sit and stare after him. Did he just skip across the courtyard?

4

ATTACK OF THE COCKROACHES

'You, you there, are you the person in charge?' I look around to the finger pointing at me, the finger that belongs to a very rotund, flushed red face with a wigwam of dyed blonde hair piled on top and secured with a pink and white ruffle. The woman gasps and waddles towards me.

'It is you, isn't it?' She says, more urgent than accusing. 'You're the one in charge of George's apartments?'

'Yes, I'm the lettings manager. How can I help you?' I pause to fish for her name.

'Karen, me name's Karen. I'm staying over there in the top apartment. I've got such a bleeding problem; I've had to run out as I can't cope anymore.'

'What's the matter?'

'It's them cockroach things. Them bugs. They're everywhere! I can't cope. It started wiv one in the bathroom, but then I opened the wardrobe and there was another one bleeding looking at me. So's I go to get a broom and – blow me down – there was another one by the flipping broom. I says to meself this is crazy, but then it got worse.' She peers at me her eyes stalk-like. 'I turns me head and there's only a bleeding flying one, flapping its wings like and coming across the room for me! Well, I screamed, a bloody good girl's scream and that was me done. I upped and left, got outta there sharpish. But I done half made a mess coz now I left me bag and everything in there. I ran, I did, didn't even look back, pick up me bag or what. Because I didn't know what to do – I was scared in case they got stuck in me hair!'

Karen ruffled her dyed blond pyramid which looked suitably matched as an ideal cockroach hiding place.

'It's given me shivers that has, I dunno how I'm gonna go back in there. I'm here on my own y'know. Since me and the husband split, it's hard now as he always used to take care of these things. He always did say I was a worrier and me fretting would be the death of me, but you should've seen 'em – those bugs they were flipping everywhere and even flying – I mean! I thought me heart would give in, that's why I'm out here now looking for you, coz you can fix this can't you? You can make them go away? Spray 'em with some special stuff or summit?' Her blue eyes were bright and watery in her shiny red face and they stared right at me.

'Of course, I can call someone...' I trailed off wondering where Jorge had put the details for a cockroach removal man, I didn't remember seeing a specific entry in the notebook.

The last few days had been a blur of busyness and business as I'd got used to the running of the holiday apartments. Managing properties was unlike any other job I'd done before – on the one hand you had quite a lot of freedom, but on the other you were on call 24/7. Managing the peaks and troughs and the spikiness of the hours was going to be something I had to get used to. In the last 72 hours, I'd managed to locate the spare key for a holidaymaker who'd locked themselves out, called the plumber to unblock a sink, changed an electric water heater so the guests could have hot water, checked-in four new apartments, checked out three, taken seven bookings – including one a whole year in advance – started a Facebook group for the apartments, updated the Airbnb profile, replied to hundreds of emails and spoken to at least a dozen people on the phone and now... a cockroach infestation.

'Let me just go to the office to check the best person to call,' I say authoritatively.

'It's not because I'm unclean y'know, it's not my fault they're there.' Karen says, her tone pleading.

'Of course it's not, they're just a part of island life,' I reply, 'as unpleasant as they are.'

I walk purposefully toward the office, Karen in tow, hoping there's a magic number in Jorge's book. I know absolutely nothing about cockroaches and despite my outward cool exterior, am panicking inside. How did the cockroaches get in? Aren't they usually found in dirty restaurants? Can they really fly? How did they get into a top floor apartment? With Karen in such close proximity I don't feel able to search these questions on my smartphone and so I make chit chat while we walk. I look across at Jorge's house, the lights are on, which means he's home with his family. I could go and knock, but I don't want to disturb him on his first week off. He's put me in charge and so I have to take charge.

The all-knowing notebook sits in the top drawer of the desk next to my computer. Given the importance of its contents I've been fastidious and scanned the entire contents and saved a digital file should anything ever happen. I flick open the notebook and start scanning through while Karen stands in the doorway sniffing.

'Bit musty in 'ere,' she says, her nose poised high in the air like some sort of bloodhound on a scent. 'D'ya still get damp out here when it's so warm all the time?'

'I, er, I...' I don't know the answer to her question and I want to try and focus on finding the right person to call to get rid of the cockroaches, but Karen is in a talkative mood.

'My Ken, that's me ex, he used to always have a nose for damp. He could smell it a mile off y'know. He could go into anyone's home, like anyone, and like anywhere he hadn't been before, and he'd be able to tell them if they had damp.'

'That's a useful skill,' I reply, my eyes scanning the note-book contents.

'Yeah, it was. He used to always have his mates asking him to pop round and check out any funny smells they had in their house. He knew a smell or two did my Ken.'

'I'm sure.' I try and respond in a friendly manner half-listening and nodding as Karen regurgitates different tales of Ken and damp houses, and people and funny stories, and laughs to herself about Ken and his nose, while I frantically search for who to call. There are no entries entitled 'cock-roach' or anything to do with 'pest removal' and so I opt to call Hans, the German builder for advice. If anything, Jorge said he was efficient and handy and so maybe he was the best solution in this current situation. I motion to Karen I'm about to make a call and like a sweet, obedient child she nods and sits on the wall outside in the courtyard and watches me intently.

Hans answers the phone with a loud Germanic grunt and I quickly introduce myself and my relationship to Jorge and the nature of the problem in hand. I'm aware my nervous disposition means I am talking far too fast for the situation and when Hans asks me again to tell him what the problem is

I try and stifle my nerves and tell him plain and simple cockroaches are the problem.

'Cock-a-racha?' He repeats in a loud guttural voice that only a German could have.

'Si,' I reply thinking I should get into the swing of trying to insert Spanish into my everyday conversation.

'Hurrr, cock-a-racha is always a very big problem on this island!' He says, I'm sure with a dispassionate shrug of his shoulders – although I can't see him.

'Si,' I reply again. 'But cock-a-racha is a very big problem in Jorge's apartments. The guest not want cock-a-racha for company.' I cringe inwardly at my grammar; what sort of sentence construction was that?

Hans laughs royally down the phone. 'No, no guest want cock-a-racha for company!' He laughs again, more throatily this time, which turns into a coughing fit borne of smoking too many high-tar cigarettes. 'I be with you in diez minutos.'

He's gone before I can say thank you.

Outside I confirm to Karen a cockroach specialist is on his way, even though I have no idea if Hans is a specialist or exactly what he is going to do. We wait outside the entry to her apartment making small talk. This time she's moved off the subject of Ken's remarkable nose and onto the topic of her sister Glenda, who was meant to be here on holiday with Karen in her apartment, but who at the last minute decided not to come on account of being too scared to ask for the time off from work. 'I mean,' Karen's saying, 'I don't understand why she couldn't ask them, you are entitled *by law* to have holidays, but Glenda's got it in her head if she don't take no holidays then when they look for who to fire in the next round of redundancies, they won't look at her. Of course, I told her that weren't the case, but would she listen...' Unsure if Glenda had told Karen the truth, I found myself tuning out to her incessant conversational minutiae and looking about hastily for Hans.

Just a few minutes later and Hans is on the horizon. Well, I assume it to be Hans as his t-shirt proclaims 'Hans Handyman' and he's carrying a large toolbox and heading our way.

'You must be Jorge's new assistant?' he says, proffering me a well-worn, scabbed and calloused hand. This was the hand of a man who did stuff with them.

I nod and open the door to the cockroach apartment. Suddenly realising my schoolboy error and that in fact my job was to try and make people's lives perfect (even when they're not), I say to Karen. 'Listen, you're on holiday. Why don't you go and get a glass of wine and enjoy the sun while Hans and I sort this for you?'

Karen looks from me to Hans uncertainly. Was she to trust the pair of us to get rid of her new found friends? 'Well, that'd be nice. Can you just grab me bag, it's in there on the side, I think on the arm of the sofa?'

I tread carefully into the apartment unsure where the cockroach critters are hiding. I spy Karen's shiny, bright red patent handbag on the arm of the sofa as directed and quickly return to the front door.

'You'll call me when it's sorted and safe to go back?' she asks, her features taking on a surprisingly cute vulnerability.

'Yes, I'll call you,' I say, stroking her arm in what I hope to be an affectionate but authoritative manner. She nods and toddles off raring to find a bar and an ear to chew.

Hans picks up his heavy toolbox and with his metal toe-tipped clunky boots clomps into the apartment. Within seconds it's clear to see there's a major cockroach problem.

'Echt!' booms Hans and stumbles back as a flying cockroach aims for his head. I quiver and duck as I sidle by the doorway not keen to enter. Hastily Hans grabs a can of spray from his toolbox and starts spraying the apartment. Within seconds the acrid fog has clogged my throat and I'm coughing and wheezing. Hans motions for me to go outside into the hallway, while he pulls a red neckerchief from his box, covers his mouth and continues to spray like some sort of power ranger on heat.

A few minutes and two bottles of pungent spray later, Hans opens the door and beckons me to enter.

'There,' he points, waggling his finger at the kitchen sink. I try and open my eyes against the haze to see what he's pointing to.

'It's this,' he repeats again, and I look harder at the kitchen sink trying to understand what he's telling me. 'The trap, the overflow is the problem.'

'Can you fix?' I ask, still unsure what the problem is but keen to solve it.

He gives me the thumbs up and ties the neckerchief around his mouth while he sets to work. I stand alongside in a semi-supervisory role pretending I know what he's doing and should be doing. He points out various bits of the kitchen sink to me including the pipe underneath and the hole in the side and shows me how the cockroaches got in. I nod and smile, appeasing and imploring him to act faster so I don't have to die in the fug that has now settled in the apartment.

With quick rapid movements he takes off the pipe from under the sink and replaces it with a long explanation as to why this would now work. I didn't understand what he was saying, but I reckoned what he was saying sounded about right. He then points to the sealant gun and starts to fill the hole in the kitchen sink to be 'extra sure.' I nod, even though with my basic plumbing knowledge I think to have an overflow hole on the kitchen sink is a good idea if we don't want guests to flood the apartment. I hold myself back before saying anything and then just as he's about to start squirting, I choose my moment to say something.

'Shouldn't we keep the overflow? I mean, if somebody forgets the tap, they'll flood the apartment...'

'It's OK,' he assures me, before sealing the overflow hole completely. 'No cock-a-racha can come in now!' I grimace at my lack of understanding if I'm storing up future problems. He wipes his hands on his dirty blue-brown jeans and stalks about the apartment with the sealant gun and starts squirting every little crevice and crack where he thinks a cockroach may enter.

'Is done!' He proudly proclaims after half an hour of sealing every possible thing that could've been sealed in the apartment.

'No cock-a-racha return?' I ask.

'Nein, never,' he says with an air of certainty I desperately want to believe. 'But, you must get air to the apartment, because this smell, this spray is not good for the health.' Hans starts to burble a little as small pods of saliva appear at the corners of his mouth.

'Yes, let me open all the windows and doors,' I declare, tugging at the balcony patio doors before Hans passes out on me.

A waft of warm breeze starts to filtrate the noxious fumes.

'You call the lady and tell her she's safe to come back in one hour when this spray finishes,' he says, as he packs up his tools. 'But, next time, you tell her either eat the food or throw it away, do not put food in the wardrobe. Is not good.' I glance down at his hands where he's holding a black plastic bag. I peer inside and spy the remnants of what looks to be a lemon meringue pie and pizza topped off with a legs-splayed-poison-induced-stiff-shocked-dark-brown-cockroach-orgy.

I shake my head as I remember how innocent Karen had looked when she claimed she didn't know how or why they'd been in her apartment. Guests, I remind myself, are guests (but that doesn't mean they don't tell porky-pies or forget things!)

5

A NEW RECRUIT

I'm not sure how or where the days slip by, but effortlessly, one sunrise leads to another sunset and another day closes.

Seriously. Life is bliss.

Yes, I'm crazy busy dealing with guests' never-ending jinxes and escapades, but somehow despite it all, the work is always good-humoured and I've been lucky not to have a guest who's popped off at me big time... yet. I know I shouldn't be saying that as I don't want to be bringing bad luck to my world or cursing my life, but I think I've got this lettings management business down to a fine art. Basically you smile: No Matter What. No matter what is happening and the things you need to do: You Smile. Even if you actually want to cry, scream, frenzy about, pull your eyeballs out and wrap them about your head: you continue to Smile, with a capital S. Smiling, I have decided, is the most powerful life-force on the planet – well after food... and water, and sunlight and that. But smiling is up there, up high. And so I do it way more often now, and it feels good. Smiles flood your body with goodness and just make you feel like life is going to be OK. Life is Good.

And today I'm smiling even more than usual because today I have a new companion. I am now the proud new owner of a fluffy, tortoiseshell guinea pig called Lilliana! Lilliana is approximately seven months old and is about 20 centimetres long. She has beautiful, what I would call triangular colouring, that is, she has white, dark brown and ginger stripes of colour shaped in triangular-like slices across her body. She has dark ruby eyes and an expression on her face of constant wonder and surprise, and she is the cutest little bundle of rectangular living fluff that ever could be!

I have to confess, I wasn't planning on getting any pets, given I've only been on the island a few weeks, but Jorge came to me this morning in such a flap because his 15-year old daughter Isabella isn't looking after Lilliana properly. After what appeared to be another fraught night, where Isabella had (yet again) not put Lilliana back in her cage and she had gnawed her way (yet again), through the electrical cables and plunged the Jorge household into a dark shell devoid of electricity, and more importantly Wi-Fi (yet again), the situation had got too much. Isabella's teenage disinterest and distraction of any other responsibility than her own life had caused so many arguments, upset and shouts of I don't know what, Jorge felt unable to cope anymore and brought Lilliana to me.

I was rather taken aback to begin with, but after he told me the gift of his daughter's electricity-addicted guinea pig was done with her blessing and after his confession that Lilliana had a special gift of 'sniffing out trouble' I was sold. Several trips later and Jorge had deposited Lilliana's cage and various bits and bobs as pertains a pet into my studio apartment.

'Jorge, I have to ask you,' I started as Jorge was about to leave on his final trip of dropping off Lilliana's paraphernalia, 'how do you know Liliana has a nose for sniffing out trouble?'

He stopped in his tracks and looked at me directly. 'Always, when somebody in my family is lying, she knows, is a skill, like a special thing.'

'OK,' I said, waiting for further explanation.

He looked at me and shrugged as though I should know what he was saying. 'That is it, she knows when things is not OK.' And with that he closed the door.

I sat looking at Lilliana in her cage. What a strange thing to say about a guinea pig, I thought to myself. Keen to start bonding, I lifted Lilliana out. Her timid body squirmed and wriggled. I picked up a small slice of carrot to tempt her with – Jorge had said it was her favourite – but she pushed the carrot away and started shrieking.

'There, there, I know it's hard to come to a new home,' I said and placed her gently back down. 'I'll give you more time.'

The next morning, bleary-eyed due to the lack of sleep on account of Lilliana's non-stop shrieking, I pondered what to do. She seemed so unhappy. Despite my busy day I felt bad leaving her alone in a strange new apartment and so I took her downstairs with me to the office where she continued to wail. All day she screeched and fussed and refused to eat a thing – not even a cucumber shaving.

'OK, it's cooler now, why don't we go for a walk on the beach, maybe the sea air will calm you,' I said. And yes, I was mindful of the fact I was now talking to my guinea pig like an actual human, but what can you do?

Clutching the handle on her cage, I gently ambled in the sand, making sure her cage wasn't getting too much wind off the sea.

'Does this feel a bit better now?' I asked in my most soothing voice. The high-pitched shriek in reply, told me not.

And so followed another sleepless night with Lilliana's non-stop squealing. Searching the internet in the early hours of the morning, I started to worry. What if there was something wrong with her? What if it wasn't just the change in environment that had caused this upset? I checked her food bowl again – still untouched. And then looked at her water bottle – not a drop had been taken. At this point, I started to panic. Liliana had been with me over 24 hours now and hadn't had anything to eat or drink in that time – not a thing. And all she had done was shriek. I opened the flap of her cage to try and stroke her – to give her some extra love. She jolted quickly away from my grasp and pressed herself flat against the bars of the cage and upped the ante on the piercing squeals some more.

'I don't know, I just don't know,' I said to Lilliana as much as I said to myself, 'I think we need to get you some help.'

Looking through Jorge's notebook I found the details listed of a vet on the upper side of town, close to the Parque Natural area.

'Right young lady, we're off to see Pablo the pet vet and hopefully he can get you sorted. I don't know what you're trying to tell me with all this screaming, but I'm hoping Pablo speaks pig.'

It takes about forty minutes to get to Pablo's veterinary practice, but when we arrive the door is locked. I look around to see any sign for when the opening hours are and notice a phone number to call for out of hours. I hunt in my bag for my mobile, only to realise in my rush to get there I've left it in the apartment.

'Yer early, 'ees jes parking,' said a curly-haired brunette stubbing out a cigarette and making me jump. I watch as she unlocks the doors, switches on the lights, puts on a white tabard, erects the vet sign outside, answers the phone and talks to me all in one go.

I pause, gently resting my bum cheeks on the sloping window sill, not daring to enter the pristine, polished whiteness of the clinic uninvited.

'Ah! Buenos Dias!' A sing-song voice chirrups from a striding, smiling man who I take to be Pablo the pet vet. 'Who do we have here?'

I part my hands ready to extend my palm, but the bespectacled man is not looking at me, his attention is focused on the perpetually surprised face of Lilliana. Effortlessly he picks up the cage and peers in.

'Oooo coochi cooo, who are yoooooo?' He says in a I'm-talking-to-a-little-baby-in-a-very-silly-but-very-cute-voice-which-makes-women's-hearts-melt-and-them-feel-slightly-moist-between-their-legs.

With a small toss of his head in awareness of my presence – insignificant though it was next to Lilliana – he carries the cage through the cool, porcelain waiting room, through a dark blue door and into an examination room where he places the cage on the table.

'She's been...' I start, until he shushes me with a look and his index finger to his lips.

'WHEEEEEEEEEEET, WHEEEEEEEEEEET, WHEEEEEEEEEEEEEEEET, WHEEEEEEEEEET, WHEEEEEEEEEEEEEEEEEET!!!!' shrieks Lilliana.

'Oh dear, oh dear, what do we have here?' Carefully, he places both hands in the cage and lifts out the squealing bundle of fur, checking in her eyes and lavishly stroking and fondling her all over. Slowly, he starts to concentrate his efforts on her underside where the fur is a silky patch of white.

'How long has he been like this?'

'Well, I've only owned her just over a day, and she's been squeaking and not eating ever since I got her. I thought maybe she didn't like the home move, but then when I checked online, I got worried and so I brought her here because I didn't know what else to do...'

'You have only one guinea pig?' He says in an accusatory tone.

'Well, I, I've only just been given her. She was a pet of my landlord's daughter, but she's been gifted to me because, well...' and I trail off, afraid my answer is insufficient.

'Guinea pigs are very sociable creatures. They prefer to be with other pigs, unless you give them a huge amount of attention and are with them all the time.'

'Oh, I, I didn't know, but, I...' I want to say something, but I'm not sure what.

Pablo looks at me sternly. 'The issue is many people get pets and they cannot take care of them. It is not fair because the animals come to harm and they get upset. Like him,' he says pointing to Lilliana, her feet splayed wide and her underside on display. 'He is not happy now because I can feel he has bladder stones.'

'Bladder stones?' I say.

'Yes, it's very common in pigs, he needs to have a diet suitable for him, and plenty of water. Cucumber is a very nice treat for the pigs and is high in water content as well,' says Pablo as he continues to massage the underside of Lilliana's belly.

'Sorry, you said *he*...is *he* a he? I was thinking *she* was a she?' I ask.

Pablo stops and looks at me. 'No, he is a he, you see here,' and he points to the intimate pink flesh just below where he'd been massaging. 'If he was a she, she would have a vulva which is the shape of the letter Y. You see here, he has not, he has a little penis and a small circle here which is his testicles.'

I feel myself inadvertently blush. How can I be embarrassed talking about guinea pig genitalia?

'It's very common for people to misdiagnose the sex of a guinea pig, especially if they were a pet from early on. Many people don't know what they're looking for.'

'I see, and now, what are you doing now...?' I ask tentatively, not wishing to pry, but wondering why he is still massaging the nether regions of my newly-discovered he-pig.

'I'm feeling if I can try and move the stones around, and if they are small enough, he will be able to pee them out. If not, then he will need surgery to remove, which is very traumatic for him and so it is best avoided, unless the stones are very large. If they are large they will block the bladder and the condition will become life-threatening.'

'Life-threatening?' I squeal. Even though I've only had Lilliana a couple of days, I already feel like s/he is a part of my life and I'm racked with guilt I didn't act sooner or know s/he was in so much pain.

Pablo presses a button and the curly-haired, overly-efficient receptionist appears. He babbles a batch of high-speed Spanish words to which she disappears and returns with a water dropper. Gently he places the dropper close to Lilliana's mouth. At first Lilliana pushes the dropper away, but Pablo strokes his furry cheeks slowly and gently, soothing him, and within minutes he starts suckling on the water teat like a new-born.

'I will try and encourage him to drink as much water as possible to flush these stones out. With the massage and this water, I hope this will be effective. But you need to make sure he continues to drink plenty of water and also eat lots of high water vegetables.'

'Yes, of course.' I say, immediately planning to stop at the shops on the way home to stock up. 'Can I just ask?' I pause, unsure if I should ask, but his expectant nod and waiting gaze means I have to carry on. 'You said guinea pigs are very sociable and like company... The thing is... I live in a very small studio flat and so getting more pigs is difficult. But, if it's about company, do you think I could take her, I mean him, to work with me?'

'Of course, why not? If you have a job where you can take your pig for company, then he would love that. Guinea pigs are very intelligent creatures. You can train them, they will listen and they understand so much. In time, if you treat him right, he will understand your voice and will recognise you as his owner. Pigs have very highly-developed senses of hearing and smell and even though his eyes are on the side of his head, he can see very well and can distinguish the difference between primary colours.'

'I see,' I reply, taking in all this new pig knowledge.

'But, you must understand, pigs are prey animals.' Pablo again flashes me his stern look. 'In the wild they are mostly preyed upon; they are not predators or fighters. If they sense trouble, or something trying to hunt them, they will run and hide, not try and fight. This can make them very timid to begin with, but once they get used to you and your handling, they can be very loving creatures.'

'So I'm OK to take him out and cuddle him?' I ask.

'Yes, you should do this. He's a very affectionate pig – look at him now curled up in my hand, he's so happy! Give him some time to get used to you, be gentle with him – he's still only very small – and you'll be fine.'

I watch my he-pig nestled in Pablo's hand and feel a well of emotion and love stirring, I feel like a new parent. I need to re-christen you, I think to myself, as I watch Lilliana playfully nibble on Pablo's finger. You need a name that's more fitting, more apt, more manly. And in a flash, the name comes to me: Mr Bob. Yes, I'm going to call you Mr Bob.

6

IS SOMETHING MISSING?

Mr Bob has taken to his new surroundings like the proverbial pig to muck. Pablo thought I was being a bit OTT when I asked to buy a special carrier to carry Mr Bob around with me, but as I reminded him, he was the one who said guinea pigs liked company and so I was just following through with his instructions.

So now Mr Bob goes everywhere with me – and I mean everywhere! I've had a basket fitted to the front of my bike and the special carrier I've got (which looks like an over-sized handbag) means Mr Bob doesn't have to spend any time at home alone, because I've learned, pigs can even die of loneliness, which depressed the hell out of me.

Me and Mr Bob have developed a nice relationship and we have our daily routines. While I eat my breakfast on the terrace, he chows down on a leaf of lettuce and squeaks away running around the tiles and trying to clamber up onto my bed. Sometimes he makes it, and when he does, I reward him with a juicy bit of cucumber. Not that I want to encourage such behaviours, but I love the sense of fun he has and so I want him to feel he can do anything he pleases.

Jorge, I think, is now a bit jealous of my relationship with Mr Bob and has taken to coming to the office more regularly than he used to and he always has a treat for him – in exchange for a Mr Bob special cuddle. In Jorge's case, this involves Mr Bob crawling up his t-shirt (always liking to go inside) and then snaking his way around until he gets to the nape of Jorge's neck and then sitting there purring for minutes on end while Jorge has to jut his head forward for fear of Mr Bob falling. It's a really funny scene with such an unnatural pose to hold – and really, a very weird cuddle to have – but the pair of them both seem to love it!

Mr Bob's also been a hit with the guests. They love that I have a guinea pig who goes everywhere, like a dog! I've had to be careful with some of the children, though, as their hands can be quite hard on Mr Bob's delicate body and so I have to teach them how to very gently caress him and make him beg for food. It's a trick everyone adores, with Mr Bob standing precariously on his tiny back legs to get a chomp of tasty lettuce, but he loves the challenge! I have to say, he's got quite the following already on the island and has become something of a minor celebrity. Now when I go out, everybody always asks me: 'How is Mr Bob today?' And they peer in my handbag as though it's full of gold, which, of course, it is because it's Mr Bob's home and I wouldn't be anywhere without him!

I think my early experience with Mr Bob has really bonded us and got us more in tune with each other. That day when Pablo the vet told me his bladder stones could be life-threatening absolutely knocked the stuffing out of me. From then on, I've made sure I always listen to Mr Bob and what he's telling me to make sure I never miss a thing again. Now, I don't know if you've ever had a guinea pig, but I can tell you, they are the most vocal of creatures. Mr Bob is always calling, cooing, wheeking, purring, chirping, chutting and chatting to me and I love it. We have the most inane conversations about anything and everything, and I obviously realise at many times it may seem like I've lost the plot. However, it really does feel like he fits a hole in my life and I need him there.

I'm happy here and love what I'm doing, but I do get lonely. I know to many of the guests I'm this loud, bubbly, go-getting girl who's living the dream life in the sun ('the escapee' they call me) but at times I do wonder if I'm doing the right thing. Admittedly, those times usually happen after I've been on Facebook or Instagram and I've seen the various images of the lives my friends are leading, but I can't help wondering sometimes if I'm missing out. Not like missing out in a work sense, because on that front I feel really fulfilled, even if it's not the best career move of my life, but I do get a sense I am missing something.

I don't know if it's because I haven't met somebody which is causing me grief, and making me wonder what's wrong with me, or if it's the fact I haven't thought about children yet and I'm getting closer to 40 than 30. Or maybe it's because I haven't got my foot on the property ladder and everybody seems to say that's what I should be doing at my age, but I just get a sense I'm missing something.

But I don't know what.

Don't get me wrong, I'm not mulling about in any sort of depressive state or moping around licking the floor. But I feel I have a hole, some sort of missing something I can't put my finger on, or find a word to describe, and this *missing* is what I'm missing. Although I don't know what it is.

Maybe it's a sense of dissatisfaction? That's what my mum said when I tried to explain how I was feeling. I don't know how she knew as I'd told her life was good and so I don't know why she started prying and asking lots of questions, but she accused me of sounding 'flat'.

'Flat?' I'd retorted. 'How can I sound flat? I'm sat here on my balcony drinking sangria and watching the sea, what can be flat about that?'

'I don't know,' she said, 'but there's something. You don't sound your usual self.'

Her comment had put me in a bad mood. I didn't want my mother's observations over the telephone from thousands of miles away. I didn't want her noticing I wasn't feeling quite as sparky as I usually was. I don't know why, but for some reason, I felt embarrassed. I didn't want to admit it, but yes, despite it all, despite my seemingly trouble-free, sun-sea-beach and wonderful life I'm living, something felt *less* than wonderful.

The thing is, I didn't want to admit it. Not to her, not to anyone, and not to myself. And so I told her there was a bad signal and I couldn't hear her very well and I put the phone down. And then I opened a bottle of local honey rum, poured myself a large measure, and turned up the radio really loud to drown out any such thoughts that didn't fit with my sunny environment. Because sad thoughts don't belong in sunshine days.

The next day, after the conversation with my mum, I realised I felt somehow torn. I was sat at the computer doing the things I needed to do for the day and looking out onto the sea when I realised it's not the place that's the problem – it's the person. You can take the person out of the place, but you can't take the person out of the person. I had problems when I left the UK. By coming to Fuerteventura I still had those same problems, admittedly different problems, but the big ones, the ones I didn't want to talk about or deal with – they were still there. They would always be there. They were inside me.

I opened up my Facebook feed to see a rush of notifications congratulating Charlie on getting a new job somewhere high-flying in the capital and the announcement of Kieran and Saskia having a new baby. Scanning through the images and updates I saw boundless stuff about people's holidays, days out, food, anniversaries, kitchen extensions, room makeovers, new haircuts, jobs, relationships, on and on, the incidentals and incidents of life in a never-ending river of needless information. But somehow I couldn't stop myself, on and on I clicked and stalked, my eyes scanning and retrieving, receiving random bits of information about these random people who I didn't really know anymore – not outside of Facebook.

My real friends, the ones who I really talked with, they were the ones who'd quit Facebook years ago in search of the real. They were the ones who'd now reverted to old school texts or WhatsApp messaging me and talking to me as an individual, a real person, for the benefit of me – not for the rest of society. 'Dark social' is the term the media use for this type of communication, apparently so-called because people can't see what you're talking about! More like, people can't spy on you and judge you for what you do and don't do in life.

'Mr Bob I feel sad,' I said out loud.

Mr Bob stopped chewing his lettuce leaf and looked up

at me, his face full of concern (I'm sure that's what he was doing and it wasn't that he'd got lettuce stuck in his teeth and was taking a break to internally floss).

'I think we should go for a walk; I need to clear my head.'

Mr Bob jumped into his carrier. He knew the word 'walk' meant it was 'going-out-time' and he was ready. The exercise for him involved very little – he was going to be carried by me. But what he did love was the fuss and treats from the locals and guests who coo-coo-ed him and fluffed his fur.

Out on the promenade, the wind felt hotter and blowier than usual. I looked across to Lanzarote, the neighbouring island I could see from the harbour of Corralejo. It was shrouded in a thick fog. 'Looks like there's a Calima,' I say to Mr Bob, 'we better make sure you don't get too much sand in your eyes, I'm going to put the cover over.'

'Yoohoo! Tarah! Mr Bob!' A high-pitched voice lilts on the wind.

'Oh hello Miriam, how are you?' I say, walking towards the source of the warble sat over on the frontline café.

'Looks like it's a good old sandstorm out there doesn't it,' she says, indicating the foggy outline of the island.

'Yes, it does feel like the temperature's increased as well. You do have enough sun cream on don't you?'

'My dear, at my time of life, it's hardly worth thinking about wrinkles – my wrinkles have got wrinkles!' She tinkles a little laugh at her own joke.

Miriam is a guest at Jorge's Place. She's been staying for the last two weeks and is halfway into her month long stay. At 82 years old, she's one of the oldest guests we have and she still insists on having the top floor flat ('for the views, my dear'), despite the fact her knees have almost given up on her and getting around is a real effort. Miriam is of the generation when women were meant to look 'like women' and doesn't go anywhere without a full face of make-up, her nails beautifully polished ('always red, my dear'), and a coiffed-up head of hair that's never heard of gravity.

'Come, take a seat and take the air with me,' she says, pushing out the chair next to her a little. 'And how's Mr Bob today? I see you've covered him up – is that because of the sand?'

'Yes, I don't want him to get any in his eyes, I know I'm probably being silly and he's more than capable of getting a bit of dust out of his eyes, but I don't want to expose him too much in case, well, in case...' I leave the sentence hanging.

'In case of what dear?'

'Well, in case he gets an eye infection or something, I don't want him to get ill.'

'No, I can appreciate that. Where do guinea pigs come from originally?'

'South America.'

'Ooh that is a long way, South America.' Miriam's eyes crinkle profusely as she smiles. 'I've never been there, but I'd love to go – it always sounds so *exotic* doesn't it! All that lovely dancing and music they do there – it's perhaps a bit, shall we say, *sexy*, for my old bones, but still, even if the body can't, my mind is willing!'

I giggle at Miriam as she winks playfully at me.

'Why do you seem so worried, my dear? You seem preoccupied today, is something bothering you? Are you having trouble with the tourists?'

'No, no, everything is fine, no trouble, no. All is good,' I reply and force a smile.

We sit in companionable silence and watch the waves crash onto the rocks in the harbour.

'I don't mean to pry, my dear, but if everything is so good and there are no troubles, then why do you look so sad?'

I can't help it, the forced smile has not reached my brain and a lone tear strays from my eye and falls down my cheek. 'I'm sorry,' I splutter, 'I don't know what's come over me.'

'There, there.' Miriam reaches out and pats my hand with her deliciously soft fingers. She reaches into her handbag and passes me a fresh tissue.

'Why don't I order us a drink and you can tell Miriam all about it.'

'But there's nothing to tell...' I implore as more tears squeeze involuntarily from my eyes.

'Of course there isn't, my dear. That's why you're sat here now in the middle of the morning crying. Now listen to me, I'm going to get us a nice white wine spritzer and we're going to have a girls' talk.'

7

TURN THAT FROWN UPSIDE DOWN!

Miriam is sat eyeballing me like some sort of specimen in the zoo. I am, obviously, sat awkwardly under her microscope and feeling very conspicuous.

'If you think you're going to tell me something I haven't heard before; you can forget it. I'm 82 years old and I've been around. I've seen so many things – too many things – and I've experienced much more in my life than most people would've, my dear.' She peers at me over the top of her glass. 'You know I think I must be three times your age and you know what that means?' I shake my head to show I don't know what that means. 'It means,' she says, with an air of puffed up pride, 'I have three lifetimes on you. I know a lot about life – three times more than you! So my dear, we are here, we have wine, we have sun, we have a sea view and now we must have the conversation about why you are so unhappy.' Miriam paused, sipped her spritzer and eyed me patiently.

'I don't know,' I began. 'I don't know why I'm so unhappy, but I just feel I don't know – unhappy – but I'm not, I'm also really happy with my life here and enjoying what I'm doing.' I avoid her gaze and stare out to sea.

'But? There's always a but...'

'But, something's missing.' I dab my eyes which I can feel are welling up. 'I don't know what it is, but I have this feeling I've left something behind. It's like I've forgotten something, like when you go on holiday and you have the sense you forgot to lock the door, or you've forgotten your passport, or something. Something important like you should've done and you haven't.'

'So you feel like you've forgotten to do something which is important?'

'I guess so,' I sigh, unsure if anything I'm saying makes sense.

'Do you want children?'

I'm a little surprised by her question, but at the same time have got used to so many people asking me, that I'm really not, not anymore. 'Honestly, I don't know,' I reply, 'I haven't met anybody and so that rules that out for starters.'

'There are many ways to have children, my dear. A man is only needed at the start, and even then, it's only the semen, not really a man as such.'

I twist the tissue in my hands, it feels strange and wrong to be having this conversation with a guest, but at the same time Miriam's wisdom and kind words make me feel so right. 'Sometimes I get really lonely and I wonder what's wrong with me and why I haven't met anyone in my life. All of my friends have got engaged, or married, or are in long-term relationships and have children and they're all OK, and then you have me here – me and Mr Bob. And as much as I love Mr Bob he's not really a replacement for a husband.'

'I believe he's probably a better husband than many, my

dear,' and she reaches down to stroke Mr Bob's nose which is poking through the carrier. 'Now, let me ask you a different question: What makes you think all of your friends are happy in their relationships?'

'What do you mean?'

'As I say, how many of your friends are in relationships that make them happy, fulfil their wishes, make their hearts jump for joy when the love of their life comes back early from work, for example?'

I struggle to see where Miriam is going with this line of questioning and the screwed-up look on my face is a giveaway.

She puts me out of my misery and says. 'I wonder, Tarah, if perhaps you've confused having a relationship with being happy. There are so many relationships in this world that continue purely out of convenience, or of fear, or of obligation, of a need rather than a want. Being in a relationship because you *feel* you have to be in a relationship is the saddest thing of all. You don't need to be in love to have a relationship – yes, to have a successful relationship you do, but there aren't so many of those around. So I ask you again, how many of your friends are happy in their relationships?'

I sit for a long time and ponder the question. Montages of my friends, their husbands, boyfriends, girlfriends, wives and children prick at my mind. I take a long gulp of spritzer and realise I know the answer, I reply, 'Maybe they're not as happy as I think.'

'That's my point, my dear. You think the rest of the world is happy because they're smiling? You smiled at me earlier, but I knew you were lying, I could see it in your eyes. Don't go looking over other people's fences and making up their lives for them, most of the time you'll be wrong with your assumptions. Life is hard for many, it's not the bowl of fizzy sweets we were promised when we were young.'

'So what are you saying?' I turn and gaze at Miriam, I want to understand how she understands, want to see how she sees, know what she knows: I want to be more Miriam.

'I'm saying to be truly happy, you first need to look inside yourself and ask: What do I need? What is it that will make Tarah happy? What is it Tarah wants? If you decide you really want a relationship and you cannot be happy until that happens then you will only find unhappiness.'

'Why?' The word pops out before my brain engages and I know I sound ridiculous.

'Because you're looking for something that first needs to exist *inside you*. How can you love another when you don't love yourself?' Miriam cocks her head and looks at me curiously, before extending her fingers and counting off. 'First, you must become accepting of yourself. Second, you must love yourself for all your flaws and faults and understand everybody else has their faults too – you are not unique. Third, you must live the life you want to lead, regardless of others.'

I involuntarily smirk, sending a shiver of spritzer up my nose. 'You make it sound so simple!'

'It is, my dear. It is when you know the secret.'

I wipe my nose with the shreds of tissue I have left and say, 'So you're saying I just have to accept myself, warts and all, love myself and do what I want and life will be all right?'

'Yes, my dear.'

'But...but...,' I tangle my words.

Miriam fixes me with her bright green eyes, there's a glint of amber running through the centre and she reminds me of a cat. 'This time, there is no but. Why make life unnecessarily hard by trying to be something you are not, by trying to be a person who you cannot be? Why spend any time whatsoever thinking about things you cannot change? Isn't it better to spend the time doing what you *can* do in life rather than dwelling on the things you can't do? If you can't afford to go to the opera, there's no point staying at home and crying about your lack of money. Either go out and earn more money so you *can* afford to go, or else accept you don't have the money and buy a CD and listen to it at home. The choice is as easy as that, my dear.'

I sit and sip my spritzer, musing on Miriam's wise words.

She motions to the waiter for more drinks and says, 'My advice: Regret what you do, not what you don't do. You'll be surprised how little you ever *really* regret the things you did do, my dear. Most people spend their time wasting their life thinking about the things they *didn't* do, and you're not one of those people – that's why you're here now living the life you are. It's time for you to get on with yourself and turn that frown upside down. No more wasting time thinking about what ifs and maybes, you're here now living, live it!'

I clap my hands together and feel a glee and a joy I haven't felt for so, so long. I stand up and hug Miriam tightly, I want to breathe in her marvelousness. I feel so inspired, so spirited, so... alive and ready to make my life right. 'Thank you Miriam, thank you so much,' I say, my arms not wanting to let go. 'I'm going to do all of these things and make a plan – a better plan! I'm going to enjoy this next spritzer and you see,' I say turning to her and pointing at my mouth, 'I've turned that frown upside down!'

'You look busy?' Jorge popped his head round the office door where I was busy tapping away at the computer.

'Yes, I've come up with an idea for the guests!'

'An idea? What sort of idea?'

'We're going to have a games night! Every Thursday evening starting at 7 o'clock – it'll be a night of games, fun and laughter.' I could feel my eyes shining with excitement and I wanted Jorge to share my passion. 'I really think it's a great idea to involve the guests and help them bond more, plus I reckon it'll give us a competitive edge over our competition. I mean, how many other private apartments also provide entertainment? I'm thinking we can hold the event on the communal balcony overlooking the sea. We'll make it free and fun and everybody can bring their own drinks.'

Jorge replied with a slow nod as he took in my idea. 'Interesting, is OK, but who will organise this? Is much work.'

'I'm happy to do it', I reply. 'I think it'll be great to socialise with the guests and, in a way, it'll be an informal way of getting feedback on their thoughts of the accommodation. So really it also serves a purpose for us to make sure we're getting things right. Plus, it's something more for people to write about in their reviews and may even give us a boost. Also, it's a shame we don't do more to use that beautiful terrace and this way it'll encourage people more – show them what's right here at Jorge's Place.'

'Hmmm, I like your thinking. You need anything from me?

'Well,' I paused, there was so much I wanted, but I needed to be careful not to be too demanding, 'if possible, and if we wanted to encourage people to use the terrace more, it would be great if we got some better furniture. The stuff we've got now is a bit old and ropey, I mean, it's not really very inviting to sit on and relax.' I watch Jorge's reaction, but his face is blank, so I carry on. 'It doesn't have to be anything fancy, but if we got some new chairs and a better table – maybe even some sun loungers. I think we could make more of that space than we currently do – and again, it's all extra things the guests can review us for, you know, by providing more.'

Jorge nods and shakes his head and I can see him calculating the costs and weighing up the benefits. 'The terrace is a good place, but I see the guests do not use. Maybe you are right, maybe the furniture are a problem and the people they not feel OK. It is pity as the view to Lobos island is beautiful from there. In the evening when the sun sets it is the best place in the whole of Corralejo.' He chews his lips before saying. 'The sun is very strong there, we will need also the umbrellas.'

I sense he's bought into my idea and before he loses steam I jump in. 'It will be great, we can really make something of the terrace with its sea views and sunny position. We can make it a highlight of Jorge's Place. I'm going to get some games organised and I'll let everyone know about the first games night, I'm going to start this Thursday – there's no time to waste!'

'Another idea,' says Jorge thoughtfully, then stops, scratches his chin, takes out his notepad, jots down some things, thinks again, looks back at his notes and hesitates to a full on stop.

'Another idea?' I nudge.

He looks at me and then back at his notebook. 'Free pizza. The guests they can have free pizza with this games night. I will ask my friend Alejandro who has an Italian restaurant to bring us food. It will be a good thing to do, people will enjoy this and maybe they will say something good in the reviews.'

'That would be amazing, Jorge!' I really want to hug him, but know it's highly inappropriate and unprofessional and so instead I settle for giving him the biggest grin I can fit on my face. 'Having a games night with free pizza really is something to shout out about, they'll really go for that! Now, I'm going to check online and see what games I can track down in time for Thursday.'

Jorge flashes me a cheeky smile and a wink 'Ah! Come with me, I can help with this thing. We go to my garage, I have many stuff from guests, they leave many things.'

Jorge's garage was an Aladdin's cave of veritable treasures, everywhere I looked he had bits of things piled up.

'What are you doing with this mannequin?' I asked, spotting a full size female pink nudie.

'Ah, a tenant they left it and so I put it here, maybe one day it is useful?'

'For what?' I asked, wondering what use a single mannequin could possibly have unless you're running a one-dress pop up shop.

Jorge shrugged and stared at the mannequin. 'My wife, she tell me many times to throw things away, she tell me this garage is mess, I should clear this rubbish. Maybe she is right, she is always right, she is wife, but I like it. I have many things here.' He cast his eyes about the stuff piled on the shelves with a guilty pleasure reserved only for those who know they're in denial. 'I have many things, too many, but maybe one day I will need, you understand?' He looked at me meaningfully and I nodded. I could see the attraction of a garage full of stuff I might need, one day, but at the same time I could see his wife's point and that Jorge might be bordering on the hoarding end of the spectrum. Still, you never know what might come in handy and if you have the space, I couldn't really see the harm.

'Jorge,' I called, tiptoeing so I could see the top shelf, 'I think I can see Scrabble up there – can you reach it for me, please?'

Jorge pulled out a pair of stepladders from behind another set of ladders and placed them against the shelf. He started slowly climbing the steps, his gaze searching, seeking, taking in all of the stuff on offer in his stacked garage. Once he reached the top rung, he leant over and began moving an inane amount of boxes which prompted a deluge of dust and rubble to fall to the floor. I stood watching, unsure if I should hold the ladder or if the unexpected solidity would make him wobble and fall off. I pursed my lips, I did feel a tiny bit guilty for creating so much work for him when he was meant to be taking time off, but still, I was on a mission and he could go back to surfing very soon, while I still got the pleasure of working.

'How many games you want?' he asked.

'Bring them all down and I can see...'

'Take this,' he grunted and passed me a pile of boxes.

I reached out and found myself grasping onto a selection of board games. 'Wow Jorge, this is amazing! I never had you down as such a big gamer! How come you have so many?' My eyes feasted on the possibilities of the boxes in front of me.

'Ah, many people leave many things, and in many years I keep. One day, I tell my wife, this things will be good, will be needed.' He stood smugly overseeing his prized finds.

I started looking through the hoard and listing out all the games – I couldn't believe the collection. Cluedo, Bingo, Yahtzee, Monopoly, Tiddlywinks, Trivial Pursuit, a dozen or so packs of playing cards. 'This is absolutely incredible, I had no idea we could even offer so many games.' I smiled up at him, my hands deep in a box. 'You know our games nights are going to be such a success, the guests are going to love it!'

Jorge buzzed with pride at his finds finally coming into use. They may've been stored for several decades, but now it was their time to shine and he was totally going to stick it to his wife later.

I got my phone out and started taking some photos of the selection. I couldn't wait to share the news of free pizza and games on the terrace. It really was an inspired idea and I knew it was thanks to Miriam. I made a mental note to stop by and tell her in person on the way back. I wanted her to know her earlier chat had done me the world of good and I was on the road to recovery.

8

GAMES NIGHT

'You're such a money grabbing capitalist THIEF!' Mrs Dennis screamed and tossed down the last remainders of her frayed notes.

'It's not my fault you passed up the opportunity of buying Mayfair,' replied Mr Dennis, a heavy hint of smugness in his tone that invited any sane person to whack him around the chops.

'But you didn't *have* to put that red hotel there and charge me the earth, did you? DID YOU?' Mrs Dennis' face grew hot and red as she glowered at her husband. 'You did that on purpose, you did it to SPITE me.'

'What are you talking about? I was using business sense, business acumen. I bought prime real estate and you gotta pay me because you landed on me. I don't know why you're getting yourself so worked up,' said Mr Dennis, disinterested in his wife's drama.

'Well, you did it on purpose knowing I didn't have enough money,' huffed Mrs Dennis, her face taking on a sweaty shine from the outrage.

'How did I know you were gonna throw the dice and land on me? I may know many things – like which are the best places to buy in Monopoly and make full use of their value – but I'm not a mind reader or Uri Geller. I can't MAKE you land on my squares.'

'You, you...' started Mrs Dennis.

'Please, please,' Graham, a chain-smoking, leather-tanned faced, sixty-something interjected, 'this is a game, not grounds for divorce.'

Mr and Mrs Dennis, suitably chided, sat silently staring at the board in the middle of the table.

'Why don't you,' said Graham, indicating to Mr Dennis, 'do an IOU so Mrs Dennis can remain in the game?'

Mrs Dennis' face boiled with anger. 'I don't need no IOUs from HIM! I don't need anything! I don't need no favours or help to win. I could've won this game if he hadn't blocked me from building by buying up all them green houses. It's HIS fault you know; he's always doing this.' Mrs Dennis inched her face closer to her husband's, gave an almighty glare and shoved her chair back. 'I'm going over there to play with NICER people, better people! People who know *how* to play rather than the blood-sucking vulture that you are. Sell your own mother, you would!' Mrs Dennis flounced, a little unsteadily from the two bottles of Cava she'd consumed, and plonked herself down at a table in the corner, where three guests were quietly working out how Professor Plum had been killed with a piece of lead piping in the library. Miriam winked at me as I passed by, she was obviously the murderer.

I watched from afar wondering if I should intervene in the Monopoly war. I didn't want my first ever games night to end in a bitter divorce battle.

'Shall we take a break and all have a game of charades?' I called to the three tables who were busily engrossed in the playing pieces.

'We're good,' came the reply from one.

'You go ahead we'll join in a bit' came another reply.

The last table – the Monopoly table – where Graham and Mr Dennis were battling it out for first place, was silent as the capitalist machinations took hold.

I sat back and mulled anxiously. My idea of a whole group cohesion exercise had been rebuffed.

'How is it? Is our games night good?' I turned round to see Jorge with his wife in tow, leaning over the wall.

'Good, good, we've got a decent turnout – 11 of us, although...' I leaned in and lowered my voice, 'Monopoly has caused some issues with the Dennises.'

Jorge laughed. 'Ah! Monopoly is always problem for people! But here, we have home-made sangria my wife made. Maybe it can be a peace offering?'

I clapped my hands and took the two jugs filled to the brim with dark red liquid and floating bits of apple and orange.

'Pizza will be here soon,' Jorge said and then startled. 'Ah! Here's Alejandro now!'

I looked round to see a handsome guy in his late twenties swaggering his way up the promenade carrying a large black box bag emblazoned 'Best Pizzeria'.

'OK everyone, time for a break. We've got home-made sangria and pizzas!' I called.

A small swell of interest trickled across the groups. Immersed in their play, most were uneasy about the spell being broken. I started to open the cardboard boxes and the aroma of freshly-baked pizza wafted across the terrace, tantalising the taste buds of the most diehard games fanatic.

'Why don't you all make a note of where you are in your games and come and join us for some food and drink?'

Muted grumbles mixed with appreciation of free food and a chance to break out of the heavy competitiveness filled the air.

Mrs Dennis sidled up to me, her glass held ready for a helping of sangria. 'I'm sorry if I got so upset earlier, but you know, he's always doing that to me.'

I nodded. 'I understand.'

'I don't know why I agreed to it,' she said. 'We always argue over Monopoly. But I wanted to play as *I* wanted to win this time, but, but... he doesn't *always* have to win.' Mrs Dennis sniffed, her sense of injustice growing.

'Playing games can sometimes bring out the worst in people,' I replied, and gave her an empathetic smile.

'He'll be crowing about it for days now, especially if he beats Graham.'

'He's a man, you know how men are with these things. They like to show off and be the ones with all the money, it makes them feel big.'

She rolled her eyes. 'I wouldn't mind so much, but I feel it's like a reflection of us, our relationship.'

'How do you mean?' I asked, abruptly aware my comment may've hit a deeper nerve.

She lowered her voice and leaned into me. 'I think since the children have grown up and I've wanted to go back to work, he's got more controlling about things. Like, he's very traditional and he wants to be the main breadwinner, be the provider. He doesn't like the idea of me having my own money or a say in things.'

'Are you sure it's like that?' I asked. 'Have you talked about it? Maybe you're right, maybe it is him wanting to stay in control, but have you thought maybe he worries about something else?'

'Like what?' Mrs Dennis edged her face away from mine ready to be educated.

'Well…' I searched for what I meant, 'maybe he likes things the way they are and he's worried about change. Maybe he's worried *you'll* change in some way.'

Mrs Dennis nodded. 'He did ask me why I was going to get a job when we didn't need the money, and asked if I was happy. I said I was, coz I am happy, but I told him I wanted to do something for me, something else. I don't know what. But now the kids have gone my days can feel very long. There's not so much to do in the house now, not with just the two of us and there's only so much time I can fill with meal planning!'

'It sounds like the pair of you need a proper heart to heart,' I said. 'Being away is probably the best time to have a chat – you're on neutral territory here and you're away from it all. So maybe this is a great time to have this conversation?'

'Although not right now, obviously!' She smirked.

'No, now probably isn't the best time,' I agreed, 'but tomorrow, why not have it tomorrow? Let him have his win, let him feel happy, and then why don't you go out and have a nice meal? You could go to Albert's, that fish restaurant right on the sea, and then while admiring the view you could have a chat about what you both want. Find out what he's afraid of, find out what it is that's bothering him – and you!'

'Yes, that sounds a good idea, thank you Tarah, I'll do that. I'm going to keep schtum now and I'll play nicely and then tomorrow I'll have THE conversation.' Mrs Dennis winked at me and wandered off to a group who were now merrily flipping circles of plastic across a table. 'OOOOO tiddly-winks I haven't played since I was a kid, can I join?' Before anybody could reply, she'd seated herself in a vacant chair and picked up a counter.

I smiled as I watched the proceedings: the laughter, the anxiety, the whoops of delight. Games night, I think it was fair to say, was a huge success. Mr Bob looked at me sleepily from his carrier and then gave me a head-splitting yawn. I chuckled as I struggled to keep my own yawns in. I checked the time and saw it was gone half-past twelve. Jorge had left hours ago, did I really need to stay up and babysit? They were all adults and could fend for themselves. I didn't have to be the entertainer for the entire night did I? Plus, I did have work tomorrow, I wasn't on holiday like they were. Deciding I was going to leave them to it, I said my goodnights and asked them to leave the games next to my office door.

'Games night was the highlight of our holiday!'

'Tarah and Jorge are very welcoming hosts, you feel you are one of the family – and the views from Jorge's place are amazing.'

'We loved our stay at Jorge's Place. They really make your holiday better with their attention to guests' needs and having fun. Games Night was brilliant! We haven't had so much fun for ages!!!'

I sat smiling reading our latest guest reviews. Just a few days on and already games night had become an instant hit. My hunch had been right – providing an evening of entertainment meant we could bond better with the guests. Also, it gave us an informal space to hear of any issues they might be having with the accommodation rather than running off to leave a bad review. Jorge's warning how bad reviews can kill a business were always at the forefront of my mind. Not that the accommodation at Jorge's Place was below standard or anything, but I knew how spiteful some people could be – and also how some people are never happy. Luckily so far, we hadn't had anybody like that, but I knew from talking to others in the holiday business, some people were 'chronic complainers' and wanted nothing less than a free holiday, or your blood.

I opened the booking page to see we'd had a flurry of bookings overnight – and a couple had specifically said they were coming to games night and to 'count them in'. I looked over at the pile of games and made a note in my calendar to go shopping to get some more. Now that games night had become a 'thing', I needed to ensure I always had a fresh stock of games to tantalise people with – can't go letting the side down when people's expectations are set so high!

The doorbell buzzer sounded. I looked at the clock, it was 7.40am. That's strange, I said to myself, we didn't have any guests checking in this early.

9

THE EARLY ARRIVALS

Opening the white gate to Jorge's Place I was greeted by four smiling faces the other side.

'Morning!' The lady dressed in white linen cooed. 'Hope we're not too early to check-in?'

I looked at the gaggle of them. Two women: one in her late thirties, dark brown bobbed hair with red highlights, and a twenty-something tall blonde who looked about as if she had somewhere better to be. The two men, both slightly overweight and dressed in matching checked shirts of clashing colours, were in their mid-to-late-forties and peered in cheekily like two naughty schoolboys let out on day release.

'You must be...' I left my sentence hanging in the air while I tried to remember who they might be from the bookings list.

'We're Patrick and Pauline, and this is Mick and Tamika,' the bob-haired lady said brightly. 'We're a little early...'.

'OK,' I replied, 'I wasn't quite expecting you yet. Can we just pop to the office so I can have a look to see which apartments I've allocated for you?'

Nodding, they picked up their enormous array of luggage and followed me down the cobbled pathway, through the swaying palms and whitewashed buildings to the office.

'Oooh, dunit look lovely, Pat, just like on the photos! We'll be all right here. I know it's the first time we've stayed on this complex, but it's looking good,' I heard the bob-haired lady say.

Entering the office, I scanned the whiteboard on the wall. I'd put this up a few weeks ago as a way to show the bookings and to manage the check-ins and check-outs. It meant everyone could see at a glance who was meant to be where at Jorge's Place rather than always being so reliant on the computer.

'You must be the Buttons and the McIntyres?' I said, turning to them with a smile.

'Yes, that's us love,' replied the man in the red-checked shirt. 'I'm Patrick Button and this is my wife Pauline,' he said gesturing to the woman with the bobbed haircut. 'This here is Mick McIntyre, my business partner, and his girlfriend, Tamika.' Patrick pointed to Mick, dressed in the green-checked shirt and the tall blonde girl, Tamika, who I thought was young enough to be Mick's daughter.

'Well, welcome all to Jorge's Place,' I said. 'I'm Tarah and I'm the complex manager here...' I hesitated while I browsed the details of the white-board. 'The thing is, I'm afraid I had your check-in down as 6 o' clock tonight, that's what I seem to remember your email saying.'

'Oh yes, sorry about that,' started Pauline, 'I got mixed up between am and pm and then I tried to put it into the 24-hour clock and Patrick said to me this morning I got it round the wrong way.'

I pasted a smile on my face. It wasn't my job to educate

guests on the difference between am and pm, but I was now having to deal with the fall-out. 'OK, I see,' I said. 'I can understand, but the only slight problem I have is our usual check-in isn't until 2pm, and I'm ever so sorry, but your apartments still have people in them, and so I can't show you them right now.'

Tamika tutted loudly and stomped out of the office on four-inch heels.

'It's OK, we understand,' Patrick said quickly, aware of the scene Tamika was causing. 'It's our fault for not telling you the correct information. Perhaps we could leave our stuff here though? We could go about and then come back later when the apartments are ready?'

'Of course, you'd be more than welcome,' I replied. 'I'm so sorry I can't do anything more, but we are fully booked, and I'm a bit stuck as I wasn't expecting you for at least another 12 hours.'

'No bother, love. We've come to get away and we don't need to be sat in the apartment. We can easily find things to do here. We know the island well, we've been here enough times!' said Patrick, his face glowing with holiday anticipation.

'Oh yes,' simpered Pauline, twirling her fingers in Patrick's hands. 'We've been coming here for years; we know so many people. In fact, this time the boys are hoping to do a bit of business on the island.'

'That sounds wonderful,' I replied. 'What sort of business is it you do?'

'We're in property development,' said Mick with a puffed up masculine pride. 'We've been in the game for years, well before any of those property programmes you see on TV. We've been doing it since we left school, no flaky chancers with us. We're the real deal and we make money coz we know how to...'

'Now, now Mick, don't go getting ahead of yourself. We've done a few deals, but we're not quite up there yet,' said Patrick, reeling in Mick's peacock strut.

'What you talking 'bout? We've made a mint,' sniped Mick. 'I'm just saying we're not some dreamer type amateurs like so many of what this young lady may've seen on TV. I don't want her confusing us with *them*.'

'OK boys, enough with the willy waggling,' Pauline smiled affectionately. 'Let this young lady get on with her work and you two can go and have a beer and discuss your latest bigwig property deal in the sun.'

'That sounds fun,' I said diplomatically.

'Oh it is,' said Pauline, as she off-loaded items from her shoulder-bag and ferreted around for some sun cream which she handed to Patrick. 'It's all a bit hush-hush at the moment, but this scheme they're planning here, *the water park*, well,' her eyes widened. 'It'd be the biggest deal of their career yet, so you can understand why they're so excited!'

'Wow! A water park?' I repeated. 'That sounds awesome!'

'Yes, but don't tell anyone, not yet...' a crease of worry crossed Pauline's face and she looked about to make sure none of the group could hear what she was saying. 'Sorry, I probably shouldn't have opened my big mouth and said anything, but I'm so excited for them. It would really put them into the big boys' game – plus it would mean I get to have even more holidays here!'

I put my index finger in front of my lips 'Mum's the word.'

I looked at the clock: 5.40pm. How on earth had the day gone so fast? I checked my messages again, I still hadn't had any contact from the Buttons and McIntyres, who'd tried to check in earlier this morning. I wonder what they've got up to, I pondered to myself.

I didn't have to wonder long. The crashing of a flower pot outside heralded their return.

I opened the door to find Mick struggling with a hot pink bougainvillaea and shards of terracotta, his hands full of soil as he tried to stuff the contents back into its pot.

He looked up at me, his face soaked with innocence and incredulity. 'I swear I was nowhere near it; it must've moved...'

'Plant pots don't move, Mick,' reproached Pauline, 'just say you're sorry and give Tarah 50 euros to buy another one'. 'Is that OK?' she said, turning to me, '50 euros would cover the cost of a new plant pot, wouldn't it?'

'Sure,' I replied, surveying the swaying and giggling of the group as Mick tried to open his wallet to retrieve a note.

'Ish de pink one, yeah?' He slurred, pressing the note into my hand, his eyes glazed with alcohol. 'Sorry, yeah...'

'Accidents happen,' I smiled. 'It looks like you've had a good day.'

'Yeah, very productive,' said Mick, his face now a sunburned and alcohol-induced red. 'We had a business meeting and well, it was a bit stressy, but fink we getting there, eh?' He nudged Patrick for a reaction, and he replied with a brief smile.

'The boys had their big *development* meeting,' Pauline interjected. 'They've had a long lunch discussing everything and putting lots of plans in action,' she said glowing with pride.

'And finding any excuse to get drunk, more like,' sneered Tamika, just loud enough for me to hear.

'I went for a massage and manicure as well down at the new place in the harbour,' continued Pauline, ignoring Tamika's comment and flaunting her taupe coloured nails for me to admire. 'What was it you were doing today?' Pauline abruptly turned to Tamika.

Tamika flicked her eyes, bored by Pauline's question.

Mick nudged Tamika, 'Yeah love, what did'ya do after you left us?'

Tamika hoisted her ripped micro jean-shorts fully so the group could appreciate the length of her ridiculously long legs.

'I been sun tanning,' she replied in a thick Essex accent and twirled her body like a stripper without a pole so they could admire her colour. Her scanty cream halter neck blouse rested lightly on her over-sized breasts, its sheer material not thick enough to cover her decision to wear a bright purple bra a size too small. She lifted her obviously fake eyelashes to me and fluttered them like a butterfly trying to escape a net.

Pauline raised her eyebrows and looked at me to share her disapproval of the lithe young girl's antics.

'Anyways,' said Patrick, seemingly unperturbed by the gnawing female politics, 'could we get our keys now as I gotta 'nother meeting shortly and then I wanna get back for your games night. We read on the internet about this – it sounds great!'

'Sure' I said, reaching in the drawer for the keys. 'I'll see you later.'

I waved them off and watched them staggering up the stairs. Mr Bob scurried to the front of his carrier for a better view and cocked his head back. 'They're going to be trouble aren't they?' I said to him.

'WEEEEWEEEEEHEEEE' squealed Mr Bob.

'Oh dear, I'm going to take that as a yes, then!'

10

THE DEATH OF A GUEST

'Tarah, Tarah... Is that you? Can you hear me?'

I wiped the sleep out of my eyes and tried to mumble a reply that it was me.

'Tarah, you must come now,' the voice urged. 'You must come quickly.' The voice softened and melted into a low, sad sob.

I listened hard as I realised it was Pauline.

'Tarah,' she repeated, 'I don't know what to do... Patrick's dead.'

I glanced at the time: it was 5.43 am. The night was still charcoal black and the moon shone out like a nocturnal blazing sun in the dark sky. I could hear Mr Bob stirring behind his star-covered blanket. I rubbed my face again with my palms and looked at my phone. *Did that really happen or was I dreaming?* I checked my phone. No, I wasn't dreaming. A mobile number had just called me.

Shit! Oh My God! Did Pauline say Patrick was dead?

My head exploded with a thousand questions. I dragged a pair of shorts from my bed and struggled into a t-shirt from the floor while trying to dial the emergency services on 112 from my phone. Having requested an ambulance and the police I dialled Jorge and explained the call I'd had.

'Dead, a guest is dead? Where?'

'5a, Patrick Button.'

'You call the police?'

'Yes,' I replied, my teeth chattering as though I were cold.

'I'll be there,' Jorge said and hung up.

My eyes danced about the room – what did I need to take? What did I need to do? I had never dealt with a dead body before and I had no clue what the protocol was.

Mr Bob squealed in his cage.

'Please, shush, I'm trying to think,' I said, rubbing my forehead trying to get my brain kick-started.

Mr Bob continued to squeal.

'Oh Mr Bob, I haven't got time to play now, I've got an emergency to deal with.'

'WHEEEK, WHEEEEK, WHEEEEEK!'

Unable to focus or think straight, I picked up Mr Bob's carrier, a bottle of water and a fistful of tissues. Scurrying down the steps and across the courtyard I hear the faint wail of a siren. *Will those be the emergency services?* Clambering up the terracotta tiled steps to the second floor apartment I knock gently on the door.

No response.

I knock again a little harder, keen for Pauline to hear me, but not so hard I wake the entire building.

No response.

Shit, did I imagine this? Was this just a bad dream?

I check my phone again, no, somebody has just called me, I'm not making this up. I dig in my bag for the keys, deciphering the coded digits on the tag to find the right one.

The lock clicks open and I pause at the threshold calling out for Pauline. A low, loud grumbling fills the echoey hallway and bounces off the porcelain tiles. I hesitate while I try and work out where the noise is coming from. I lift up the carrier and see Mr Bob is vibrating, his body trembling. The deep growl is coming from him. He jerks his head back just as I am reaching in to try and stroke him to quieten him.

'Shhh,' I tell him with more force than I feel, I've never heard him make a noise like that before and I'm freaked. This whole situation is freaking me out.

I continue down the hallway calling for Pauline, reaching out with my spare hand, trying to find the light switch.

'Pauline, Pauline?'

I can hear a muffled cry at the far end of the apartment. I walk gently but quickly, trying to be as quiet as possible. Suddenly, the carrier lurches, I look down and see Mr Bob is frozen still.

'What are you doing?' I whisper in a half-scream at Mr Bob, whose body has now frozen statue-like. I raise his carrier so I can look at him closer.

'Oh please, not now... what are you doing? What are you doing?' I can feel my voice begging, desperate.

'Stop playing around, c'mon move, don't do this to me, what are you doing?' I can feel my eyes filling with tears, the rounded globules of water on the brink of my lids and about to spill over. 'Please... please don't do this to me.'

I shake the carrier. 'C'mon stop playing now and move, don't do this, don't you do this to me!'

The front door bangs open, the handle bouncing off the wall. Jorge strides in with two ambulance crew directly behind him. He stares at me shaking Mr Bob in the carrier.

'The bedroom through here,' he tells the waiting paramedics.

I quickly manoeuvre myself out of their way and the three of them head off to the front of the apartment.

I look into the carrier again; Mr Bob is staring directly at me. He does a frantic blink and runs into his little house.

Pauline is in the lounge. She's sat on the beige sofa, her hands grasping a cup. The curtains are drawn. The standing lamp emits a warm glow on the shiny white surfaces. The paramedics and Jorge are in the bedroom trying to resuscitate Patrick. Pauline and I sit looking at each other, listening to the noises emanating from the bedroom. It's all in Spanish. There's a lot of grunts and shouts and feral sounds. My stomach twists and empties and shoves itself back inside my throat as I realise there's a dead body just beyond the wall.

'Do you understand what they're saying?' Pauline says to me, her eyes red.

'I think they're trying to get him to breathe again...'

Pauline's face erupts into an avalanche of tears. I cross the room to sit next to her, put my arms around her and hug her as closely as I can. I don't know what to say. I don't know what to do. I know nothing about death.

'They're doing their best,' I say as soothingly and gently as I can. I can't tell her everything will be all right, because I'm fairly certain from what I can hear and translate, things are not all right, things are far from all right.

'I don't understand it,' Pauline begins, her lips trembling. 'Last night he was fast asleep and snoring, and then this morning, I woke to have a wee and I saw his body was locked solid, like he was a cut log or something. I went to him and when I touched him, he was cool, not like cold, but his skin, it didn't feel like skin, it felt... I don't know...' she begins to sob, her voice cracking. 'I put my ear to his lips, I wanted to feel his breath, but I couldn't feel it and so I tried to find his pulse, but I couldn't remember where you felt the pulse from. And then, then... I touched his skin, it was so, so, cool, not right. It was waxy, clammy... and... and I tried to dial 999, but then I remembered I'm here and it's not 999, but I couldn't remember the number, or what I was doing or who to call. Then I saw your number from earlier and so I called you...' She looks at me forlornly, her face wet with tears, her shoulders sagging.

I take her hand and put it in mine. 'You did the right thing. I called the ambulance and Jorge is here with them now helping.'

'But what are they doing? Why is he not breathing?'

'I don't know,' I say. 'Was Patrick ill at all, or taking any medication?' I have no clue about these things, but I seem to recall in any medical drama they ask those sort of questions.

'No, no he was fine. He had a bit of a cough, but I've got a cold so I've got a bit of a cough. And yes, he was a bit overweight, but show me a middle-aged man who isn't!'

'And he's not had anything like this before?'

'You mean where he's stopped breathing?'

I froze. What was I saying? What sort of crazy thing had escaped from my mouth? I open my mouth again about to say something and close it. I don't trust myself to not say something stupid that may upset his distraught wife who is looking to me for support, not dumbass questions.

'I'm sorry, I didn't mean it like that,' Pauline says, 'I know you're just trying to help, I just... I just...' The tears flow freely and the scraps of wilted tissue in her hands start to break away in little chunks of shredded fibre.

'I'm sorry,' I say, 'I really am.'

We sit in silence for a few minutes, listening to the jolts and voices from beyond the closed door.

'I'd like to pray.' Pauline places her cup on the coffee table and kneels in front of the sofa, her back to me. She lowers her chest, rests her elbows on the cushions and brings her hands together in front of her face.

'Dear Father, who art in heaven, hallowed be thy name, thy kingdom come, thy will be done, as on earth as it is in heaven. Oh Father, please help me, you must bring Patrick back to life. He is a good man, a very good man and he loves you a lot. I love him a lot. He's very young and has so much more life to lead...' She breaks into a sob, which she stifles to continue. 'He's always been a very good man, and while he hasn't always believed in you, he knew you were there really. And so God, I'm praying to you and asking if you could please find it in your heart to save Patrick. I promise if you do I will make him to go church more and donate more money to charity, and to see his mum more. And I will be good as well. I promise. Please.'

Pauline remains in the prayer position whispering incoherently into her hands. I sit awkwardly on the sofa, aware my presence is too close, too intimate for this, but too scared to move in case I break the spell.

A knock on the lounge door rips the noiselessness of the room. A man dressed in a white shirt and navy blue trousers enters. He is the chief paramedic. His facial expression says everything before he even opens his mouth. I try and listen to the words he's saying above Pauline's wailing.

'I'm sorry, we did all we could, we tried, but he has gone. I'm sorry there is nothing more, we think it was his heart.'

I try and hold Pauline, calm her howling. She wriggles and screams and bangs her fists on the table, the spindly legs of the IKEA construction threaten to give way at any moment.

Jorge enters and heads straight for the cupboard above the fridge freezer. He takes out a bottle of honey rum, pours a large glugging measure into a glass and hands it to Pauline. She flicks his offer away and buries her head in her hands. He goes to her, strokes her upper arm with his palm. Her lips widen again into a hollering cry. Jorge gulps back the rum, stands, returns to the cupboard and pours another. He returns to the space next to Pauline.

'Take this,' he says, stretching out his hand holding the amber liquid.

Pauline takes the glass, sniffs its contents and glugs back the entire lot in one go before coughing violently.

Jorge stands up and returns to the bottle pouring another glass full. He returns and gives it to me to drink.

'For the shock,' he says.

The police arrive not long after the ambulance has left with Patrick's dead body. They understand his wife is distraught and unable to answer any questions, but it is routine. They just have a few.

Jorge stays, sedating Pauline with sips of honey rum and acting as translator between her and the police. No, Patrick had not been ill. No, Patrick had not been taking any medication. Yes, Patrick had been a bit overweight. Yes, Patrick had been drinking. Yes, Patrick was probably a little bit drunk. Yes, it was likely Patrick died of a heart attack. Yes, it was a surprise. Yes, it was their wedding anniversary tomorrow.

I'm so torn, I have shedloads of things to do and more guests to check in soon, but I daren't leave Pauline on her own. Jorge has gone to the hospital, or maybe it was the police station, I don't know, I don't remember. Either way he has gone to one of those institutions to sign the death certificate or do whatever is necessary in these situations in a foreign country when somebody dies. I'm sure it's a paperwork nightmare. There's always loads of paperwork anyway with stuff, even though we're meant to be digital, but in these circumstances, in these countries, when you've got a dead tourist abroad, I think it complicates matters.

Pauline hasn't said anything for the last thirty minutes. We are sat here in an awkward silence buffeted by the noise from the locals going about their business outside. I want to make small talk, but nothing seems appropriate. What topic of conversation do you bring up when somebody has just lost their husband? And so I sit here, waiting. Mr Bob is still hiding in his house. He hasn't come out, but I can hear him scuffling about in the straw bedding. He's being unusually quiet, but I think maybe he can feel the oppressive silence even inside his little house.

Pauline has drunk three-quarters of the bottle of honey rum. Its sticky residue is leaving trace marks on the coffee table. I resist an urge to fetch a cloth and wipe it.

'I feel numb,' Pauline says, her tone flat.

'It's a big shock,' I reply.

'Is this really happening?' She looks at me, her eyes wide, searching. 'Or am I dreaming?'

I want to cry. I cannot bear the sadness of this situation. 'I'm sorry', I say, and place my hands on hers. 'Yes, this is real.'

11

THE MOURNERS ARRIVE

The knock on the door is rapid and insistent. Pauline looks at me vacantly. I stand up to open the door to Pauline and Patrick's holiday apartment. Alejandro rushes in, practically pushing past me to get to Pauline, who is still sat on the sofa.

'I came as soon as I heard.' Alejandro grabs Pauline's hands and holds them close in his. I loiter in the background, unsure what's happening. Why is Alejandro the pizza guy so torn up about Patrick? Did something happen at games night last night that I didn't see? I wind my mind back and try and recollect the night. I remember Alejandro and Pauline and Patrick being friendly, but not overly so, not like this display of emotion that's going on right here.

Pauline holds Alejandro's gaze for an impossibly long time without blinking, then breaks down in choking, chesty sobs. He pulls her close like a father comforting a child, stroking her hair, stroking her shoulder. I watch from afar. They haven't noticed I'm still here. They're caught in their own bubble, their own world of personal emotion.

I stand awkwardly, not wanting to make my presence known. Their gestures, their bonding, it seems too intimate for me to be here, but I don't know how to leave. And so I stand and wait, trying not to stare, trying to focus my gaze out of the window. I hope if I don't look, they won't see me. It's childish I know, but I like to keep the dream alive that sometimes I can become invisible.

A sudden galloping of feet on the stairs outside and banging on the door makes me jump. I dash to the door and find Mick, his face red, his breath heavy and panting. He stares at me in the open doorway.

'So it's true? It really is true?' His face collapses inwards.

I nod and open the door wider to allow him in. Tamika, dressed in a skimpy floral jumpsuit breezes past in a haze of just-showered scents. Mick bounds into the apartment, almost running down the hallway to the lounge. He stops dead when he sees Alejandro comforting Pauline on the sofa. His ruddy face turns darker, puce, veins pop to the surface in his temple and his lips grow thin and whiten as he clenches them together. I can tell he's holding in a tirade of abuse. Tamika, sensing his anger, deftly slips her hand into his.

'What happened?' he says, defiantly, his tone commanding, his body taut with anger.

Pauline disengages from Alejandro's comforting embrace, takes a deep breath and looks directly at Mick.

'I don't know what happened, one minute he was there asleep, the next he was dead.' Her tone is calm, matter-of-fact.

'But how can that be? How can he be alive one minute and dead the next – it doesn't make sense!' Mick bawls, shaking his head.

‘They say it was his heart,’ Pauline replies.

‘What was wrong with his heart?’

‘I don’t know, they said it stopped, it was likely a heart attack.’

Mick’s face crumples and he covers his eyes with his hands as big, racking, gut-wrenching spasms heave through his body. His shoulders shudder and he turns away from the group staring at him, his face hidden behind his hands. Tamika and Pauline move to comfort him but he pushes them away. He walks alone to the patio door, unlocks it and slides the glass across. He stands on the balcony looking out to sea. We sit watching him. Nobody says a word. Nobody exchanges glances. All eyes are on Mick. Slowly, he takes his hands from his face and places both palms face down on the railing. A cool sea air flutters the curtains and in the distance the waves can be heard, pulsating on the shore. A far-off child’s shriek of happiness curdles in the breeze, its joy mutating to misery as it ploughs on through the air and into the room. The atmosphere is stifling and I’m grateful for the small gusts which blow in.

Mick’s silhouette on the balcony throws off looming shadows into the room; one movement by him is emphasised several times over in shades of near-black. His arms stretched like thick string, wrap across the sofa and the wall. His sudden unfurling of his fingers and swinging round to walk back into the room is magnified colossally in shade.

‘I’ve got a meeting, I’ve gotta go...’ he declares to the room and stalks out. Tamika watches him and when the door is closed, trots off behind her shadow who has left the building.

‘I think it’s probably time I left as well,’ I say, quickly grabbing my chance to leave while everybody else is making their exit.

Pauline sniffs and looks at me with red-ringed eyes. She holds out her hands to me. 'Thank you so much for everything you've done Tarah, I appreciate it, I really do.'

'It's nothing, honestly. I'm sorry,' I reply and gently lift her hands from mine and retrieve Mr Bob's carrier from the unit.

I don't have a good feeling. I don't want to be starting rumours or seeding gossip, but as Hamlet would say, 'Something is rotten in the state of Denmark', or in this case, Fuerteventura. I can't decide if it's because I haven't had much sleep or maybe the drama of the past few hours has addled my brain, but something to me doesn't feel right. I switch on the kettle and make a tea, the seventh I've had already this morning. I'm waiting for the kettle to boil when I hear the roar of a car. I peer through the shutters and see a bright red Maserati pulling up outside. I look back at the whiteboard on the wall for some clues to the visitor – there's nothing written up.

Curious as to who may be visiting the complex in such a fancy car, I make my way across the courtyard to the gate in preparation for the doorbell to ring. Except it doesn't ring. I loiter in the courtyard, busying myself with pulling dead flower heads and brown palm leaves. A parakeet squawks from overhead and soars across the blue, cloudless sky. I stand and watch as the bright green bird circles and dives out of sight. Just as I'm about to return to the boiling kettle inside, I sense the presence of a person on the other side of the gate. I cock my ear, listening intently for the shrill of the bell chime. Nothing.

Fuelled by paranoia, I lurch to the gate and swing open the white wooden panel separating us from outside. A man with designer sunglasses dressed casually cool, but expensively tailored, is standing with a mobile to his ear. His skin is burnished with sun; his dark brown hair, freckled with specks of grey matches the morning stubble lightly sprinkled across his square, strong jawline. He turns to look at me as I open the gate.

'Can I help you?' I ask, in my most polite but authoritative voice.

He smooths his hair, gives me a suave smile revealing professionally whitened teeth and says he's looking for Mick. He has a strong local accent and something about his face looks faintly familiar. I tell him Mick has gone out and suggest he call him. He waggles his mobile in front of me and explains he's been trying to call him, but he hasn't managed to connect.

'We were supposed to be meeting here. I was to pick him up,' the man says.

I catch a scent of just-showered fragrance and Tamika struts into view.

'Oh Lucas!' she calls, seeing the man. She rushes and extravagantly air kisses him. 'Let me go and get Mick for you! His mobile ran out of battery and he's been trying to find the charger.' She sashays off aware of our gaze on her long limbs barely contained within her short dress. Lucas and I exchange uncomfortable smiles while we wait for Mick to appear. A few minutes later and Mick lumbers into view, dressed now in a crisply-ironed white shirt and cream chinos.

I smile a greeting at him (even though I only just saw him) and nod to them both as he and Lucas exit the complex and get into the red Maserati. The engine revs into life and fills the street with its overwhelming growl. I wait by the gate until I can no longer hear the car.

Back making my tea I'm struck by the change in Mick. When I saw him earlier he looked devastated by the news of his dead friend and business partner. But now, just half an hour later, he was like a changed man – a man who'd never heard anything bad in his life. Business as usual, appeared to the order of the day. Can people really bounce back so quickly? I flicked on my computer ready to sort through the emails and bookings, but my mind was distracted. I couldn't get the image of Pauline and Alejandro out of my head. They were way closer than any pizza guy and his customer would usually be – but was it really like that? Was something going on or was I seeing things that weren't really there?

I stroked the lip of my cup, deep in thought. *Lucas*. Where had I heard that name before? I opened my search browser and typed in 'Lucas' and 'Fuerteventura'. The screen filled with information and news items. I nodded to myself, that's where I'd seen him before; Lucas was a big shot developer on the island known for his flashy lifestyle. I clicked on the various images: Lucas with his car collection, Lucas with his yachts, his family, on holiday, at parties – his life screenshotted like a movie star.

Just then Jorge pops his head around the office door. 'You OK?' he asks.

'Sure, I've left Pauline upstairs for now, I'll check on her again later,' I reply, purposely leaving out about Alejandro, I don't want to appear bitchy or gossipy.

'The red car was here? Was Lucas in it?'

'Yes, he was collecting Mick.'

'Death keeps no calendar,' he replies sagely. He picks up a stapler from the desk, inspects it and places it back down. 'Lucas is quite famous, he has many cars and money, but the people, they not like him so much now, they don't really do the business with him.'

'How come?'

Jorge moves some other bits about on my desk before replying. 'He is like a hungry shark, a very hungry shark who only fish one way. They say he is successful and has plenty of money, but he is not a trusted man. He upset many people and no more they want to do the business with him. Now, he find more foreign people.'

'How did he upset people? What did he do?' I know I'm fishing and feel bad not sharing the business plan Mick and Patrick had talked about, but this doesn't feel the moment to share.

'Ha, people like Lucas, they have their own rule book; his cars and houses don't grow on a palm tree. No, he trod on people, upset many people to take what he wants. This is his character.' Jorge surveys the office and then makes to leave. 'Today I promise to take my family to the beach, is OK? Or you need me?'

I look at Jorge and feel a bit bewildered. I don't really need him here, but at the same time it would be nice to have him around. It feels a strange day, a day when you need someone, *just because*. I think he senses this as he goes on to tell me how this whole business with Patrick has reminded him why he was taking a step back. That today was the time to spend with his family, to go to the beach, to do all the things he's been meaning to do. Who knows what may happen tomorrow? When he says this, I can't really say much against it, so I nod and smile, and tell him to have a lovely time and an extra sangria for me. But I can't help feeling a bit odd, a bit abandoned, a bit lost.

I try and get back into my work, but my mind is distracted and I struggle to focus. Mr Bob stares at me from his carrier. I scoop him out and cuddle his soft down in my hands. He rests gently on my thigh while I stroke him in long swipes. I don't know why I'm so bothered, but I am. Something isn't right about Patrick's death. Is Pauline really an innocent wife? Is Mick really a good business partner? And how can the pair of them carry on with their lives just a few hours after Patrick's death?

I stand up startling Mr Bob into a squirmathon up my arm. I tickle gently behind his ears and he purrs happily when I take him back on my lap. 'The thing is', I say out loud, 'did Patrick die of natural causes or did he get a helping hand?' Mr Bob freezes, his whole carcass stiff and solid. My breath catches. *I must not panic. I must not panic.* I quickly rub his body trying to get movement into his torso. A few seconds later he relaxes and melts back into form. I caress his fur gently, trying to slow my hurried heartbeat. These seizures have become too frequent now. I need to speak to Pablo the pet vet, but I'm afraid what he may say.

'You'd tell me if you were in pain, wouldn't you?' I say, holding Mr Bob aloft so we can peer eyeball-to-eyeball with each other. He stares at me and then blinks. I'm sure he'd tell me if there was a problem. I cross my fingers and give him a little kiss on his nose. Yes, everything's going to be fine, I tell myself.

The phone rings and makes us both jump. It's Jorge calling to say the coroner has recorded a verdict of natural death for Patrick, he died of a heart attack. I hold Mr Bob close enjoying his furry warmth and reprimand myself for my bad thoughts. Nobody wants bad juju; only bad things can come from bad thoughts. I must think good thoughts to bring good energy and good things into my life.

Think positive.

12

SUSPICIOUS MINDS

Feeling restless and out of sorts I head to The Ship where I know Kris will be doing his karaoke gig. It's not my usual sort of scene, given the place attracts mainly English tourists who want cheap beer and food, but the crowd is laid back and a good laugh. And that vibe can get strangely contagious – especially after a couple of drinks. Plus, entertainment wise you never know who's going to get up on stage. Admittedly, it's usually the drunks larking about, but every-so-often a real songbird hits the stage.

Kris, or as he would prefer to be known, Kris 'Karaoke' King (not that I even think his surname is King), is a late fifties wannabe popstar. Despite his advanced years and gravelly smoked-too-many-fags-for-too-many-years voice, he still thinks he can *make it*. Between the fags and the explosive phlegm-stuffed coughing fits, Kris talks endlessly of his 'almost made it' moments. The time when he was 'almost' a singer for the Rolling Stones; the time when he 'almost' got signed by Polyphone Records, and most famously the time when he 'almost' met Elvis Presley. Kris' stories are legendary. Most people have heard them, or a variance of them, at least six times. It's a fact Kris is well aware of, but pays no heed to, even when his audience starts yawning and informing him he's already told them the same story, five times before.

A casual, happy-go-lucky fellow, Kris is a dreamer who mainly dines out on stories of the past. This makes him easy company. Whatever your mood, Kris has a story, a song, or a something to tell you – so much so you don't have to think about what to say when you're with him. And that's the reason why I enjoy his company. He's not serious or intense or challenging. He doesn't poke you for questions you don't want to answer and he's always entertaining. He's always got a story to tell – even if it is the same one you've heard several times before.

As I was feeling so preoccupied with the death of Patrick, I thought Kris would make good company in my present mood. I didn't want to think bad thoughts any more. Also, I was reminded I needed to catch up with him on the latest about him entering a talent show. He was still obsessed with being 'discovered' so he could finally get his 'long overdue' multi-million-pound record deal.

The Ship is, as the name suggests, themed on a ship. Great wafts of once-white, nicotine-stained sails bloom from the ceiling and are pinned to the wooden panelled interior to make the punters feel they are in the middle of a ship from some bygone era. To aid the nautical ambience further, portholes are placed strategically to give the impression of being 'at sea', along with various hanging fish, a pirate's flag and a host of other expected marine paraphernalia. Tacky and welcoming at the same time, The Ship is a main staple of the Corralejo strip on account of its cheap beers, which at happy hour are just one euro a pint. Of course, Kris and his karaoke machine are also a well-known feature and draw of the place, especially after the aired soap operas have finished at 9 pm and people are in need of light, live entertainment.

Walking in I see Kris sat on his usual tall stool by the bar. He sees me and waves me over. Pulling myself up into the neighbouring seat, mindful of the full-size replica wooden steering wheel jutting out, we exchange greetings of the day.

'It's a bad business over at Jorge's Place,' says Kris, leaning in closely so I can feel his breath on the underside of my ear.

'Yes, it's really sad about Patrick, not something anybody expected.'

'Yes, sad, but bad as well,' he says, looking at me with a there's-more-to-this-than-what-you-think look.

'Have you heard something I haven't?' I ask.

'Depends what you mean on what I've heard...'

'Don't be so coy will you, just spit it out,' I say, a flutter of annoyance entering my tone.

He lowers his voice, leans even closer and huffs into my ear. 'Are you really sure it's natural causes?' He leans away from me and looks directly into my eyes after his question and then leans back in, his voice wheezy from the strain of whispering loudly. 'Patrick was as fit as a horse. There was nothing wrong with him, and yet he comes here for this big ass business deal with his partner Mick and then suddenly, or should I say *conveniently*, dies in the night?' Kris screws up his face in a sneery veneer of doubt. 'I'd say that's a bit weird, don'cha think?'

I pull away from the closeness of his breath and the glare of his eyes.

'The coroner says it was a heart attack. I'm not sure what

you're implying, but even someone who appeared healthy beforehand can die of a sudden heart attack,' I reply neutrally. 'Plus, Patrick was a bit overweight and he'd been drinking heavily all that day, it's never a good combination.'

Kris snorts derisively. 'How many tourists come here, to the island of cheap tax-free booze, and don't take full advantage? If I had a cent for every tourist I've had to send home too drunk to walk I'd be a millionaire. You're not seriously telling me you think it was the drink to blame?'

'I don't know,' I shrug. 'I'm not a doctor or a coroner, I'm telling you what they said. They're the experts, so they should know.'

'Yeah, they should, but I'm not sure they're bothered to ask the right questions,' he says with overdone enigma and a tap on the side of his nose.

'So what questions do you think they *should* be asking?' I say, not wanting to get involved in the topic of conversation, but unable to stop myself from asking more.

He looks at me long and hard like I'm an abstract art piece, takes out a cigarette, lights it, draws heavily and in a cloud of smoke says, 'I think they should look at who benefits from him being dead. I get what you're saying about sudden heart attacks, but I've known him for a while and he was fit, his job kept him fitter than most gyms. Yeah, he may've been a bit overweight, but I don't get it, it doesn't stack. If that were me, I'd be wanting to know who stands to benefit before they close the case and say job done.'

'But, that's the thing,' I say, 'as the case is closed, I'm not sure what *can* be done.'

He shoots out a plume of smoke and rolls his tongue in the remaining fog. 'I've heard they're not flying his body back for another day or so. I would've thought that was time enough for them to at least investigate more, check on those things. Obviously it's a bitch on the paperwork and it gets in the way of siestas, but I'm just saying, you know.'

'Hmmm,' I reply non committedly, 'I'm just not sure your suspicions are suspicious enough for it to be looked at as a *suspicious* death.'

Kris smiles at me, a deliberate self-righteous smile. 'We'll see.' He presses several buttons on the karaoke machine and Elvis Presley's dulcet tones fill the bar. I give him a raised eyebrow in return as the lyrics to 'Suspicious Minds' plunders on.

The crackle of the ancient speaker and the piercing feedback as Kris grabs the microphone and attempts to sing along, draws winces and groans from the audience.

'What happened to your new kit?' yells a greying man with a union jack t-shirt to Kris, who's busy fiddling with an array of buttons resulting in a cacophony of increased squeaks. Kris says nothing, but I can see his face growing redder. He must be under a lot of pressure, I think to myself as I watch his exertions and grapples. The Ship audience can be great, but they're not the most patient of people, especially not when they've got a pint in their hand.

I look back at the equipment Kris is struggling with. The old guy in the audience has a point, this is the stuff Kris used to have a few weeks back, before he upgraded to some fancy new digital stuff. He was all over it and how it would revolutionise his karaoke business. I remember at the time feeling unsure how he intended to revolutionise a business that'd been dying for years, but it felt unkind to say anything. Kinda like saying to a dinosaur: don't you know you're living in the Ice Age?

Deep in thought, I sipped my sparkly cava and watched

the crowd. Carefree, glowing faces sat expectantly waiting for the entertainment to restart. Bronzed and sunburnt knees and shoulders visible through skimpy tops and shorts shone with lotion in the bar lights. A gangland of questions bubbled in my mind. Who did stand to gain from Patrick's death? What was going on with Mick and Lucas and this property deal? What was going on between Pauline and Alejandro? Did Patrick really die of natural causes? Were the police making a mistake closing the case so early? On and on, over and over, my mind frothed and fizzed to over-flowing. I watched Kris as he served customers and cajoled them to sing. Why was he so obsessed with thinking Patrick's death wasn't a straight-forward heart attack? What did he know that I didn't?

Without a proper plan, I found myself striding down the high street to Jorge's house. I wasn't sure yet what I was going to say, but somehow I wanted to strike up a conversation to get a 'read' off him. I wanted to try and understand this situation better without saying anything, daft as it sounds. Pausing at the gate, I decide to collect Mr Bob from my apartment. The Ship is one of the very few places I can't take him on account of the loud music and his sensitive hearing. Opening my door, I'm glad to hear his welcome home squeaks and rustling of paws as he scrabbles to see me. I treat him with a quick tickle and a crisp, cold lettuce leaf from the fridge and set off to Jorge's.

Jorge is a little surprised when he sees me standing on his doorstep with Mr Bob in tow.

'Sorry to bother you, are you busy?' I ask, spying the time has just gone 9 pm.

'No, is fine, come in, is everything OK?'

'Yes, everything's fine, I think I'm feeling a bit weirded out by the events of today.'

Jorge nods. He gestures for me to sit on the shiny, brown leather sofa while he goes to the kitchen and uncorks a bottle of red wine. I can see from the used glass on the table he's already been drinking. He fetches me a wine glass, and without asking, puts it in front of me and pours it to the top. He then does the same with his glass.

'Is not a good thing for us what happened in the apartments,' he starts. 'It's best we say little about it... is for the best.' He clasps his hands together as though our conversation is already concluded.

I pull my eyebrows together and give him a questioning stare.

'I must think of the business, of our name. A guest death is not good for business.' He pauses and looks at me, his eyes a little moist, pleading. 'This business is for my family, not only me. It pays for them, for you. A bad review... it is all bad for business, bad for the pocket.'

'A bad review?' I look at him unsure what he means. 'How could we get a bad review from this?'

'The people they are strange, they do and say strange things.' He takes a long sip of wine and pats his lips.

'But,' I say, 'Patrick died of a heart attack, that's not a strange thing. Obviously, it's not a good thing, but sadly it does happen pretty often to people.'

'Ah, yes.' Jorge shrugs, his face sagging with defeat. 'But he was here on holiday in our apartments... and now, he's dead.'

'And? I'm not following?'

'The people don't like it, the people don't like to go on holiday and then die.'

'No,' I say, nodding my head. 'I s'pose not, but in Patrick's case, it's pretty straightforward isn't it? I mean, they've already closed the case, so what's the big deal?'

Jorge hesitates, he's staring at Mr Bob. I follow his gaze to see what my errant guinea pig is doing.

'Is Mr Bob OK?' Jorge asks, going over to check on the furry face staring out of the carrier.

'As far as I'm aware,' I say, 'although he's been acting a bit weird today.'

'Like how?' Jorge leans in to inspect Mr Bob.

'I dunno. Earlier he was growling – a sound I've never heard him make before. Then he's been jerking his head and now he's got this new thing where he keeps freezing his body, making it like stone. I don't like it,' I say shaking my head. 'I may have to take him to see Pablo.'

Jorge stares eyeball to eyeball with Mr Bob.

'He doesn't look ill,' he declares, like he's an expert on guinea pigs.

'No,' I agree, 'but there's something not right.'

'Maybe he playing a game with you, testing you?'

I laugh out loud at Jorge's ridiculous notion. 'I know guinea pigs are intelligent, but I'm not sure mind games are their thing!'

Jorge picks up his glass of wine again and rubs his chin. 'I told you something before and I don't think you believe me. I told you then, I tell you again now. He smells trouble. Is a gift he has.'

I check Jorge's face for signs of a wind-up, but his expression remains serious.

He carries on. 'I tell you this because I know it for myself. My daughter Isabella, when she lied to me – told me she not have boyfriend when I knew she had – Mr Bob he do the same thing. He freeze, he jerk, he act strange.'

I stare at Jorge unsure what to say.

'I know is strange thing he do, make his body like stone, freeze like ice lolly. I said he must be ill; I will take him to Pablo. But then I watch, I watch him and I see he only does this thing – this stone thing – when he hear the sound of Isabella's boyfriend's name.' Jorge motions me to observe. 'Rafael' he says. Mr Bob, who until that point had been merrily twitching about, pauses statue-like. 'See, see, he do it now!' exclaims Jorge, his face set in righteous satisfaction.

I get up from my seat and stand in front of Mr Bob's carrier. 'So you're telling me he does this every time you mention Rafael's name?'

'There, there!' Jorge points excitedly. 'He do it again. He was moving and now he stop because you said the name!' I glance at Mr Bob and then to Jorge, confused by the revelation.

'Maybe he used to be called Rafael?' I suggest, unsure how to explain the connection.

Jorge shakes his head. 'No, we had him from baby and thought he was a girl, that's why we call her Lilliana.'

I sit back down and take a sip from my wine glass trying to gather my thoughts. 'So, if I understand you right, you're saying Mr Bob reacts to names?'

Jorge nods. 'Something like this, but not all the names, only names he thinks is trouble.'

'You do know how crazy you sound?' I say, checking how much of the wine bottle Jorge has consumed.

He shrugs, unbothered by my accusation. 'I speak the

truth, is like sixth sense. He did this freeze thing when Isabella was lying about the boyfriend. He was the one who gave her away.'

'OK,' I say, 'so why's he doing it now?'

Jorge's face darkens and he twists his mouth uncomfortably. 'Is Patrick.' He shakes his head sadly as Mr Bob freezes into his lifeless pose. 'That is his problem, he smells a trouble.'

13

TROUBLE

Jorge was silent as he selected another bottle of wine from the wooden drinks cabinet in the far corner of the room. He was deep in thought and I could tell he didn't want to talk, but I couldn't leave it.

'When you say *trouble*, do you mean the death of Patrick? Like...maybe it's not as *natural* as what we've been led to believe?' I ask, my voice wavering as I say the words out loud.

Jorge clenches his jaw, biting hard into his molars. 'I not want trouble,' he says, his face gripped with a glumness I'd never seen before. 'But, I not want the people to say anything bad, or the police to say we did a wrong thing.' He traces his fingers over the bottles, lost in wiping the dust from the necks. 'This whole thing, it make me feel sick.' He turns to me, his arms folded, a streak of fear etched in his features. 'How can I sleep at night? My children, my wife are here – next door. You are there, other guests are there. Who else is there?'

I sit back into the sofa cushion and say nothing. I am

stunned by Jorge's admission. From the very start he'd been so practical and seemed to know what he was doing. I thought he had everything in hand. He seemed to treat the whole unexpected death of a guest as a thing that happened every day – like a blocked sink. But here now, he was admitting he didn't feel like that at all and what was worse, he seemed to be suggesting it wasn't even a normal death.

Jorge breaks the awkward silence and says we need to get more information and look into the death. Perplexed by this I tell him we should call the police, until he reminds me, without proof it looks like we're criticizing them for not doing their job properly. Plus, it runs the risk of Jorge's Place being named as a potential crime site and negatively affecting the reputation – something he's keen to avoid.

My head feels full, jammed with an overload of thoughts I didn't want to think. For most of the day I'd felt uneasy about the circumstances surrounding Patrick's death, but never did I really consider the implications of this sort of thinking.

Jorge tells me we need to formulate a plan to find out more and sets out his idea which involves his plumber Diego (who doesn't speak English) secretly turning off the water at the mains and me and Diego going round to see each guest to check if they have a blockage (which, of course, they won't). The point is for the maintenance issue to look believable and give us a chance to speak to people about their movements and what they may have seen. To be fair, as a plan, I think it's pretty cunning and tell Jorge that. He looks uncomfortable in my praise and replies: 'I see Patrick at games night, he was fine, not a man to die. This morning when I see his body, stiff and grey, I say why? Why is this man dead now?'

I nod uncomfortably, there's nothing more to discuss, we

need more answers. We agree I will meet Diego at 8 am to go round the apartments. There is no time to lose.

Back at my apartment I double lock the doors, close the shutters and pull the catches for the first time since I've been living here. The uneasiness is overwhelming. I've not felt like this here before and I don't like it. This island is safe. This island is warm. This island is full of good people. This island isn't a place where bad things happen.

The incessant knocking on my apartment door was like a drum roll finale. I sat up in bed, my skin pricking with fear.

Who was at the door?

I clung onto my light summer duvet trying to shield myself. On and on, the fist continued pounding the door. Scratchily I tried to find my voice, to say I was coming, but nothing came out.

I sat in the bed shaking, my heart jumping in fright. If I didn't move, nobody would know I was in. My lights weren't on. There was no noise from my apartment. As long as I kept quiet, quiet and still, no one would ever know I was hiding inside.

I sat still. Very still. My palm on my chest, my breath shallow and light, dusting my lungs with just enough oxygen to survive.

I could hear movement and low voices outside. I cocked my ear waiting for the footsteps to depart. Nothing.

Two minutes passed. I sat upright in bed waiting. Waiting and waiting. I checked the clock: 1.07 am.

My legs shook as I tiptoed my bare feet across the tiles to peer out of a tiny crack in the door. Holding my breath, I squidged my eye to the wood as it met the frame to try and see if anybody was outside. My body trembled as I tried to make out a shadow, an outline, a presence the other side of the closed door. Unable to see, I backed away and took tight, deep breaths trying to calm my pounding heart. I closed my eyes and tried to focus on what I could hear. Could I hear if somebody was still there? I stretched my ears close to the wood and focused on the sounds. Was there a presence?

I checked about the room. *I'd definitely locked all the windows and balcony door hadn't I?*

Then suddenly I heard a rush of footsteps. It sounded like two or three people. I could hear them across the courtyard. It sounded like they were coming back. They were coming back for me.

I stood, terror coursing through my veins as I tried to think what I could use to defend myself. *A knife from the kitchen? A hammer from my toolbox?*

'Tarah! Tarah! You there?' Jorge is knocking urgently on my door.

Confused and relieved I quickly grasp for the key, turn and open.

'Jorge, it's the middle of the night, you scared me!'

'Sorry to wake you, but Mick he try to find you and when he couldn't, he come for me.'

I turned and realised Mick was standing next to Jorge, alongside Tamika in a silky purple dress, it looked like they were dressed for a night out.

'Sorry I was asleep, what's the matter?'

'It's Pauline...' Mick started. 'She's not at the apartment.'

'What do you mean *not* at the apartment?' I reply, trying to get my head together.

'We came back about ten minutes ago, and I went to check on Pauline and she wasn't in her apartment,' he said.

'Maybe she's asleep? I replied, not wanting to admit I'd been too scared to open the door to their earlier hammering.

'No, she's not *in* the apartment.' Mick shakes his hands and moves a step closer. 'She left her door unlocked, I went in and she's not there. Her bed's not been slept in and her bag and mobile's gone!'

'And you've tried calling her?'

'Yeah, loads of times and it rings and rings and then goes to answerphone.'

Unlike the trio outside my door, I am not panicked by this news. Guests go wandering all the time. 'Maybe she's gone out? Does she know anybody else on the island? Is there anywhere else she could be?'

Mick shakes his head. 'Don't think so. Thing is, she was in a bad way earlier. I tried to convince her to come with us, but she said she was gonna have a lie down. I don't reckon she would've gone out, not the state she was in.'

'Has anybody called Alejandro to check she's not there, with him?' The three faces stared at me agog. 'Well,' I said, 'let's not get coy about this now, she knows him and if she's not in the apartment it stands to reason to ask anybody she knows if they're together?'

Jorge nodded and took his mobile out of his pocket. He dialled Alejandro's number and after several rings the caller picked up. Jorge exchanged a few words of Spanish and then hung up.

'She's not there, he not seen her since the afternoon. She told him she want early night.'

'And you're quite sure she doesn't know anybody else

here at all? I mean they have been coming for a quite a few years now,' I asked.

'Nobody I can think of,' replied Mick with a shrug, 'but if she was going to have an early night – and that's what she told us – then where is she now and why's she left her door open?'

'But you say she's taken her bag and mobile?'

Mick and Tamika exchanged glances.

'That's what you said?' I asked impatiently, trying to get to the hard facts.

'Yeah, but,' Mick looked uncomfortable, 'I can't say I looked *everywhere*. I mean it's not my place to go snooping. I saw it weren't on the coffee table where she normally keeps it.'

'OK,' I said, unsure on the veracity of their account. 'Let's go and check the apartment again, maybe she's come back now or maybe we can see if there's anything else she's taken to give us some clues. Give me a couple of minutes to put something on.'

Pulling on a pair of shorts and wrapping a fleece around me I slip on some flip-flops, tap on Mr Bob's carrier and join them again. Leading the way, I marched the trio across the courtyard and up the steps to Pauline's apartment. I hesitated as I drew close – less than 24 hours ago I'd made this very same journey after Pauline had called me about Patrick's death. Jorge seized my dithering and gently pushed past, saying he should go first. He tried the door, it was open and unlocked, as Mick said.

'Pauline? Pauline? You here?' He called before stepping inside and beckoning us in. Anxiously, we made our way in, checking, scanning, looking for any signs of anything.

Walking into the bedroom, my stomach dropped. The

bed had been stripped. All of the nicely prepared linen and matching cushions I'd laid out was gone, leaving the mattress bare apart from a large dark stain. This is where Patrick had died. This is where his life had ended. Looking around I saw the wardrobes full with his intended holiday clothing: colourful short-sleeved shirts, nicely ironed and ready to wear; light summery trousers and shorts; sandals and deck shoes, all casual, easy footwear designed to be worn and enjoyed in the sun.

I opened the neighbouring wardrobe, its contents were bursting with vibrant dresses and skirts, shawls and scarves, sheer shirts, tops and cardigans and at the bottom, piled several pairs high, a collection of heels, sling-backs and pumps in a variety of colours with matching handbags and purses. I stared at the stuff, did anybody really need this amount of clothes and paraphernalia for a two-week holiday?

'Anything?' Jorge asked as he entered the room.

'She's got a lot of clothes, shoes and handbags!' I spread my arms widely to show the innards of the wardrobe.

'Mick,' I called. He rushed in from the lounge. 'Which handbag has she taken?'

He peered inside. 'Oh God, I forgot how many bags she has. She does love her clothes does our Pauline.'

I bent down and started looking through the handbags. All had remnants of different nights out left in them: chewing gum, mints, lipsticks, tissues, pens. I'm clutching a patent green multi-pocketed number when Mick said, 'I'm sure that's the one she had with her today.'

'This one?' I said, looking down at the handbag. He nodded and I poked my fingers around inside, searching the various pockets and crevices. Its contents were pretty much the same as the others, apart from this one had a small child-like wallet inside: a stitched fabric affair with a yellow and blue owl face and moving beady eyes. I open it to find a bunch of euros and one credit card.

'That's the purse she uses when we go away,' Mick said. 'I know coz I take the piss out of her having a kid's thing like that, I mean it's a bit... innit?'

I glance down at the colourful little wallet. 'So this is the purse she should've had with her tonight?'

Mick nodded.

'So where's her other purse, the *bigger* one?'

Mick looked at me confused. 'A bigger purse? I dunno. Why would she have another one? Beats me what you women do with all them purses and handbags. I've got one wallet and it's always in my pocket.'

I put the little purse to one side. Any woman, but especially a woman like Pauline, would have another bigger purse with the rest of her cards in. I find it odd to think she would travel with just the one card and a few notes. Reaching under the bed I pulled out the over-sized hold suitcase they'd arrived with. I unzipped the case and flipped open the lid, there's nothing inside except a collection of used carrier bags.

'Mick, can you call her again?'

He dials her number and holds the phone to his ear.

'DEEE-DEEE-DEEE-DEEE,' a ringtone bleeped from inside the bedroom.

Jorge began opening the bedside drawers, while I hunted in the handbags searching for the phone.

'It's here,' said Tamika, holding the bleeping mobile aloft.

'Where was it?' I asked, taking it from her.

'In that jacket pocket, on the back of the door.'

Mick hung up and plunged the room into an eerie quiet.

14

A MISSING PERSON?

'She's probably gone for a walk,' I heard myself saying. I have no idea why I would say anything quite so clueless and based on nothing whatsoever, but I'm desperate to remain upbeat and positive about this crazy situation.

Mick nodded at this suggestion, although I could tell he didn't believe me.

'Can we go to bed now then?' asked Tamika, elegantly over-doing a stifle of a yawn. She looked bored, bored and disinterested. She tapped the heel of her stiletto ever so slightly against the tiled floor.

'We can't go to bed; we don't know where Pauline is!' said Mick, a hint of annoyance edging into his voice.

'Tarah said she's probably gone for a walk,' replied Tamika with a petulant pout.

'*Probably*, but not *definitely*!' Mick said, his voice louder and more emphatic than it needed to be in the close confines of the bedroom.

Jorge stepped forward. 'Maybe is getting too excited now, I think...'

'I'm not, I'm ready for bed,' yawned Tamika, her jaw opening wide, emitting an unruly exhalation of air.

Jorge waved his hands to call for attention. 'I know today is difficult day, we must be kind and focus. *Tranquilo*. Now, if Pauline not here we should look for her. Maybe she get lost, maybe she…' He didn't finish his sentence, but instead told us we should split into pairs and look for her because it was late and dark. He instructed Mick and Tamika to go south on the promenade, while he and I would go north. We were to check the side streets, the main streets and anywhere we could think to look to find Pauline. He informed us we had five minutes to change into warmer clothing while he fetched the torches.

Back outside the sky is sooty-black, wafts of wispy feathered clouds pass over the moon and lightly veil the starry brightness. A gentle breeze is building, carrying grains of sand from the Sahara, whistling and whipping at our hair. Tamika has gracefully tied her long blonde hair into a loose topknot, she's holding a long black over-sized cardigan against her and has changed her heels for a pair of silver ballet pumps. Mick has now put on a slim-cut navy bomber jacket. The zip line is swollen from his protruding belly; a body shape the designer never anticipated the wearer to have. I've now got a hoodie and have changed into some trainers.

Jorge hands us torches and double-checks we have each other's numbers. Routes agreed, we estimate to meet back at the apartments an hour from now: 2.45 am.

Out on the seafront the wind whips my hair and I pointlessly try and tuck windswept strands behind my ears. Searching in my pocket for a hopeful scrunchie or hair band to tie back my hair from my eyes I give up and shove my shoulder-length hair into the hood of my top. The sea at night looks black. White crusts form, foam and crash down onto the shore. At any other time, I've always thought the sea at night looks beautiful, but tonight, it looks menacing. The crests and troughs look savage and wild. Where before the sea had signalled freedom, adventure and a force of nature, now all I can see is a fierce, rampant monster smashing against the sand, pulverising and pummelling anything in its way.

The streetlights bordering the walkway of the seafront promenade throw off a yellowish-orange glow, illuminating the path in a low, cloudy, candlelit way. Their dim radiance throws off enough light for visibility, but not enough to see. I switch on my torch and the white beam feels harsh in contrast to the darkness all around. I'm tempted to turn it back off again for the light feels too abrasive, but then I remember the reason why I'm out here in the middle of the night.

Jorge nods to me to turn right and keep walking. The usually busy town is stiflingly quiet at this hour. There is a stillness and nothingness of everybody sleeping that makes it feel eerie, wrong even, to be walking about at this time. I search the darkened buildings for any sign of light, any sign of life.

Preternatural. I want to use that word. It feels weird. Nothing feels like it usually feels. It's like something has shifted, like the tectonic plates have collided into each other and a new order has taken over. Everything looks the same, but it isn't.

Uneasy, that's how I feel. It seems like in the last twenty-four hours my stable life has become unstable. What I thought I knew, I don't. My life feels stripped bare of the assumptions I've made. Now I feel I need to question everything, everyone. I don't know who to trust, what to believe, who's lying, pretending to be something they're not.

'You're quiet,' Jorge says, interrupting the colossal noise in my head.

'I was just thinking…' I reply.

He says nothing, doesn't prod or pry. I wonder if he feels as unsettled as me.

We walk along the promenade slowly and deliberately, but making good progress. Our torchlights beam and bend down alleyways and across buildings. To the outside eye we must look like a couple of watchmen, security guards doing their regular patrol. Perhaps I could feign it, tell myself this is a perfectly normal thing to be doing at 2 am.

'I'm scared,' I hear myself saying, the words spilling out before I want to vocalise them.

Jorge rubs my arm in a brotherly fashion. 'Is OK, I'm here.'

I laugh out loud, the notes twanging off the empty spaces. It sounds hollow. I want to tell him how angry I feel, how ripped apart my world is. I want to tell him how before all this shit started I thought I'd finally got my life in order. I knew what to do, how to live – and that now, now I don't feel I know any of the rules any more. That now I feel scared again. Nothing feels right and I don't want to feel like this, I want to feel safe again.

'I'm sorry,' Jorge says.

'Sorry, what are you sorry for?' I say, perplexed by his apology.

'For this.' He shrugs. 'Maybe I am wrong.'

I stand and stare at him in the dim, orange glow of the streetlight. 'How can you be wrong? How is this the *wrong* thing to do? What we're doing is the right thing.' I surprise myself with my confidence, my belief in what we're doing. 'I mean; how can this *not* be right when... when... where's Pauline?' I don't say anything more about the rest of the mess, and maybe where Jorge could be wrong. Now's not the time to open the closed conversation from earlier. We made a plan, and I'll stick to it.

Jorge returns my stare, then turns his head to the sea and quickly back to me. 'Her passport, where is her passport?'

My eyes widen at the question. 'I don't know, I didn't look.'

Our eyes lock like midnight lovers. I chew the inside of my cheek. Jorge gazes, assessing the distance we've walked. 'We go to end of pier then come back, if she already gone we too late. But maybe... we should check, be sure.'

I nod and we walk on in silence. The pier is lit with brighter bulbs, the glare fanning across the concrete path and skimming the surface of the sea. In the daytime when the sun is shining, this pier is a thronging, bustling place. Fishermen sit cheek by jowl throwing their lines while ferries bound for neighbouring islands pour in. Catamarans of day-trippers and power boats chop and loll in the deep, blue waters alongside manic jet-skiers and gliding windsurfers. At the end of the pier stands a magnificent basalt sculpture, some five metres high, of a lady looking out to sea. I've always presumed she's waiting for her sailor to return. She has a wistful patience about her, a longing and a loving that is so beautifully carved. I can see her shadowy outline at the brink, but in this light she looks more lonely than lovely.

The tread of our feet is a dull thud. The lights from Lanzarote glitter across the 12-mile stretch that separates the two islands. The lady sculpture stands waiting, watching. As we round the end of the pier towards the front of her gaze, the outline of a person can be seen sitting at her base. My heartbeat quickens, a shiver of fear in my blood. The person is sat very still, knees tucked up under their chin. I cannot tell if it is a man or a woman, their body nestled into the shadowy skirt folds of the carving.

Beside me Jorge has hastened his pace. I pick up my tempo until we're in front of the person, who I can now see is Pauline.

He gently rests his backside on the curve of the statue's carved bare feet. I slink alongside, leaning slightly, so we form a human sandwich with Pauline in-between. The three of us sit there looking out to sea, sheltered by the magnificent maiden on the shore.

'You OK?' Jorge says, his face still gazing out.

Silence.

I survey her profile as best I can in the dim light. She's wearing knee-length shorts, perhaps beige or taupe, or maybe cream. Her blouse is dark, maybe burgundy, or dark-red, its armless with a loose tie detail at her waist. Her pale skin looks luminous, but even in the shadow I can see the goose pimples – erupting, small, hard, raised pimples topped off with shafts of fine hair that ever so slightly catch the light. Her feet are bare, toes polished, her flip flops, have been cast aside.

Her face remains still, her expression impassive. She has a fine nose with a strong, straight line. Her chin is delicate, a small peach below her plumped lips. They don't look natural, but she hasn't overly done the filler. Her skin looks mature, but well-kept with expensive moisturiser. She strikes me as a good-looking lady who knows it and wants to keep it. Strands of finely cut hair blow about her face, but she lets them be, unmoved, unfazed.

We all three sit watching and waiting.

'I was going to have an early night,' says Pauline, her voice flat. 'But when I got to the bedroom and saw the bed all stripped like that...', her voice falters and tears slip down her face. 'I, I just remembered.' She coughs a little, her voice sounding huskier and more nasally. 'All I could see was his body. But he's not here anymore, he's gone. It's just me...and I, I wanted to get away, away.' The sobs choke her voice and I put my arm around her to comfort her. Her skin is frigid to the touch. Her posture unaltered.

'I couldn't... I can't bear the thought of this.' She breathes so deeply and so quickly I worry she may pass out. 'I can't bear that this is happening, that this is my life. I've come on holiday with my husband and I'm going home a widow.' Her wails pierce the peace.

I try and hug her tighter and Jorge strokes her arm. She cradles her head in her hands, her body consumed with grief. I feel so inadequate, there's nothing I can say. We sit for a long time coddled like three children trying to keep warm. We listen to the rush of the waves – every ebb and flow makes me realise how insignificant we are. The ocean, the vast, great watery wilderness is soothing, but scary. We are mere specks of life in comparison; a grain of sand will probably live longer. I can see the steady flow of tears tracking her face. I want to cry, also.

'We were married for 16 years you know; it would've been our anniversary today.' Pauline's voice is wistful. 'I was just 21 when we married, 20 when we met. It was, what they'd say was a *whirlwind romance*. He was 32 at the time, 11 years older than me. My parents weren't best happy as they thought Patrick was a bit common – he was a builder, 'a manual labourer' my dad used to say. They wanted someone with better career prospects, but he'd done OK for himself, he had his own house, his own van and a car. And he didn't have any baggage. He didn't have kids or an ex-wife from before. He'd had a couple of girlfriends, but he'd been more interested in trying to build his business. We met at a bar – back in those days you could meet people at bars! He asked me out while I was buying a drink, and when I saw his smiley, cheeky face and twinkly blue eyes I said 'maybe'. I wanted to say 'yes' straightaway, but I didn't wanna make his life too easy. I always wanted to keep myself a bit of challenge, you know. I don't want to be such an easy catch, that's what I told myself. Within a month of us going out he'd proposed, and six months later we married at my local church. It was a beautiful day.'

I squeeze her shoulder.

'Married life wasn't always easy. He could be hard work, especially when he got stressed. Money used to be his big thing, he was always worried about overdoing it and losing his shirt. He'd seen quite a few of his friends in the business lose everything and he didn't wanna be like that. He knew he'd done OK for himself, *for us*, and he was a bit precious about it, you know. We had a good life and he wanted to protect that, keep it going. He didn't want to overstretch and be on the street. Bankruptcy, I mean the threat of it, was a big deal to him, it's that sort of industry. He didn't want to be a boom-bust guy, or feast or famine. He was steady; he wanted steady money, a steady life.'

'Do you have children?' asks Jorge.

Pauline sighs before replying. 'Oh he desperately wanted children, he couldn't wait for us to start with the little-uns as he called them. I didn't really feel the same as him. I've never ruled it out, but I've never ruled it in – I mean once you have 'em you can't change your mind and give 'em back! I know he'd have helped, but still I knew it would be me looking after them all day and all night, and I, I guess I'm a bit selfish.'

'Children *are* a big responsibility,' I say.

'Too late now, ain't it?' A dollop of anger enters her tone. 'I should've thought of that before, I shouldn't have been so selfish, always looking out for me and what I wanted to do.'

'You can't be so hard on yourself, having children is a big ask, you need to feel ready.'

'Is it? Is it really?' She turns to face me and I can just make out the whites of her eyes as she glowers at me. 'All my life Patrick has given me so much – everything. No woman could've asked for more. All he wanted was a little piece of me and him to carry on, to bring up and have a family.' She shakes her head and covers her face with her palms. 'I wish I'd done things differently. I should've been a better wife. Things could've been different. Maybe if we'd had kids, we wouldn't be here now and he'd still be alive.'

15

A STRANGE COINCIDENCE?

The morning came around too quickly. By the time we'd manage to settle Pauline and explain to Mick and Tamika where we'd found her, it was gone 4am when I got to bed. Jorge told me Diego would come a bit later than planned, but still, 9am felt a cruel early start today.

The day was already hot, 23 degrees and counting, it was going to be a scorcher. Dousing myself in tepid water I washed my hair, even though I'd only washed it yesterday, just to try and wake myself up more. Mr Bob had been agitated when I'd returned last night/this morning. I think he was concerned by me being away in the middle of the night. I cuddled him and tried to calm him, but still he fidgeted and his bustling about in the straw bedding meant I hadn't really got into that deep dreamless sleep that makes you feel you've actually had some sleep! Turning the shower to cold I felt the goose pimples spiking up all over my skin. Even though I've barely slept it feels like I'm in some sort of bad dream. It's a weird sensation – something between sleep walking and hallucinating, but with a realistic edge. It's as if you know life is actually happening and you're a part of it, but at the same time you feel apart *from* it. I don't know how to explain it – things feel real, but not real, and there's like a surreal mist shrouding me.

Shivering from the too-cold water, I turn the shower off and wrap myself in a towel to dry. Am I really doing this today? Am I really going to try and work out who killed Patrick? The thought sticks in my throat, did I really just think that?

I look at myself in the mirror, my eyes are saggy and my skin has a greyish hue. Who am I? Who am I to be doing this and to be asking such questions? I sit on the edge of the bath and the sick feeling in my tummy turns. My throat tightens and I wretch. My head is pounding like I've been drinking all night. God, I can't believe my life has come to this, how have I got myself into this? This can't be happening; this isn't real life. Real life is checking customers in and cleaning up their mess, it's not this, it can't be this.

Shaking my head, I look about the seaside-themed home I've created, the hard work I've put into creating this dream life in the sun. How can I allow bad things to happen here? This place is my sanctuary, my home, my happiness. I've spent months creating the perfect holiday life that is my *real* life, and I'm not about to let some bloody person come in and take that away from me. I need to feel safe in my own place, on this island. I want to feel happy again, settled. I can't allow someone, some stranger, to take that from me. I need my life back.

Mr Bob gazes at me with his wide-eyed stare and wheeks for some attention. Lifting him out of his carrier he nestles comfortably in my lap and starts licking my finger. Stroking his soft, downy fur I feel myself becoming grounded. 'What are we going to do, Mr Bob?' I say to him. 'Do you know who killed Patrick?' Suddenly, his body freezes in my hand. I can feel all of his ligaments taut, stone-like – it's as if he's holding his whole body, his whole being, waiting for me to understand. Almost a minute passes until he fixes me with his wide eyes and then scurries away from me and clambers back into his carrier.

If ever I needed proof, this was it. Every mention of Patrick's name made Mr Bob shudder to stone. This was his hallmark behaviour of signalling trouble. No matter how crazy, this had to be done. There was a wrong that had to be put right. I didn't know how, but I would try my best. I've watched enough murder mysteries to know what I need to do – now I just need to find my suspects and put it all together. I will find Patrick's killer and I will make my island, and my life, safe again.

'Morning, my dear,' calls Miriam, as I'm heading across the courtyard trying to dodge the swaying palms. The sun may be out and shining brightly, but the wind is flowing freely, Fuerteventura isn't known as the windy isle for no reason!

'Morning Miriam, how are you?' I'm delighted to have Miriam staying again, she's fast becoming a regular at Jorge's Place and has already booked her next stay in two months' time.

'Can I have a word, my dear?'

'Of course, how can I help?' I about-turn abruptly, the motion so quick Mr Bob's carrier swings like a pendulum and he scoots to the opposite side at breakneck speed.

Miriam gestures to me to come closer. I take another pace

forward. She beckons me again. I move even closer, so close I feel I'm going to hug her. I can smell her powdery lavender perfume and the old-fashioned hairspray she still uses after six decades to keep her wispy bouffant in place. 'It's about this business with Patrick,' she says, in a voice barely above a whisper.

'Yes, it's a very sad situation, did you speak to him much?'

'Not really my dear, but it's not what I spoke to him about, it's what I *saw*.'

I jerk my head back. 'What did you see?'

'My dear, I don't want to be starting rumours, but on the day... on the day when later he was found...' she pauses, searching for the right word, 'dead. I saw him and I thought he was looking very, shall we say, stressed.'

'Stressed?'

'Yes, you see the reason I noticed, was because he was one of those happy chappies in life. You know the sort, always smiling and saying hello and waving to me. He was always very charming and complimentary and would take the time to talk with me. He'd say something about the weather, or make a lovely comment on my outfit, or my hair. He was a good sort, my dear, always had a smile for me, for anybody.'

'OK?' I say, waiting for more.

'Well, the matter is my dear, on that day, you know *that day*, I saw him *twice*, and *twice* he didn't even look up or say anything to me. He looked very much as though he was in his own world. What I found most strange, was on both occasions when I called out to him in greeting, he didn't respond. Not *once*. It was most rude of him and most out of character!'

'Perhaps he didn't see you Miriam?'

'Well, you say that my dear, but I was practically *right in front of him*! And,' she sucks in her breath for amplified effect, '*I was wearing a bright orange dress!* It was the same summer dress he'd complimented me on only the day before, but that time I was wearing the yellow version. You know how these things are when you find a style that suits? Anyway, I found it most strange, he's always smiling and he's here on holiday, and to be so... so distracted. Don't you find it odd?'

I pause, unsure how to react. Miriam is watching me, waiting for me to reply. 'So what are you thinking?'

'Well, my dear, as I say I don't want to start rumours, but have you considered maybe something may've been *bothering* him?'

'Bothering him?' I ask, tilting my head to the side.

'I hear they're saying it was a heart attack, but I can't help but wonder about the timing.' Miriam shuffles her feet in her lemon-patterned espadrilles. 'It seems – how should I say? – awfully convenient.' She pauses to check my reaction (I keep a poker face) and continues. 'My dear, every day he's been the sunniest and smiliest man and *then*, then on *the very day* he suddenly and most unexpectedly dies, that's the *same* day I saw him and he looked so preoccupied?'

I keep my face blank and my tone neutral. 'So then, given what you saw, what do you think I should do?'

'Well, as I say, I don't want to interfere, but I really think you should start asking some questions of the guests. Perhaps it's just me and I've been reading too many books, but it doesn't seem right, does it?'

'So I should start by asking *you* questions?'

'My dear, I think you're testing me now,' Miriam looks at me, a knowing gleam in her eye. 'You know *exactly* who you should be asking questions of.'

I scrutinize her face. 'Who? Who should I be asking questions of?'

'His wife obviously, and that business partner of his, running about town in that fancy, noisy car while his supposed lifelong friend and associate lies in the morgue. It can't be right, can it?'

'No, I s'pose not.'

'If you need any help my dear, you know where I am.'

I turn and smile, and she winks, crinkling her long, thickly-applied mascara lashes against her perfectly made-up face.

Jorge is waiting for me with Diego outside his house busying themselves with some sort of machinery I don't know the name of. As is the case with every tradesman I've ever met, Diego's got a large toolbox next to him overflowing with gadgets and gizmos for fixing any number of things. He smiles shyly at me. We know each other by sight, but I don't tend to use Diego as my go-to man on account of him not speaking English, but Jorge trusts him implicitly and if ever there's a plumbing issue, he calls Diego to sort it. Diego is in his mid-thirties with a strong Canarian suntan and thick mahogany eyebrows. He's wearing a once-was-white t-shirt, with grubby grease stains and dirt stuck firmly in the fibres. His navy blue cargo pants are smeared with grime and debris and the pockets look stuffed with plumbing paraphernalia. I watch his gaze fall onto Mr Bob's carrier. He says nothing.

Jorge motions for me to come closer so he can speak to me quietly. 'Diego, he stopped the main water from the tap in the street.' He motions with his eyebrows to the manhole.

'The people, they have enough for one flush, but then... kaput. If they try wash their hands or have shower, nada.'

'The guests will go crazy,' I say, pursing my lips.

'We put a notice, a sign to say we have problem and must to use the outside tap.' He indicates a faucet on the wall of the terrace. 'They have access to water, but in apartments, no, no water. I bring buckets, people they can use them. We say there is blockage in system, you, you and Diego look into, you need help to talk with the people, to understand maybe they put something accidentally, or no, but we talk with them to find blockage to fix. You tell them we cannot take apart whole building, so we must to talk with everybody in the apartments and then we find and we fix.'

I marvel at Jorge; anybody would think he's done this gag before. I look over at Diego wondering what Jorge has told him we're actually doing. He was the one who stopped the water in the first place, so to now be pretending to find out why the water has stopped seems pretty nuts. He stands patiently waiting while Jorge explains all this to me and nods when Jorge looks at him.

Conscious I'm talking about someone when they're stood right in front of me, I lean in to Jorge and lower my voice. 'Can I ask, what have you said to him about what we're doing?'

Jorge gives me a small smile. 'I tell him money gone missing. I say we not know if missing or maybe stolen. I tell him I not want to make wrong accusations, you and him you look in guest apartments to see and talk. With no water you have reason.'

I gawp in wonder at his ingenuity. Now with Diego being told this story, he will also be on the lookout for how people react and looking around for anything that may be out of place. Admittedly, he'll be looking for different clues, but still, he's primed and looking for something that may be amiss.

'I tell him you bring the pig because he's sick and you afraid to leave him alone.'

I laugh. 'Was that better than the truth? You didn't want to admit we're both bloody crazy?'

Jorge winks at me and pinches me on my shoulder. It's mental. This whole thing is truly mental, but for some reason I'm still in.

16

WHAT TAMIKA SAW TODAY

Even though Diego doesn't speak English, I find myself wanting to talk to him. I try and convince myself it's a companionable silence, but it doesn't work, the guy is a stranger and walking along in silence with a stranger is awkward. I string together some words.

'Bwenos deeass!' I say, trying to put on a strong Spanish accent to hide my Englishness.

He nods at me congenially and raises his thick eyebrows.

I smirk as I realise all I've managed to say is 'Good Morning'. I try again. 'Ess ooon bwenos deeass,' I say, hoping I'm now explaining it's a good day.

Diego nods again and chatters something back very quickly and I pause to stare at him and have to ask him what he's said again (more slowly), 'mas slower', accompanied with hand gestures of what I believe is a slowing down motion.

He repeats himself slowly this time and I catch he's saying something about the sun and it being hot. I reckon this on account of his pointing at the sky and the bright, blazing sun that's burning my face. I don't know how to reply and so

I tell him in English about how I've put suntan lotion on this morning because I didn't want to burn, and I do have my hat on – which I point to. I have no idea if he understands any of my gestures or words, which I try and pepper with some Spanish, when I remember, or think I remember.

He nods.

I nod back and we continue walking, in silence. But now, somehow I feel less awkward, I've *broken* the silence. It may only have been a small exchange about the day and the weather, but I think we're bonding. We feel less like strangers now and more like people off on a strange mission.

Rounding the paved walkway to the main entrance of the apartments, the beach is packed with swimmers and sun worshippers. I scan the golden yellow sands and take in the multi-coloured umbrellas, bikinis, shorts and bodies. So many people having so much fun. I glance at the gleaming aquamarine of the sea at the shoreline, casting my eyes to the dark, navy blue, deep waters as it meets the clear, pale blue horizon. I never tire of so many views of blue.

I check the time on my phone and shudder as I see it's already ten past ten. We only have a few hours until Patrick's body will be repatriated to England.

Diego points to a rusted iron square in the ground just outside the white boundary walls of Jorge's Place. 'Agua,' he says.

I nod, this is where he's turned the water off for the whole block.

Entering the seafront terrace, I see Tamika sunning herself on a lounger. She's pulled across the umbrella from the other side of the terrace and is using a chair as a table. I note the almost-finished bottle of wine and the lipstick stains on the glass. A half-full ashtray is nestled next to a folded-up pink dress. Her skin, bronzed, oiled and glistening in the sun, looks airbrushed to perfection against her shockingly whiter-than-white-too-small-to-be-decent bikini. I can tell she's watching us as we enter, but she doesn't acknowledge us through her large shades.

'Sorry to bother you,' I say, crouching down on my knees so I'm at her eye level, 'but we have a water problem – actually we have *no* water.' I wait for her to respond and when I get nothing, carry on. 'I'm talking to everybody to understand when their water stopped or maybe if they remember anything or heard anything that happened before...' I trail off as she scowls at me.

She sits glaring at me through her sunglasses.

'I'm sorry, you're probably very tired after the late night last night,' I offer meekly.

'You could say that,' she replies.

'It was good we found Pauline though,' I say, trying to inject some cheer and positivity.

'If you say so,' she replies, her tone deadpan, her face sullen.

'Well, it's got to be good news. We don't want people going missing!' I say, forcing my jollity out.

'Frankly, I don't care what the woman does or where she goes, it's got nothing to do with me.' Tamika stretches her lithe figure to reach for a cigarette, lights it and blows smoke in my face, on purpose. 'To be honest, the further away from me that woman goes, the better, it means I don't have to deal with her or her shit.' She drains her wine glass and looks about for a refill. Eager to please, I grasp the bottle and empty the remains into her waiting glass.

'Want me to get you another?

'Why would you do that?' she asks, eyeing me suspiciously.

'Well, because it can't be easy, being here on holiday and then all the upset with Patrick, and then the late night looking for Pauline, then all this stuff about the property deal with Mick and Lucas and...' I leave my sentence hanging and motion to Diego to get me a bottle of wine from the supermarket next door, stuffing a 10 Euro note into his hand.

The conversation stops awkwardly while we both watch Diego scuttle off and return with a chilled bottle of wine. I quickly fill her glass. She sips deeply and considers me while readjusting her glasses. I can feel her gaze weighing me up. She pouts and then spurts, 'No, you're right, it ain't been easy. I mean, I came here for a bit of R and R and to tie this deal up, which I'd already sorted. So far, all I've had is non-stop fucking hassle. If it ain't this, it's that and if it ain't that, it's this.'

'I can understand,' I say.

'Can you?' She ups her tone, challenging, she wants to fight. I soften my features into the most passive, willing expression I can muster and reach out to her with a gaze that is so sympathetic, so beseeching, I can feel myself dripping on the floor. Her prickles subside and she continues. 'Don't get me wrong, I *wanted* to come here – this deal with Lucas is a game changer. I mean, it's really epic stuff. How many people do *you* know developing water parks?'

'I don't know anybody at all!' I reply in an instant.

'Exactly my point! That's what I told Mick. I told him opportunities like this don't come along ever, like *ever*. And so the fact it came along meant he *had* to do something with it. He *couldn't* leave it, not a deal like this, it's a life changer, absolute life changer.'

'Was there a reason why he was thinking to leave it?'

'If it was up to Patrick, they would've. He didn't have a business bone in his body, that man didn't. He wouldn't know how to see a good deal if it came up and sucked his cock off. He was a plodder. I don't know how Mick put up with him for so long, must've been pity. Obviously, they only made the money they did coz of Mick, and that's what I told him. Mick's the money man, he's the one who knows how the world works. He understands what a big ticket opportunity this is, despite what Patrick was saying.'

'Oh? What was Patrick saying?'

'He was mithering like an old woman. He got himself all worked up 'bout the risks and things that could go wrong and *would* go wrong, and how they needed to allow for *this* to happen and *that* to happen. Honestly, you'd think the world was gonna cave in the way he went on about things.'

'And what did Mick say?'

'He told him to get a grip. Told him they'd come here to meet Lucas, this was a deal of a lifetime and he hadn't lived all his life to *not* do a deal like this. Between me and you, I think he was getting really fed up with Patrick holding him back. Mick's got a new lease of life now, he don't wanna be acting like an old geezer and not earning what he's due.'

'I thought their business was doing well?' I say tentatively, conscious I might be straying into prying territory.

'It was, it is, but like with anything, you gotta keep moving forward else you go stagnant and then you're going backwards. And thing is, Mick's ex, Jesus she's a bitch!

Demanding this and that and how she wants this property and that money and y'know, *typical gold digger*.'

'Does she know about you two?'

Tamika snorts a laugh, lifts her shades and looks at me directly. 'Know about me? Hun, he left *her* for *me*! Course she knows about me!'

I deign her reply with the light-hearted and appropriate chuckle she expects and ask how she met Mick. Although I struggle to hide my surprise when she informs me they met at work. 'Oh, you're in the building trade too?'

She arches her eyebrows as though I've just shat in her lap. 'Do I seriously look like I work on a building site? No! I was doing a piece on a renovation they were doing. I'm what's known as an *influencer*. I've got a social account 'What Tamika Saw Today'. I go round and check out the latest property stuff that's going down, take photos, get a tour, do interviews with the developers, get the low-down and that, y'know. People love it, they can't get enough of it! They love it even more when the guys, as it's always guys, have a decent car collection as well. I've driven a few Porsches and even a Lambo in the last year y'know.'

'That's impressive.'

'Yeah, I've also had a TV company contact me about a show and done a screen test. But y'know I earn well with all the ads, so I dunno really if they'll make it worth my while. It's all about profile. You should see the free stuff companies send me – I could fit out an entire house!'

'So with your channel 'What Tamika Saw Today', do you have many followers?

'Bout half a million.'

'Half a million followers?' I repeat, trying to keep the admiration out of my voice.

'Yeah, but now I wanna grow it more and focus on the big ticket stuff, you know the *real* money. I'm not one-a-them people who pretends they don't like money – I love it! People wanna be rich and I'm good with that, nothing wrong with it. So I'm like on my channel I talk a lot about that. People get scared of money and talking 'bout it, but that's rubbish – we need it, we want it – not a problem. I get the answers for my viewers.

'Sounds like you know your audience.'

'Yeah, they don't wanna be hearing 'bout the toil, they wanna see the rewards – the fun stuff – like when you've made it and you're living your best life. Lucas is a prime example, he's made a mint and is like a fucking movie star!'

'I saw his red Maserati,' I say keen to find a connection.

'You wanna see the rest! He's got a G-Wagon, Lambo, Ferrari, Porsche GT, you name it, he's probably got it!'

I make suitable oohing and aahing noises to show I'm impressed. But despite my enthusiasm, Tamika's gone off the boil. I hesitate wondering how to spark her interest, but she's twiddling intently with her cigarette packet and seems to have pulled up a glass wall. She finishes ripping the cellophane off and throws it on the terrace. A waft of wind picks it up and I grab it.

'I see Pauline's strutting round like she's the sad widow,' she says.

'Well, she has just lost her husband,' I reply.

Tamika leans into me, her tone lowering conspiratorially. 'You mean you don't know about her Facebook *friends*... or her *history*?' She picks up her phone and rapidly swipes and taps and passes it to me. 'See there,' she declares as I scroll down. The screen is filled with loads of photos of Pauline and Alejandro, sometimes with Patrick in the picture, but most of the time not. 'You seen the dates? Over 10 years some of them are – look how much younger they look. I reckon Alejandro must've been a boy when it started!'

'When what started?' I ask, pretending I'm not making the obvious connection.

'Are you looking at the same pictures?' Tamika stares at me like I'm dumb. She takes the mobile out of my hand and jabs at the photo on the screen. 'Look at 'em, they're obviously together! I dunno how she got away with it, Patrick was either too blind or stupid to see!'

'So you're saying Pauline and Alejandro are together, like in a relationship?'

'What else do you call it?' She doesn't wait for me to answer. 'What gets me is how little pride she has with all this flaunting, I mean it's so disrespectful to your husband, ain't it? If you're gonna have a dirty secret, at least keep it *secret!*'

I was about to start asking more, but then Tamika's phone starts to flash and she motions me to hush while she answers.

17

ABOUT THAT NIGHT

I didn't really want to hang around while Tamika chatted to her friend on the phone, but I had to stay. Her tongue was loose on wine. The interruption of the call gave me the chance to switch subjects.

'About *that* night...' I started, topping up her glass again to keep her jowls slick. 'Do you remember what happened?'

'You mean the night Patrick checked out?'

I nod.

'What can I say? I wasn't there, I thought he was in bed with Pauline when he died, his heart wasn't it?'

'Yeah, but before then... weren't you all at games night together, here on this terrace?' I spread my arms indicating the same place we're sat now.

She looks about, her eyes taking in the features of the tiled patio area. 'Yeah, but you were there as well.'

'I know, but I wasn't sat with you *all* the time. I was here, there and everywhere with so many people. I was just wondering what you might remember about that night?'

'I dunno really. I'd been shopping and was wearing a

new Desigual dress. Mick was getting a bit naggy with me coz he wanted to get to games night and was moaning I was taking too long to get ready. Anyway, I told him to go on ahead coz I still had to blow-dry my hair. You know with hair like this,' she flicks her long blonde locks for emphasis, 'it ain't gonna dry in two minutes. So I joined them, I dunno, maybe half an hour later. They were playing some shit game I wasn't interested in so I sat that out. And then Mick wanted to play Monopoly. I wasn't really interested, but he was going on a bit and I wanted to keep him happy, so I did.'

'OK,' I say, urging her on.

'Well, I was the hat, and Mick he was...'

'I don't need to know about the game.'

'So what *do* you wanna know?'

'Well, how did Patrick seem?'

'I dunno, I wasn't really paying attention to Patrick, but he was there, he was playing the game. Pauline had a cold and was spreading her germs everywhere with her crappy tissues. I didn't wanna hold the dice after she'd touched them – I mean, how'd you come down with a cold in this heat? Anyway, I moved away from her as I didn't want to get ill, I mean, really, she should've stayed at home rather than passing her lurgy to everyone.'

'And Mick?'

'He was a bit overly excited y'know coz him and Patrick had been drinking most of the day, lairy really, like how they get after a few too many. He was messing about a bit, winding Pauline up and calling her Rudolph coz her nose was all red.'

'And Patrick?'

'I didn't really talk to him, he was there, he was drinking. I was just biding my time till the game finished.'

Aware I was bombarding her with questions, I gave a small smile and topped up her wine glass, waiting for her to take a sip before continuing. 'Do you remember we had some food? Did you have any?'

'That soggy pizza – no way! The rest of 'em weren't minded and were proper filling their faces. It was pretty disgusting the way they were shovelling down like they hadn't eaten for days!'

'And then?'

'There was the homemade dessert, a really eggy one which I didn't like. Dairy's not good, especially that sort of dairy.'

'Did anybody else eat it?'

'As I say, free food frenzy – they were like flies to shit.'

'And then what happened?'

Tamika lights another cigarette and gulps a large mouthful of wine before replying. 'I dunno, Mick wanted to carry on with the game, they got some more drinks, then Patrick started coughing, think he got the germs off Pauline. They decided to call it an early night and Mick and me went to a cocktail bar on the strip.'

I hesitate as I try and piece together everything Tamika's told me.

'Do you think it could be possible Patrick could've had some sort of food allergy? I ask.

She shrugs. 'How would I know something like that? I barely know the guy, let alone what he's allergic to.'

'Yeah, I understand,' I say, 'I guess I'm just thinking out loud. Anyway, if he did have an allergy Pauline would've stopped him from eating it.'

'Would she?' Tamika eyes me brazenly and twiddles

with her hair. 'I don't wanna get involved or say anything out of order, but maybe it would've been in her best interests?'

I give Tamika a puzzled look waiting for her to continue.

'I'm just saying, if Patrick wasn't around Pauline would be a free agent and then she could get with her toy boy, collect the cash. I mean, people have done worse things for less.'

I try and keep a neutral look on my face, I don't want to be seen to be agreeing with her line of thinking, but I can't help but wonder. Miriam also said something similar, but I find the idea to be so at odds with how Pauline is, it just doesn't seem right. Can you really play-act such devoted love?

Bored with my constant questions, Tamika picks up her phone and tosses her head as if to dismiss me.

'I'll leave you in peace, thanks for the chat,' I say.

I rejoin Diego who's been patiently standing, waiting, not saying a thing, just being a part of the background like a lick of paint. I nod a greeting at him and open the door to the main entrance hall. I need to speak to Pauline. If Patrick did have an allergy, why would she let him eat something that could harm him?

18

BUSINESS AS USUAL

Pauline is folding clothes and packing them into a suitcase when Diego and I arrive at her apartment. I eye her things and wonder how I can bring up the subject of not having any water, it doesn't seem like she's sticking around for this to affect her.

'I know, I'm checking out early,' she says, in reply to my gaze. 'I can't stay here any longer, not now Pat's not here, and certainly *not* with the amount of things I've got to sort back home.'

'Yes, I can understand,' I say, nodding sympathetically.

'Also...,' she begins, but then stops as the words catch in her throat. She swallows loudly, her face pulling inwards, fighting against the impending tears. She wipes her nose. A dribble of watery mucus clings to her scrap of tissue. Her wet, tear-sodden eyes fix on mine. 'I can't bear the thought of him travelling all alone on the airplane tomorrow. I've asked if I can travel with him, but they... they've told me he has to travel in the hold and I can't travel there.' She quickly inhales and exhales and blurts, 'I can't bear the thought of him being there all on his own in a box. All on his own in a box!' The pent-up tears pour down her face into a shuddering sob. 'Pat would hate it. He always wanted me to keep him company, even when he went for a shower! He'd ask me to follow him round like a lapdog. He loved my company, he always loved my company – that's why we did so many things together.' She gazes at me with her heavy tear-filled eyes. 'Today would've been our 16-year wedding anniversary.' She shakes her head, the misery coating every word. 'We did *everything* together, we had so many plans, so many dreams...'

I nod and stare at the floor. I feel so overwhelmed by her emotion I can't believe I'm here suspecting in any way she could be involved in Patrick's death. She clearly adored her husband and is devastated by his passing. Just what am I doing? I'm making a mockery of her grief. I watch as Pauline picks up another dress and starts to fold it away into the suitcase. I want to ask her about Alejandro and all the things Tamika said, but it's so inappropriate. I don't want to insult a bereaved widow. I cower awkwardly, waiting, watching, wondering.

Pauline holds up a petite peach-coloured bikini to show me. 'I bought this just last week to wear on this trip. Pat loved it, wanted me to wear it the same day I got it! He was so cheeky... I told him I was saving it for the sun and he had to wait.' She casts her gaze out of the patio door to the sea where Tamika is lying back sunbathing on the terrace. Pauline turns and stares directly at me. 'Some people don't give a shit about other people, but then what did I expect?'

'Are you talking about Tamika?' I ask.

She shoots a little parp of air through her nose and kicks her jaw like a bad-tempered horse. 'All she wants from Mick is his money, if he didn't have any, he wouldn't get any from her. She's so transparent I don't get why he doesn't see it, but then that's men for you. Jesus, he seems to think she *actually* likes him, wants to be with him! I mean, can you imagine? Men are so stupid. They think young, beautiful women want to be with old, fat, balding men because of *what*? Because they think a young woman couldn't get it anywhere else? Give me a break!'

'Have they been together long?' I pounce into this new conversation with gusto.

'Must've been a few months now. You know he left his wife and two young kids on account of her? Broke up the family good and proper she did. Poor Natalie, she was beside herself. Her and Mick had been together since forever, so when he dumped her for a younger model she went to pieces, poor thing. I mean, can you imagine one day he was there playing happy families, then the next, he's gone, taken everything and hooked up with that!'

I look over to the lithe frame of Tamika lounging on the sunbed. 'That's really tough.' I shake my head in disdain and involuntarily wonder what Natalie, Mick's ex-wife, looked like.

Pauline moves to the window and studies Tamika's form from afar. 'Yeah, nobody saw that coming, that's for sure. Within five minutes of meeting her he'd upped sticks and moved into a hotel with her. But, men and their dicks – what can you say? He's smitten with her, thinks the sun shines out of every hole she's got – doesn't see she's playing him. Pat tried to talk with him, make him see sense, but they just argued. Mick's got this thing right now about how he isn't getting any younger, you only live once blah, blah and he wants to be with her. I guess it's a classic mid-life crisis isn't it?'

'And the wife and kids?'

'They're still at the marital home. You know he hasn't been back since? It's crazy, it's like one day he was living this normal family life and the next he's shacked up in a hotel with a young girl. Like how can you just flip overnight like that and change so dramatically?'

I twist my face in shared confusion.

Pauline's tone softens. 'It did make me think, you know, worry a bit; the suddenness, the quickness of how someone you thought you knew and loved can change so... so quickly. I mean, it just brings it all into question doesn't it? Like how can you trust someone, know someone?' She lowers her tone more. 'Me and Pat, we had times, when things didn't *you know*, and I was worried. I wouldn't want him to leave me for someone else on account of that. So I've always tried to keep myself in shape; I go to the gym, get manicures, I try and look after myself. This growing old lark is no fun, and it's hard on women. Women *age* while men *mature*. And even when you've done all you can, you've still got the risk of a younger model coming onto the scene.'

I'm struck by Pauline's vulnerability, she didn't seem the type who was bothered by competition, but as I look at her well-groomed hair and perfectly manicured nails, I realise it's all a veneer. I want to say something supportive, something that defends the role of ageing women, but all I can muster is, 'Well, that doesn't happen all the time.'

She gives such a derisory and sarcastic smirk that I wince. 'No, maybe not, but men are so easily led. Their dicks rule their life! Mick's a prime example. That girl can tell him anything and he does it. She just has to jiggle her boobs, give him a flash of bum and he's there panting asking how high should he jump. You probably don't know, but before she met him she was working in a local bar, then *bam* she meets Mick and now she's got a new car, new tits, new clothes to wear in them videos she puts online.' Pauline screws her face further and practically hisses with contempt. 'She says it's a 'look behind the scenes at property', but it's practically *porn* with the little clothing she does wear! That's why she's got such a big following. I mean, climbing up ladders with such short skirts on! It's disgusting, it takes women's rights back at least five decades!'

'I had no idea it was *that* sort of channel,' I squeak.

'Yeah, don't go believing the hype, that's the one thing she *is* good at, but check it out, see for yourself. Once Natalie saw it she got down the solicitors so bleeding fast. She's making a beeline for everything Mick's got, she doesn't want her to get anything and I can understand. She's given up the best years of her life to support Mick and the kids. He's in cloud cuckoo land if he reckons he can try and keep 'em all happy. I mean, the financial demands of her alone would outstretch most men, let alone an ex and two kids!'

'But I thought the business was doing well?'

'Yeah, I'm told it is, I don't really get involved, but I know they've been at loggerheads these last few months. Mick's really changed and he's started taking some big risks. Pat was stressing about it coz Mick wasn't thinking through everything. He didn't want to lose everything over a stupid mistake.'

'I can understand, it's difficult when you're working so hard...' I don't really know what to say.

'Thing with Mick, he used to a be good, reliable guy, but now he's got all money-obsessed and he doesn't look at the detail, that's what Pat said. They had a big barney coz Mick forgot to pay the VAT bill and they ended up with a fine last month.'

'So what was the whole deal with the water park?' I ask.

Pauline hesitates, purses her lips and frowns slightly. 'Listen, as I say, I try not to get involved, my role is to be supportive and be positive, but if I'm honest, even I was worried about this. Excited? Yes of course I was. Who wouldn't be when you're talking about making millions from such a mega deal? But it didn't come without risks. Maybe for somebody like Lucas it's all par for the course, but for the boys, it's a different level to what they're used to. If that went wrong we could lose everything, so Pat was worried.'

'I see. So what's happening now? Are Lucas and Mick still going ahead or is it all over?'

She shakes her head and smiles wryly. 'Nothing stops Mick! He's become unstoppable. Even if his supposed best friend and business partner of three decades has died, he still carries on business-as-usual. That's what I say, he's *changed*, he's not *Mick* any more. He's not the guy I used to know, the guy who *used* to care.'

I try and contain the surprised extra octave in my tone. 'What? The deal can still go ahead without Patrick being around?'

'I guess so,' she shrugs. 'I mean it's a business, so I guess the business can still do things even if one of the directors isn't around anymore. To be honest, I don't know the ins and outs, it's not really anything to do with me, it's up to Mick now and what he wants to do.'

'But surely you're still a part of the business?'

She shakes her head. 'I'm nothing to do with the business, it's a separate entity – that's between Mick and Pat, nothing to do with me.'

'You mean Mick would inherit all of the business from Patrick?'

She picks up a thinly-knitted taupe cardigan and stuffs it into her bag. 'I honestly have no idea and don't really care – he can have the lot as far as I'm concerned. My only concern right now is sorting Pat.'

19

THE ALLERGY TEST

'AICHOOO!'

I'd completely forgotten Diego was with me until he sneezed, and I don't think Pauline had noticed him until then either.

'Oh I'm sorry, I didn't see you there. Bless You!' she smiles at Diego. 'Sorry, I've been blathering all this time. Was there something you wanted?'

Diego gives Pauline a polite head nod as if he's a waiter, and Pauline turns back to me.

'He doesn't speak English,' I say, by way of explanation for his silent presence. 'The reason we were coming by is because there seems to be some sort of blockage in the water system and so we're checking with guests...' I trail off as I'm reminded by Diego's sneeze there was a far more important question I wanted to ask. 'But, there was something I meant to ask you about Patrick. Did he have any food allergies? Like dairy?' I try and keep my face normal, but even I know my conversational topic-switch is way weird.

Pauline doesn't seem to notice and blithely says, 'No, he was fine with dairy, it was cinnamon he was allergic to.'

'Cinnamon?' I repeat.

'I know, weird isn't it?' She grins at me as if she's sharing a joke. 'We had no idea either, but apparently these allergies can develop later in life, that's what Carol told us.'

'Who's Carol?' I ask, unsure if I'm meant to know her.

'Carol's the allergy testing lady who told us Patrick was allergic to cinnamon. She's got one of those mobile stands, like a pop-up. She was running a buy-one-get-one-free promotion and it seemed a good idea. You read so much about how people are allergic to things.'

'So what happened?'

'Well, it turned out I was allergic to some grasses and pollen, which I already thought, and then she said Pat had an allergy to spices. She did say it was rare and we'd have to do other tests for a proper diagnosis, but she suspected it'd be cinnamon coz apparently that's well known for causing allergic reactions.'

'So how bad was Patrick's allergy?'

'Well, it turned out Carol wasn't really set up for more serious things and told us we needed to get referred to a specialist by a doctor.'

'OK, so what did the doctor say?'

Pauline pinches her face. 'I tried to get an appointment sorted, but Pat wasn't a doctor's man. He had like a phobia when it came to seeing doctors or dentists, you know medical people. He reckoned you got more ill from the germs in the waiting room than what you went in for. He told me he'd avoid cinnamon and that was that. I tried to push it, but he could be such a stubborn mule.'

'So you never got it checked out?'

'No, we just cut cinnamon and some other spices out of our life. It wasn't too hard, although I did miss our weekly Indians. At the time it didn't seem worth the aggro.' Pauline turns away and looks about the room, checking for any forgotten items. 'I may as well give you the key now, and then I don't have to worry about trying to find you later.'

'You're checking out now?' I ask.

'I can't stay here, there's too many memories. Plus, we don't even have water, so I can't have a shower or wash my hair. I'll go to The Bay hotel and sit there for a bit before I head to the airport.'

'But you can't leave...' I blurt.

She looks at me sharply. 'Why ever not? The bill's been paid and I've given you my key.'

'Because, because...,' I clutch at words anxiously, 'because, I don't trust Tamika.'

Pauline half-snorts and laughs. 'That horse bolted a long time ago! Of course you shouldn't trust her, she's a gold-digger.'

'But I, but I...' I fumble around for words. I feel desperate. I don't want her to leave, but how can I make her stay? I know she seems like the devastated wife, but how do I *really* know she's not involved? 'And I'm worried about Mick,' I say, shaking my head frantically. 'I don't think he's coping well. He's putting on this show of everything being OK, but you know what men are like – they pretend everything's OK when inside they're falling apart.'

'Mick's big enough and ugly enough to look after himself, and anyway he's got his resident slapper here, he doesn't need me.'

'But what about this deal with Lucas? The trouble he may be getting into?' I'm grabbing at anything.

'That's his call, it's up to him what he does, it's nothing to do with me.' Pauline folds her arms and stares at me directly. 'Tarah, I know you're trying to help, but I'm leaving. Being here is very stressful for me and I hope you can understand. Please let me finish my packing so I can get out of here.'

I look at her tensed face. Within 24 hours she's aged by ten years. Faint wrinkle lines have become deep grooves, and despite her sun-kissed skin, a grey pallor shines out. I realise I've overstepped the mark. 'Of course, I'm so sorry. I just... I'm trying to do the right thing.'

She nods and gestures to the door.

Outside of the apartment and out of earshot I call Jorge and fill him in with everything I've learned so far. He says I'm doing a good job and we should continue to talk to more guests to find out more things. I feel a bit spun out by Pauline leaving, but Jorge tells me he'll pop by and offer her a lift and that way we can keep tabs. I'm not really sure how we're keeping tabs, but I agree with him anyway.

20

BIGGER FISH TO FRY?

There's no answer at Apartment 4, Mick and Tamika's holiday rental, but I already know that; Tamika's outside on the terrace drinking, and Mick's out at lunch with Lucas. Still, something tells me I should go in and look for some sort of clue. I don't know what, but I feel a need to see.

I unlock the door and let myself in. Diego trots after me like a weaning puppy. It's so odd to have a silent shadow following me about, but I've got used to it by telling myself he's my secret security guard. That gives me a funny thrill, like I'm important or something. I place Mr Bob's carrier on the kitchen worktop surface. He's been very quiet the last hour and I peer in to check he's OK. He gazes back at me and gives me a quick blink. I think he's soaking it all in, like a little rodent sponge.

I stand scanning the room; it's spotless, immaculate even. I pause – have they really unpacked all the ginormous bags they brought with them? I want to start opening the drawers and cupboards, but my arms are glued to my side. My mum didn't bring me up to be prying about in other people's things. If she knew I'd let myself into a guest's empty apartment to snoop, she'd go ape. I pull my bottom lip in concentration and can feel Diego waiting for me to do something, anything.

I walk into the bedroom and am relieved to see the bed made, cushions plumped, the turquoise throw adorning the bottom of the bed, like in an interior homes ad. Seeing the stripped bed in Pauline's apartment reminded me of the thin line we traipse between life and death, how one minute we're here and the next gone. My heart flips. What am I doing? Why am I standing in this bedroom? My breath hurts in my chest and I feel a desperate need for air. I slide open the glass doors onto the balcony and lean on the ledge, my head pulsating. Diego stands next to me, reaches out his hand and touches my arm. He's asking me if I'm OK. I don't know all the words he's stringing together but I can tell from his worried expression that's what he means. I give him the thumbs up and say I need a minute and gesture towards the sky to say I want fresh air.

My mind is on overdrive. The lack of sleep and too much craziness is driving me insane. Just what the hell am I doing? Why am I even doing this? Why am I seriously trying to interview people, pretending I'm doing what, for what? Patrick died in his sleep next to his loving wife and his body is being flown home. People die. These things happen. Yes, OK, so Mr Bob seems to be acting weird when we say Patrick's name and Jorge hasn't had this happen before, but really after all these years he's chancing his odds if he thinks something like this will *never* happen when people come on holiday. Life, and death, do happen, that's the way things are. I need to call him. I need to tell him not to follow Pauline, she's a widow in pain. Are we really going to chase her around Corralejo because we think she's topped her husband? What kind of madcap vacation place are we? What sort of reviews are we going to get for behaving like demented *Poirot* wannabes? No, I've got to be the sensible one now, Jorge has lost it. He's obviously acting out some kind of weird murder mystery thing because he's having a mid-life crisis. That's it.

A noise in the bedroom makes me spin on my heels. Diego is at the patio doors before me and he's shouting loudly in Spanish at somebody. I join him at the threshold of the bedroom and see Lucas swiftly closing a drawer.

'Can I help you?' I say.

'I don't know why I'm being shouted at.' Lucas shoots Diego a dirty look and smooths the lapels on his expensive looking burgundy suit.

'Why are you in this apartment?' I ask.

'Mick asked me to come and get something for him,' he eyes me suspiciously. 'What are you and this man doing here? Don't you need your guests' permission before you enter their apartments?'

My skins crawls at his accusation, he's totally right, but I'm not letting on. 'It's an emergency situation,' I reply, 'we don't have water and we're checking to see if there're any blockages. Diego here is a plumber.'

Lucas casts his critical eyes over the pair of us and I can feel my hair receding from his gaze.

'Is there anything else I can help you with?' I ask, keen to break the death stare.

'No, I have what I need,' Lucas turns to leave.

I don't want to engage the man in any more conversation but I steel myself and say, 'Sorry to be a pain, but I needed to speak with Mick, can you let me know where he is?'

'Now's not a good time,' he says, his tone flat.

'Sorry,' I say, injecting a heap of begging into my voice, 'but it is urgent, it won't take long.'

He fixes me with a long glare. 'You'll find him at Los Amigos, tell him to call me when you're done.' His manicured fingers preen his suit again and he stalks out of the apartment clacking his expensive-soled shoes on the ceramic tiles. The door slams and the entire building winces in pain.

Diego turns to me and speaks rapidly in hushed tones. I'm not sure I'm following what he's telling me, but I think he's saying Lucas has stolen a pair of Tamika's knickers (red) and stuffed them into his pocket. I stare at him confused, unsure how to reply. Why the hell would Lucas do that?

Mick's sat under a faded ice-cream branded umbrella shading himself from the sun. His feet are bare, toes dug into the sand, drinking beer from a chunky glass tankard while reading some printed documents. He looks up as I approach, smiles warmly in greeting.

'Hi Tarah, how are you?' He puts down his documents and waits for me to reply.

I twist my lips and share I'm a bit stressed about the water blockage, then quickly switch the conversation back to him. 'Enough about my hassles, how are you? Looks like you've got yourself a lovely spot here.' I glance at the cresting blue-green waves on the sun-drenched gold of the beach.

'Ah! What's not to love? Look at this place! Here I am sat in the sun, drinking a beer, feet in the sand – don't think I've ever had a business meeting like it!'

'Oh, so you're having a business meeting?' I ask, keen to keep my tone light but inquiring.

'Yeah, I'm meeting Lucas here. I'm just genning up on some details beforehand.' He picks up the documents from the table and flaps them in my direction. 'There's loads of things to get to grips with when you're developing in another country, not as easy as back home. Luckily, Lucas knows most of what to do – he's a right successful guy.'

He may not have meant it, but Mick gives out an aura of inferiority. Maybe it's the tiny maternal bone in me, but I want to gee him up. 'Now, a little birdie told me you're a pretty shit-hot developer in the UK?' I smile encouragingly, hoping my praise is complimentary rather than patronising.

It works. He looks up at me shyly and bats his short, mousey eyelashes, in what I suspect is meant to be a flirtatious move, but looks more like he has something stuck in his eye. 'Yeah, things have been good, but it's time to step up. This water park project is a different league, like *big time stuff*. Get this right and it'd be like a lottery win!' He inhales noisily through his nose and joggles his head.

'Wow! That big? Really?' I wince at my overdone excitement, but Mick doesn't notice. He's peacocking proudly.

'Seriously, I don't wanna brag, but this sorta deal is mega – it's like the stuff of dreams! That's why I gotta keep going.' He looks at me, tears filling his eyes. 'Patrick would've wanted me to do this. If I quit now, when we're so close, it'd be shameful. Anyway, the best way to honour his memory is to have a slide named after him – I'm gonna call it the 'Petrifying Patrick''. He laughs at his own joke and looks lost in memory. 'He would've liked that, would've made him smile, God bless his soul.'

'That's such a lovely gesture,' I say soothingly. 'He was a bit worried about this project, wasn't he?'

'Worried?' Mick huffs. 'He was always bloody worried about everything; he was one of *them* people. If he didn't have anything to worry about, he wouldn't be able to function. Worrying to him was as natural as breathing is to you and me. That's why I was so surprised he got into that crazy venture with Kris and his karaoke thing.'

I feel my eyebrows shoot up and instantly try and maintain a poker face. 'What was the deal with Kris?'

'That guy, you probably know him, runs the karaoke gigs at The Ship?' I nod a little to show I understand who he's talking about. 'He said he needed some new digital equipment, told Patrick if he got some new stuff he could do more gigs, get more clients, roll it out and make a killing. Sold it like an investment opportunity, though I dunno how Patrick thought he was gonna get his money back, sounded a bit of a con to me.'

'So what happened?'

'I talked Patrick out of it.' Mick screws up his face as though he's just smelt a bad fart. 'That Kris is a washed-up drunk. And why's Patrick gonna spend so much time trying to make pennies with bloody singing machines when he's got the opportunity of a lifetime and millions with me? Patrick had bigger fish to fry – that's what I told him.'

I nod as I listen, but I feel bad. I like Kris, but can see Mick's point, even if he's being a bit overbearing.

'Anyway,' Mick's still talking, 'everything would've been fine, but the bloody fool bought all the fancy gear before Patrick had sealed the deal. When Patrick told Kris, he went ape, said he wasn't able to pay the loan back, said he was gonna lose his home yada yada.'

'Oh, so did it get a bit heated?'

'You could say that. I may've stepped in and said a few choice words – like to bring home reality. That Kris likes a drink and he's got a bit of a temper. It's not Patrick's fault if his life's shit. You gotta take some responsibility for your decisions!'

'Hmmm,' I reply noncommittally.

'Anyway, I reminded Patrick about priorities and the big business we're here to do.' Mick puffs up his chest and twitches his biceps as if readying for a strongman competition.

I feign a slight expression of awe at his overflowing display of masculinity. 'Of course, and I've already taken up enough of your time, so I better let you get on.' I twist on my heels about to leave and then turn. 'Oh, one other question I wanted to ask Mick, do you know if Patrick had any allergies?'

'Yeah, I think he did,' he squeezes his lips in thought. 'It was some sort of spice, an exotic one, maybe cinnamon I think. It was the one where loadsa people were filming themselves trying to eat it and coughing up their guts. I remember Tamika did a video, crazy challenge it was.'

I thank him for his time and wish him a successful business meeting. I walk back along the shoreline pondering how many other people knew about Patrick's allergy and did this have something to do with his untimely death?

21

A MAD DASH

Back in signal range my phone buzzes rapidly with a load of notifications. I check the screen and see a mass of cancellations of upcoming reservations. My hand shakes as I press on each message informing me of a guest pulling out of staying at Jorge's Place. I stare at my mobile. What on earth is going on? Something's wrong, something's very wrong.

I motion to Diego I'm going to the office. I need a bigger screen to see what's happening. Turning on my laptop I see a bunch of people have cancelled their upcoming stays, but there's no reason, just a notification from the sites. I curse, that's the issue with these websites – they're brilliant for advertising and getting your name known – but customers can cancel at the drop of a hat. The site still takes its 'admin fee' from them, but we as the business get nothing.

I click through to the sites to see if I can get any extra information from the messages. There's nothing, no details or anything as to why so many people are now withdrawing. I open the latest news website. Has something happened in the world I don't know about? Has there been a bomb, a major currency crisis or an airline gone bust that could explain this rush of behaviour? Scrolling through I can't see anything out of the ordinary. The world's still in a mess and so people should still want to come on holiday to escape.

I open the sites again to check our listings, maybe a link has broken or we've been hacked or something? Managing multiple tabs on the screen I check through the photos: Jorge's Place still looks stunning. Whitewashed apartments, glittering turquoise sea in the background, big, blue skies, golden sandy beaches. No random pictures or links that could put people off. I read through the descriptions, my eyes scanning for anything that could possibly deter people. I purse my lips, everything was as it was.

Then I notice a flashing icon in the top right hand corner, we've got some new reviews. I scroll down, open them and gasp at the latest.

** AVOID IF YOU DON'T WANT TO DIE**

Jorge's Place is under investigation for the death of a guest. If you want a holiday and not a funeral, stay somewhere else!!!!! This place is not safe

What the heck? Who the hell has written this? I read the username: Jonesy_1978. I check the guest book; nobody has got any name similar to that. I scan my white board to see who's checked out in the last day – maybe it was a disgruntled guest? My eyes scan the names looking for clues. Only Ethel and Brian have checked out recently, and they were in their seventies and didn't have a clue how to work the internet, let alone leave a bad review. Plus, they didn't even know anything about Patrick.

I suck in my breath. Fact is, nobody outside his inner circle really knows anything about Patrick. We'd been pretty good at keeping his death under wraps, not that we had anything to hide, but we didn't want to cause any unnecessary upset or anxiety to our other guests. Unless they knew him, we didn't feel it was compulsory to make an announcement. Need to know basis was how we'd played it.

I sit and stare at the screen. Was that the right thing to do? Did it look suspicious we didn't make it public knowledge? What do other places do? What about big hotels? Do they make announcements if a guest dies?

I try calling Jorge. It rings and rings and goes to voicemail.

Who else might know about Patrick? I drum my fingers and crunch on my pen anxiously. The plastic weeps with my saliva and within moments I've chewed the blue lid into a misshapen mould of my teeth. Mr Bob stares at me, his face screwing with irritation at my incessant nibbling. I eyeball him back – he's such a hypocrite – he keeps me awake many a night chewing and chatting. Diego remains an ever-faithful discreet presence, playing quietly with his phone (volume off) while waiting for me.

I look at the review again my blood boiling. Shit, no wonder so many people are now cancelling. But this is so unfair, we can't be held responsible for the death of a guest. It wasn't our fault. We didn't cause it, we weren't negligent. I stare at the screen searching for answers. I don't get it, it was so early in the morning when the ambulance came and nobody was even up by the time they left, so I'm not sure who would've seen anything. Most people were asleep. And anyway, with the exception of Miriam, nobody's asked me about Patrick's death. It's not like I'm trying to keep a secret or hide anything.

A gnawed piece of plastic catches on the side of my cheek mid-chew. I poke my tongue on the rough spot trying to sooth the scratch. Unless I've missed something? Unless there was something we *could've* done? Something we *should've* done. Was Patrick's death somehow avoidable or preventable? Was there something somebody knew that I didn't and we *could've* done something? I resume my manic chomping, my mind going over all the events from that night and the morning when Pauline called me. Was there something we'd overlooked; a really important detail we'd forgotten?

I really need to talk to Jorge. I call again and let it ring out. Still no answer.

I don't know what the right thing to do is, but I know I need to take action to protect us against this review. We're not on trial for this and apart from Jorge and me (and Mr Bob), nobody's even treating Patrick's death as suspicious.

Deciding to take action into my own hands I file a complaint against the review with the holiday websites. I don't know who's behind it, but I want to stop this. I'm sure this has got to be slander or libel or something illegal. You can't go shooting off your mouth like that when things aren't true. These 30-odd words have already cost us thousands of pounds in lost bookings - who knows how many more people may see them and choose not to book. I start to complete the online form and link to the comment. Then I read the report I'm writing and pause. Was it untrue? Was the feedback incorrect? We did have a guest death; does that mean what they're saying is true? Can I argue against this person? My hands slither away from the keyboard. What can I actually say?

I copy and paste the contents of my form into another document and stare at the words. Perhaps I better talk to Jorge first, I don't want to do the wrong thing and cause any reputational damage – even if right now we're being hammered unfairly and blamed for a death that wasn't our fault. I better tread carefully.

Shutting down the computer I decide to head off and find Kris. He never said anything to me about the investment Patrick was going to make in his karaoke business, or the argument they had. And I mean, well, suspicious minds and all that. I want to know his side of the story.

Crossing the sun-filled courtyard, I'm surprised to see an orange tuft lying on the floor the other side of the complex gate. Suddenly I feel Mr Bob jumping up and down in his carrier, wheeking wildly. I look in at him and his face is full of terror.

'It's OK little one, don't worry about those nasty cats, I'll look after you. Nobody can get in to hurt you,' I coo soothingly. I know how much the local cats scare him. At five times his size, he's potential prey – or a plaything – and he wants to be neither. But Mr Bob is not to be comforted.

'WHEEEEEEEEEEEEEEEEEEEK!
WHEEEEEEEEEEEEEEEEEEEEEEK!'

Diego looks at me questioningly while Mr Bob continues to jumps up and down, his screams getting louder and louder. I point out the orange tuft to Diego and his eyes follow my finger. His body jolts into action and he swerves off to investigate. Meanwhile, I try and calm Mr Bob. I feel like an overly-anxious mother as I tell him how Diego will scare away the naughty cat and everything will be fine.

Except it isn't a cat.

I look over to where Diego's gone and see he's on his

knees cradling the orange tuft of hair attached to Miriam's head. I rush over and lift her arm, my hands trembling as I try and feel for a pulse in her weak wrist. I struggle to count the beats; my own heart is thudding too much. Her head is nestled between Diego's arm and knee, his shoulder hunched on his mobile as he talks rapidly to the operator telling them he needs an ambulance.

'Miriam, Miriam, can you hear me?' I stroke her arm, her skin thin and crepe-like to my touch.

I take some water from the bottle in my bag, pour it on my fingertips and gently wipe it on her forehead. She's sticky with hot sweat; her usually perfectly made-up skin is congealing in the concoction of pale powder, perspiration and cold water. Her lips look tacky and dry.

'Miriam, Miriam, it's Tarah here...' I coo.

Her face twitches a little, her closed eyelids flickering. I continue to stroke her arm and cool her temples. Her eyes bright and blue open and focus on me.

'Oh Miriam, Miriam, are you OK? Can you hear me?'

'Oh, my dear,' she starts, her voice frail and feeble. 'I was wanting to... I was wanting to...' the exertion of trying to talk is too much, her eyes tremble shut.

Diego motions at me to try and lift her upper torso into a sitting position. Gingerly we try and manoeuvre her upwards, careful of her delicate frame. Despite her slight appearance, her body has taken on the weight of dense concrete. Diego shifts me out the way, carefully puts his two muscular arms under her armpits and hauls her to sitting. She flops forward, I wince at her jelly-like spine. Diego heaves her back and holds her against his strong thigh. I try and encourage her to drink some water. But she's not responsive.

Diego signals to hold her while he fumbles in his pocket and dangles his car keys in front of me.

'But I thought an ambulance was coming?' I ask, my hands holding tight on her bony shoulders.

He shakes his head, gestures to Miriam and his watch, and gabbles in Spanish. I think he's saying the ambulance will take too long and we'll drive her to the hospital. He starts to stand and engineers a switch so I can take over from his holding place. He says he'll be back in two minutes. I focus my body-weight, centring myself so I can keep Miriam erect. The noise of jolty wheels fills the courtyard; Diego is pushing a wheel barrow in our direction. I look from Diego to Miriam to the wheelbarrow.

'No, we can't do that!' I shriek.

He shrugs and grabs the blanket off the top of Mr Bob's carrier and puts it in the wheelbarrow. It's barely any cushioning for her frail bones. Motioning for him to take my place holding her upright, I run to the office and grab the cushions off the small two-seater sofa and the hand towel from the toilet. I line the metal interior of the wheelbarrow with the eclectic armful of soft furnishings.

'Miriam, we're going to take you to hospital,' I explain. 'But, we've got to get you to the car, so we need to put you in the wheelbarrow so we can move you. OK?' Her eyes are closed, but I'm sure I see a gentle nod of her head. We don't have time to waste. 'It's just to the car Miriam, won't be long. Diego's about to lift you. Ready? One. Two. Three.'

Within a flash, Diego's hauled her up like a ragdoll and dragged her inanimate form, disgracefully, and most unladylike, into the colourful padded wheelbarrow. She doesn't fit whatsoever. Her head is dangerously crooked, hanging down as though every vertebra in her back has broken. Quickly, I plump the support behind her and try and straighten her head. Her legs dangle at awkward angles from the lip of the barrow. Oh My God, if she could see herself now she'd die of embarrassment. I try and re-arrange her poking-out hanging-off bits, but Diego shoos me away, pointing to the car parked only meters away.

I wince as the wheelbarrow smacks into every hard round stone of the cobbles and Miriam's body is thrown convulsively around its tinny interior. Diego's navy blue estate car is parked just outside the gates. He clicks the remote button to unlock and I open the rear doors. I can barely watch as he manhandles Miriam across the back seats, propping up her head with the lining from the wheelbarrow. I want to sit next to her, but there's no room, so I opt for the passenger seat and twist myself gawkily so I can hold her hand and narrate what we're doing.

'Miriam, we're going to hospital, you're in Diego's car. We'll be there soon and everything will be all right.'

I cross my fingers and say a little prayer to any God who's listening.

22

TEMPERS ARE RISING

The hospital is stark, white and clinical. The cool interior is a blessed relief from the hot sunshine outside. Diego grabs a nurse and explains about Miriam in the back of his car. Within moments a team of strong men and a trolley are being dragged to the rear doors. The men exchange curious glances as they pick amongst the ragtag of kaleidoscopic textiles stuffed in to make Miriam's journey more comfortable.

Miriam is still barely responsive, although a quick double-take reveals what I'm sure was a gleam of a grin, at the tanned, ripped muscles gently moving her delicate features from the car to the gurney.

A voice from inside the waiting room surprises me. 'Tarah, what are you doing here?' I spin on my heels. Jorge is standing, staring at me, clutching his arm.

'What am *I* doing here? What are *you* doing here?' I say, checking out his arm.

At that moment, the nurses bustle pass, wheeling Miriam, her lifeless form atop the blue plastic trolley. Jorge's mouth flaps open but he says nothing. He turns to me wide-eyed with questions.

'We think she must've fallen in the courtyard, that's where we found her.'

Jorge nods and quickly chases after the nurses, talking and walking as they guide Miriam's gurney down the corridor. He rejoins me a few minutes later, patting his forehead with a tissue.

'They think probably is heatstroke, but the doctor will check. She is old so best to be safe.' He says.

I exhale a little sigh of relief, I know heatstroke's not good, but it's not as bad as what I was thinking. With some hydrating fluids and bed rest Miriam will be on the mend in no time. I stretch out my neck and rotate my shoulders, trying to ease out some of the built-up stress. As I'm doing so I notice Jorge is still clutching his arm and ask him what happened.

'Something flew into the road, I turned to avoid it and went into a speed sign! The problem is I cannot move my arm; the doctor think is broken. I wait now for x-ray and maybe the cast.' He makes a sad face at me.

'Oh no, that's terrible! So where's your car now?

'Still at the sign! Luckily another driver he saw me and stopped to check if I'm OK and brought me here. And then when I'm here and I go to call my wife I realise I forgot my mobile in the car.' He gives me a pained look and I'm unsure if that's due to having forgotten his mobile or having to tell his wife about the car.

'Ah, that explains why you weren't answering,' I say.

He turns to me, a new worry crease forming on his forehead. 'Is there a problem?'

I hesitate. Is this really the time to be telling Jorge about the review? He's already in pain from his own car accident and anxious about the health of an elderly guest. Does he really need more to be stressing about? His dark brown eyes search mine, the copper flecks of his irises shine brightly in the reflection of the fluorescent light. I decide he has a right to know and tell him. His tanned face sets hard and a deep reddening glow spreads across his features. I can see his anger bubbling, ready to explode as I tell him how I was going to lodge a complaint and then didn't because I wasn't sure on the grounds of my complaint, what with it being the truth that a guest *had* died. 'The thing is,' I say, finishing off, 'do you think there's anything we missed about Patrick's death?'

Perhaps it wasn't the right thing to say. Or perhaps it wasn't the right moment. Or maybe it was the way in which I said it, but Jorge leaned into me and hissed his reply which was something along the lines of me not doing my job properly, how he's put all his trust into me and how I'd let him down and I was destroying his business. I don't know exactly, the words rush up to me and I struggle to take them in. His lips are thin and angry and flecks of saliva are pipping onto me. I stare at him trying to understand how I'm being blamed for something I've been trying to fix.

Unsure how to react, I leave. Perhaps I shouldn't have, but I want to get away. I don't trust myself and what may come out of my mouth. I need time to think. I need time to try and take in Jorge's attitude and work out what I'm doing. My eyes search around looking for the toilets. My feet clatter loudly on the tiled flooring, echoing thuds of annoyance. Pushing open the door it swings violently against the wall and bounces back at me, almost hitting me squarely in the face. I dodge the force and duck into the small room fitted out with two toilet cubicles and two sinks. Luckily there's nobody else around. I breathe in the heavy, cloying scent of bleach and chemical cleaning agents.

I don't need the toilet, but out of habit I find myself squatting trying to pee. A tiny trickle bursts into life and wets the inside of my thigh. Tutting in anger I grab a handful of paper from the dispenser and swear angrily under my breath. *What the fuck has happened to you when you can't even piss straight in a toilet bowl?*

I pump the soap dispenser and take comfort from the soothing action of the suds as I foam the liquid in my hands. Remembering the germs in a hospital, I wash my hands again and very deliberately take my time scraping under my nails and scrubbing my knuckles for any ingrained bacteria. Pulling the green paper towels from the holder I watch the water soak deep, dark patterns into its dryness - anything to occupy my mind.

I turn my back to the mirror and lean against the sink. I don't want to think anymore. My head is sick of thinking. I came here to escape stress and now I've got more stress than I've ever had in my life. This whole situation is crazy.

My phone buzzes a reminder. It's 3pm. I'm meant to be meeting Hans about some work. I text him to apologise, say something's come up and I'll be in touch. I turn and look at myself in the mirror. My face looks strained and tired. I tug on the loose creases of my cheeks and try and smooth out the lines. *Where's the carefree girl who used to greet me in my reflection?* I peer closer, my bluey-grey eyes clouding with the hyper-proximity. My pupils are little pinpricks, blacks dots in the mirror. I can feel my childhood stigmatism kick-in, my gaze collides and crosses and I step back disorientated.

I feel like I'm back at primary school. I can see myself at

the little wooden desk in the classroom. Miss Bettsworth is at the front writing with chalk. I'm trying to read the board, but the words are just lines. The letters swim and merge into indecipherable symbols. I squeeze my eyes hard, trying to eke out some sort of vision, some semblance of sight. Miss Bettworth's mouth is moving, opening and closing like a feeding shark. I can't hear what she's saying, I'm too focused on trying to read the letters, the words, the sentence on the board. I mentally push my eyeballs forward, as if getting them closer I'd be able to see.

'Tarah, what are you doing?'

Miss Bettsworth is talking to me. She sounds angry, annoyed. I shrink into my small, wooden chair. The seat is hard; the solidity has no give against my six-year old bottom. I want to tell her I'm trying to see what she's writing. I open my mouth to tell her I can't see, but then I notice every head has turned to look at me. I feel hot. Really, very hot. I don't want everybody to know I can't see. I don't want to be different. I want people to like me.

Her stride is strong and powerful. Her steps vibrate and echo on the beige plastic floor. She stands over me, her stature towering. I want to melt into the wood, to be a splinter in the chair, or a knot, or a stain. Anything but here and being me. She's talking to me now. Her voice booming and accusing. She wants to know why I'm not doing the work. Why I haven't copied down the words from the board. My eyes well up. I want to tell her I would if I could, but I can't. I clutch my tummy. Tell her I don't feel well. She huffs and glares. I hold my breath. I think I may be sick. Everybody's staring. She tells me to go to the school nurse. I pack up my pencil case, take my bag and scamper from the room.

I pick up my coat hanging in the cloakroom and don't go

to the nurse in the main school building. I get to the gates and I turn right. And I run. I run all the way home. My mum looks up from watching television as I knock on the window. I tell her I'm sick, my eyes don't work and I'm scared. She puts me in the car and she drives us into town. We go into a brightly lit store and a nice lady with big, brown, shiny hair tells me I'm going to have some special power glasses. I don't understand what she means until she places some glass discs on a giant frame which doesn't really fit on my nose. She asks me what I can and can't see. Some letters are fuzzy, some are OK and I tell her this. Afterwards, she talks with my mum and they choose me a pair of pink plastic glasses. The lady tells me I need to wear them every day. My mum calls the school and shouts very loudly.

'Stand up for yourself'. I can hear my mum's voice urging me on. She of the steel-coated skin variety. I've never been very good at confrontation. I don't like upsetting people. I don't like people not liking me. I'm such a coward when it comes to arguments. I study my reflection. *Aren't you old enough to know better?* I wish I could be stronger. I wish I didn't care what people think. *You don't, that's why you came here.* The internal voice pricks and pinches my frontal lobe. *I can do this.* Jorge's being a knob because he's frightened. He didn't mean to blame me, he's just lashing out in fear, frustration, fucked-off-ness.

I take a deep breath and pat my face with some damp tissues. I don't have time for mucking about and being angry at myself. I need to be able to sleep at night and the only way I can do that is by getting to the bottom of what happened to Patrick.

23

A DITCHED DEAL

We drive to The Ship in silence. I could tell Diego was torn between whether he should've stayed with his boss at the hospital or come with me, but Jorge shrugged amiably enough when I asked Diego for us to leave. Jorge and I now seem to have some sort of uneasiness going on that neither of us has spoken about; I'm annoyed with him and he's annoyed with me. Well, sod him, maybe I could've done things differently, but I didn't. We are where we are and that's it.

A few hardened drinkers, fag in hand (no smoking ban here), glass in the other, are dotted about The Ship. In the mid-afternoon, when the sun is at its strongest, most normal people would be sat in the shade, but not these lot. These seasoned pros bask in the rays putting their two-fingers up to skin cancer. Their skin is ragged, ravaged by years of smoking, drinking and too much ultra-violet light. I smile at the regulars, many of whom I know by sight, even if not to talk to.

They prop up the bar most nights with their saggy skin and alcohol-soaked limbs until they tumble back home to sleep and start all over again the next day. Leathery and lethargic, these are the lushes that keep bars like The Ship in business.

Kris is at the back of the bar, eyes watery and red-rimmed from another long night and day on the lash. I wave to him in greeting and join him next to where he's trying to plug a cable into a speaker.

'Hey Kris!' I say with a forced happiness I don't feel but manage to paint onto my face.

'Ah, Tarah, you missed a good craic here last night. You should've stayed. We got so many of 'em up on stage I didn't have enough microphones!' He laughs and coughs smoky phlegm at the same time, his grin widening and splitting his face.

'Business better now then?' I ask, lightly trying to steer the conversation.

His face clouds. 'Well, it *could've* been better, if it hadn't been for having this crappy equipment.' His face screws up as he looks over at the dated console.

'I'm not sure I'm up to speed?' I lie, searching his face, waiting for him to share more.

'I didn't want to say anything before, y'know I don't want to talk ill of the dead.' Kris takes a large glug of his beer and looks at me directly. 'But Patrick deciding not to invest at the last minute really fucked me over, scuse my language.'

I don't say anything, but murmur and nod empathetically waiting for him to share more.

Kris spreads his arms out wide to showcase the equipment as though he's a karaoke salesman. 'He was meant to be my business investor; I was going to take this big time.' He turns to look at me. 'Not with this shitty stuff, obviously. No, with the digital stuff. I was gonna franchise the model, train people, get karaoke all over the island! That was the plan.' The sparkle in his eyes dies and they droop like a basset hound. He gulps another large mouthful of beer and lights a cigarette. 'He was gonna invest fifteen k, meant I could buy the equipment, get people lined up. I was stupid, I believed him when he said he'd come good, told me he'd had enough of the stress of all them risky property deals.'

'So what happened?'

'I reckon it was his business partner got to him. He's a loud-mouthed beast. Come in here all effing and blinding and telling me how I was a drunk waster. I mean, can you believe it? He got all uppity. Patrick at least, had the decency to look a bit sheepish. Anyway, he said the deal's off and that was that. They left.'

'Oh, that's such a shame,' I say.

'More than that love, I'd already bought all the gear!' Kris cranes his eyebrows and slaps the bar. 'Patrick told me he'd bring the money out this time and then just like that, he's not! I said to him 'Mate, I only did this coz you said you were investing'. Told him I was crippled by the payments, that I couldn't make my rent and was now homeless coz of the bloody stuff. But he wouldn't listen.'

'Shit, that's so shit.'

'You can say that again – I've lost the lot now.' Kris hangs his head dejected, the top fluff of his dyed yellow-gold hair almost touching the bar. 'I weren't able to return the stuff so I had to flog it at less than half what I paid, and I *still* got a ton more payments to make. Broke my heart it did.' His eyes tear up a little. 'It could've been something so big... Anyway, I guess Patrick thought this water park lark was a big thing.

Just goes to show eh? None of it really matters in the end, not really.'

'No, I guess not.' I nod sadly in agreement and ponder if I should let slip Mick's still in on the deal. 'Sounded like it was going to be a game changer?' I say, testing the water.

'The water park? Maybe... but who knows if they'd ever have got their money outta the deal. It needed a stonking investment and that Lucas, let's just say I wouldn't trust him to look after my pint.' He cackles a smoker's cackle and slurps at his beer. 'I was always surprised how he ended up doing a deal with a couple of brickies from England, seemed an unlikely pairing to me. I mean, how did they even meet? They don't strike me as people who move in the same circles.'

'Apparently it was Tamika, Mick's girlfriend, who made the introduction to Lucas.' I clamp my mouth shut. I can't believe I let that slip.

He doesn't flinch, treats this new information as normal. 'Yeah, makes sense, she seems to be the sort to move in the sorta worlds he would.'

'But, I don't think she's got any money,' I say, teasing him for information.

'She doesn't need to, not looking like that.' Kris smirks and then sensing the disapproving look on my face, says, 'I'm sorry to say it love, but men, well: men are men. They love with their eyes and think about anything else later.'

As if on cue, a leggy brunette wearing only a bright pink bikini top and cut-off faded jean shorts sashays past the bar. All eyes follow her and her backside as she parades along the street, well aware of the attention, but deviously coy enough to hide it behind over-sized sunglasses. Keen to switch the subject back and acutely aware of the ticking clock, I tap the bar to get Kris' attention and barrel on.

'So with all this karaoke business and Patrick's broken promises, it sounds like he left you in a bad place, a place where maybe you might not think about what you're doing... you know things can escalate.' I can feel myself redden. I can't believe I'm taking this line of questioning. I want to try and backtrack, but it's too late, I've blurted it out and the intent of my meaning is...

'You accusing me of murdering him?' Kris looks at me, his face full of (to be expected) astonishment.

'I'm just saying... you said yourself the other night it seemed a bad business.' I honestly cannot believe how off-the-shelf I'm taking this and I have to grip the underside of the bar so I don't fall off the stool.

He stares at me like I've got a mushroom growing from my forehead and pushes himself back from the bar so I can see him more fully. 'When I said that I wasn't meaning *me*!' What would I have to gain with Patrick being dead – he's no bloody use to me now is he? I was meaning this lark with the water park! Ain't it weird he comes here, ditches me, meets Mr Fancypants and is dead the next day? That's what I was getting at!'

At this, Mr Bob pipes up with a high pitched squeal. Kris looks across at Mr Bob's furry face pressed against the wire meshing. He nods at Mr Bob and looks back at me. 'He knows, he does. Just listen to your hamster and he'll tell you what's what.'

I take a deep breath and stop myself from reminding him Mr Bob is not a hamster. No point getting petty now, even if it does wind me up that he does it every bloody time. I need to move on. I draw my knees up ready to make the drop to the ground. 'By the way,' I say, 'did you know Patrick was allergic to cinnamon.'

Kris pauses before he answers. 'I dunno if this is a trick question, but yeah I do know that. And the reason I do, was because it was an ingredient in a cocktail I was gonna make him and he said to leave it out. I remember it coz it's a weird thing to be allergic to, takes all types though, don't it?'

'Don't it just,' I reply and take my leave.

24

WHERE'S THE WATER PARK?

It would be difficult *not* to be curious about this water park. After all the talk I've heard about it, I'm expecting great things. Obviously, I know it's not built yet, but still a little part of me feels I'd know a potential water park site when I saw it. Mad with nosiness, I ask Diego where the water park is going to be. He wags his finger and tells me it's not built yet. I nod and gesture and go through the whole charade in pidgin Spanish, how I want to see the land where it's going to be built.

I can tell he's puzzled by my question, but reels off a bunch of street names and gestures with his arms in a direction I struggle to follow. For the second time today he dangles his car keys in front of me and I nod enthusiastically. The atmosphere in the car feels different, somehow charged – like we're off on a mission. Diego turns the radio on and Europa FM blasts out its happy pop. He smiles at me and taps his fingers on the steering wheel in time to the beat.

I feel ignited. I don't know what's happened, but

somehow the awkward stench has left us. Maybe it's me, maybe it was my perspective on stuff? I don't know why but somehow it's like a mist has cleared and I feel freer, more able to do what I'm doing without tiptoeing about so much. I glance across at Diego, he's lost in the music and concentrating on the road. I'm pretty sure he knows there's something more than the alleged stolen money going on, but I don't know how much he can guess. Even if he doesn't speak English, the guy's not a moron, this whole situation has got to look weird. Anyway, whether he understands or not, he seems to be up for an adventure.

I look out of the window and survey the landscape. It's funny how I can find beauty in the barren, volcanic views afforded by our little island. I love this island so much. It's got a spirit and an energy to it I've never found anywhere else. People call it the land of 'eternal spring' because it has such a constant warm temperature and never gets cold. But, I think it's something more – I think it's also about the vitality of the place. There's a wish, a desire, a *need* to be outdoors, to be sucking up, hoovering up all the goodness from the sun and the winds. Right here, we're in the middle of the Atlantic Ocean, miles away from anything. Just a little volcanic rock in the sea, coursing with life and lava. Maybe it's the force from the earth's core, the molten heat leaking up, but this place makes me feel alive – and that I want to be alive!

Diego pulls off the main road onto a dirt track some four miles north of Corralejo. The road is unmade and the car bumps and jolts across the rocks. He continues driving, unbothered by the threat of the tyres being shredded. The Euro pop tunes blaring from the stereo sound disturbingly loud against the quiet backdrop of the nothingness, and I have to restrain myself from turning the volume down. To the right, a huge mountain looms large, its jagged peak piercing the blue of the sky. To the left, a barren plain peppered with occasional knee-high wiry shrubs, their mass of dead-looking stringy branches breaking the continuity of the arid bleakness. I look behind me to the town in the distance. From here, Corralejo looks like a little Lego town or an urban game of Tetris. Low-rise white blocks form the base, interspersed with terracotta, dark red, green and yellow infilled like some other player playing the game.

The car comes to a halt in the middle of a dirt patch. I look about me, trying to find something of significance – a border, a marker – anything which suggests this place is something more than what I can currently see.

Diego gets out of the car and I follow his lead. His feet scratch the dirt and a scuffle of dust billows into the air. I scan the land, wondering why this place would be good for development. I try and visualise how this parched, infertile patch could produce the fecundity and riches people have been promised. I squint and squinch my eyes trying to locate some rose-coloured lenses. I can't see how this is a place to make millions – it all looks pie in the sky to me.

I turn to Diego, my face full of confusion, and ask him what's special about this place. He stretches his arms wide indicating the size of the site. I don't fully understand everything he's saying, but it sounds like the water park is the smallest bit of the development. He's talking about what sounds like a new village with hotels, houses, shops, bars and restaurants. The whole thing sounds epic – like something a multi-national would develop – not something a couple of small-time builders would be capable of.

The distinct, deep, thick growl of the engine approaching

makes me flinch. I don't know if this is private land, but I'm sure we're about to find out. I look around and see Diego's already in the car, beckoning me to hurry. I fling open the passenger door and within seconds we're bursting our way across the rough ground, coughing up dust clouds as we race across the arid terrain. The wheels jolt on a small rock and I pray we don't get a puncture. I'm not sure where the boundary of the site is and where we need to get to, but I'm willing for us to get there quick. From the perspiration on Diego's normally unruffled brow, I can tell we're obviously not meant to be here.

The red car flashes into sight up ahead and drives menacingly close to us. It slows as we approach waiting for us to pull over. I check across at Diego unsure if he will obey what is obviously a command from Lucas. His eyes are focused straight ahead and we continue to accelerate. The red car downshifts and roars its Maserati holler, wheels spinning, as it thunders after us and pulls alongside, Lucas pressing hard on the horn and gesturing for Diego to pull over.

Diego ignores him and carries on driving, speeding up to make it to the main road. Lucas accelerates, shooting plumes of dry dirt behind him. Diego's hands are tense at the wheel, his knuckles pale with the strain of keeping the car straight at speed on this mishmash of uneven ground. We slow as we pull onto the tarmac, there's a rough ramp about thirty centimetres high, and rushing onto it at speed is likely to shred to the tyres. I breathe a small sigh of relief to be back on the main road, back in civilisation.

Diego slows for an upcoming left bend and then slams on the brakes. Lucas is parked across the road blocking both lanes. We crawl nearer. Diego's eyes flit about taking in the road edges, the pavements, the palms planted along the roadside. There's no easy way of getting round Lucas without smashing up the car. We stop. Lucas steps out and gestures for us to do the same. He leans lethargically on his driver's door as though he's waiting to be photographed for an ad campaign. Diego says nothing. He sits, stares straight ahead and keeps his hands on the wheel.

I open the car door and walk towards Lucas. He fixes me with a thin smile, but his eyes are hidden behind mirrored sunglasses.

'Is there a problem?' I ask, my voice unbetraying of the trembling terror I feel inside.

'What were you doing on *my* site?' His tone is accusing and spiky.

'We're just having a drive,' I reply.

He cocks his eyebrows at me and folds his arms. We're going nowhere until I come clean.

I give him what I hope he'll take as an innocent, sweet smile. 'Well, the thing is, Mick's made this water park sound very exciting so I thought I'd have a look where it was going to be.' I force myself to sound sunny and brimming with enthusiasm. Anything to appease his glare.

'Nobody but me and Mick know where the site is,' he deadpans me.

'Well,' I twist uncomfortably, 'must be a lucky guess then.'

Lucas stares straight at me. I can't see his eyes, but I can feel them boring into me, eating me alive. He rubs his lips with his forefinger, takes his keys from his pockets, opens the car door and starts to get in. Then he turns and with a pose I've only ever seen in a gangster movie, says, 'I don't want to see you or him up here ever again.'

'Sure, sure thing,' I say and give him a cheesy thumbs-up.

He starts the car, revs the engine to overload and thunders off.

I rejoin Diego. He gives me a look which seems to say 'I told you so' and 'what the fuck are you doing?' both at the same time.

'It's OK,' I say, but I know nothing's OK.

25

A HOLIDAY THING

I ask Diego to take me to Alejandro's pizzeria. He must now realise this has clearly got nothing to do with any stolen money, but as he's not asking me any more questions, I'm not offering any more information. *Need to know*. That's how Jorge and I said we should run this investigation and that's what I'm going to stick to. *Investigation?* I think I may be getting ahead of myself there, but I can't think of a better word for it.

As we drive I muse on Lucas' reaction to us being on the future water park site. We've obviously touched a nerve, but I don't see what the big issue is. The land isn't fenced off and they haven't started construction so I'm not sure what harm it can do. It's open for anybody to visit, so why the big showdown? Perhaps I'm being too suspicious, but if there's nothing to hide, why or what is he trying to keep secret?

I'm so caught up in my thoughts we almost miss the pizzeria and I have to shout out for Diego to stop. He shakes his head, pulls over and reverses. I get out of the car and wait for Diego to join me, but he stays sat, his hands firmly on the wheel. I gesture for him to follow, but he says 'No' and shakes his head. I try and gee him up, but he's not moving. I'm torn between leaving him in the car and going it alone, but it feels wrong.

He stares at me and asks in a smattering of Spanish and broken English, what the hell is going on. I stare back. How can I explain what I don't even understand myself? He switches the radio off. The silence is oppressive. I look at the time and calculate in a little over five hours Patrick's body will be hauled onto a flight and leave the island. Then it'll be too late. Too late to know if anybody was to blame for his death, too late to know if a murderer is on the loose – and too late to know if it's safe to sleep at night.

Honesty is the only way forward. And so I tell him everything I know including my suspicions. I have no idea how much he understands, but he watches me intently and pulls at his wrist hair while he listens.

'OK,' he says, when I finish my confused ramblings.

'OK?' I ask, surprised by his easy willingness to remain on board.

He taps his heart with his palm. 'Justicia.'

I want to hug him; he knows what we're doing is the right thing: we're fighting for justice. His reaction makes me so happy I can feel my heart inflate and sing a song. I mimic his gesture with feeling and place my palm on my heart. 'Justicia,' I say.

Alejandro is busy wiping down tables when we arrive. The pizzeria is one of those standard Italian take-out places where it's better to take-out than eat in. The plastic red tables, which have seen better days, are adorned with papery thin white covers and small green vases with a fake single red rose poking out. The walls, a rich tapestry in devotion to all things Italia, scream out the pizza and pasta dishes available, along with a badly drawn mural painting of what appears to be Mount Vesuvius through a vine-covered open window. Diego and I pause by the door, waiting for Alejandro to finish his duties. He moves to wipe another table, senses our presence and looks up.

'Oh hello, sorry I did not see you.' His face is open, welcoming but distracted. 'I make the tables ready, come in, welcome. We not so busy now, is early, the people, they are still on the beach.' He looks around apologetically at the empty restaurant.

'That's no problem,' I say, venturing into the vacant space. 'In fact,' I pause, this is uncomfortable, 'we haven't come here to eat, we, well... we wanted to talk to you.'

'You want to talk to me?' Alejandro twists his mouth thoughtfully and pulls out two chairs motioning for us to sit. 'Well, come in and sit. You want something to drink?'

We both shake our heads, but take a seat at the table he proffers. He sits down opposite and gazes at us quizzically. 'How can I help?'

I clasp the edge of the thin tablecloth and toy with it between my fingers. *Really am I doing this?* I feel nervous under the weight of Alejandro's patient gaze, he looks so young, so innocent – and what I'm about to say, to ask...

'Look, I'm sorry there's no easy way to say this, and I hope you won't take offence by me being direct, but I have to ask... you see Patrick... and Pauline, and you know...'

Alejandro wilts. 'It is very sad; he was too young to go.'

I chew my lip. 'The thing is, and I'm sorry if this sounds wrong, but people are getting suspicious. Stuff's been written online about Jorge's Place, they say we're covering up the death of a guest – which we're not – but still, people, they want to know what happened.' I pause and stare at the crepe-like qualities of the cheap table-cloth. 'Anyway, the thing is... people are saying you were in a relationship with Pauline, and well, people are pointing the finger.' I admit, I may've embellished a bit, but I had to find a way in.

Alejandro coughs, shifts in his chair a little, exhales and leans forward. 'Patrick, he had a heart attack. I do not understand why anybody is asking any questions?'

'Yeah, but you see, Patrick was fine, didn't have any heart problems and then he comes and stays here and now he's dead. You can see how it looks?'

Alejandro's face clouds with confusion. 'I do not follow; how can it be your fault if a tourist dies of a heart attack? You provide tourist accommodation; you are not a hospital. Unfortunately, people die, that is the nature of life.'

'Yes, but now people are saying about the relationship between you and Pauline, it's got more complicated.' I stare at him squarely.

Alejandro returns my gaze. His eyes are molten brown like a deep bowl of chocolate. He blinks his extraordinarily long lashes and nibbles gently on his plump, pink extremely kissable lips. He stands up and fishes his mobile out of his pocket, he swipes and presses and shows me a photo on his screen of a strikingly gorgeous young female all hair, lips and eyes holding a young baby.

'This is my wife and our new-born son, Mateo. We've been together for almost one year and half now.'

Diego reaches across the table to take a look at the screen and gives Alejandro the thumbs up. I glance again at the idyllic photo. Why would he be playing away when he has such a beautiful wife and new child?

'So, I don't understand then about you and Pauline?' I say.

Alejandro screws up his face a little as though he's swallowed something dubious. 'In truth, I don't know either,' he looks away and then down, 'but Pauline, she is... what can I say? She is like a sex kitten.'

I can feel my jaw start to gape and I quickly close it. Out of all the replies I expected him to say, this was not one of them.

'It is like an animal attraction, whenever I see her I cannot get enough of her, but it is only for holiday. My life is with my wife and my son.'

'OK,' I say, and pause playing for time, 'but now Patrick isn't here you can be with Pauline all the time?'

Alejandro sits back in his chair and the plastic scrapes on the tiles. He spreads his hands wide on the table. 'I do not want to be with Pauline. I like being with her and the things we do when she is here on holiday, but that is it – nothing more. My life is with my wife and my child, they are everything to me.'

'Clearly not *everything*...' I say, raising my eyebrows.

A glow of embarrassment flushes his features and I wince as I realise it makes him even more handsome, vulnerability is a good look on his face. 'It is very difficult. I tried to finish this thing with Pauline last year when I met my wife. I told her we couldn't continue; I didn't want to lie. She keep coming to see me and I tell her 'no'. It was not easy, but when my wife she told me she was pregnant that was the end, no more. No Pauline.'

'So when did you last have a thing with Pauline?'

'I think maybe one year, I told her I was going to marry and no more, but she keep coming in. It was difficult, she wanted to see me, talk to me, but I tell the other waiters to serve. I smile and say hello, but I stay away from being alone with her.'

'Did Patrick know anything about this?' I ask.

Alejandro shifts awkwardly and I note the look of shame. 'I don't think so. He was a very trusting man, a good man. It is a pity what happened, he was too young. He treated her very well, like a princess, she could tell him to do anything and he would do it for her. He was a good man, a good husband.'

'So what happens now?'

'I don't know,' he shrugs, 'for me it doesn't change anything. For Pauline, many things will change... but,' he hesitates and looks at me directly, 'Pauline, I am sure, will soon find another husband. She is the sort of woman who needs a man to look after her.'

'And that man isn't you?'

He shakes his head and looks at his screen again stroking the photo of his wife and son. 'No, they are my world; to me they *are* everything.'

I give him a small smile and thank him for his time and hold out my hand in a gesture of gratitude and to ease any tensions. He clasps it beneath his two hands, they are hot and dry. I hang onto his touch a little longer and add, 'Can I just ask... did you know Patrick was allergic to cinnamon?'

He snorts a little puff of air. 'Yes, he told me every time to not put it on his cappuccino. I told him the world is going crazy with so many allergies. The tourists they come and one year they cannot eat bread, then no tomatoes, then no cheese – so many problems! But you know the one thing they have no allergy to? Beer! Beer they can drink all the time, anytime – no allergy to beer!'

26

MR BOB'S GREAT ESCAPE

The tow truck outside Jorge's house had recovered his smashed up car from the side of the road and was depositing it in his driveway. The silver Opel, some crossover SUV model, was dangling on the end of the chain, its bonnet and driver door crushed inwards revealing the car's mangled upholstery. I took a sharp intake of breath as I realised how lucky Jorge had been to escape with just a broken arm. It was the sort of damage you saw and wondered how the driver even got out alive.

Diego's gaze is transfixed by the metal mess the recovery vehicle is placing on the ground. I tell him we should speak with Jorge.

We cross the road and approach the boundary of the complex. The usually closed and locked white gate is open. We walk in and I purposefully close it behind me, ensuring the latch is sealed. Open gates are an invitation for visitors and given we're a private complex, I prefer to keep our entrances closed. I'm not keen on strangers wandering about thinking they can use our sea view terraces unless they're guests. Just as I'm walking away, the gate snaps open again. I go back and shut it and notice the latch isn't quite fitting. I bodge it as best I can, and make a mental note to get Hans the handyman to sort out.

Despite it being gone five o' clock in the afternoon the sun is still high in the sky and hot as hell. At this time of the year, sunbathing is an all-day-round experience until the sun sets, and even then the temperature will only fall a few degrees. In fact, sunbathing is pretty much an all-year-round experience. We're on the same latitude as Florida and Mexico which means it never gets cold, just a bit cooler. In the winter months I'll still wear t-shirts and shorts and in the evening I'll put on a jumper or a cardigan, but there's no need for thick jackets or central heating. Fuerteventura really is the island of eternal spring!

Making my way across the cobblestoned courtyard I feel a twinge of guilt I didn't pop in and see Miriam at the hospital. I make a mental note to call by later and update her, but for now I need to focus. I need to ensure Jorge is on side and we get to the bottom of why Patrick is dead. I'm deep in my thoughts musing over everything, when I realise Diego is yelling and flapping his arms.

'La rata! La rata!' he shouts, gesticulating widely.

I look around trying to see the rat he's talking about, but he's pointing at Mr Bob's carrier and making running motions. I peer inside the carrier to see Mr Bob is no longer inside.

'Dónde?' I shout, spinning round to see where he may have gone. My heart drops when I see the gate has come open again. Running to the entrance I scan up and down the street, if Mr Bob gets out on to the main road it's unlikely a car will see him, and a battle between him and a speeding lump of metal will not end well. Diego exhales loudly as he joins me scouring the roadway.

'Mr Bob! Mr Bob' I call, my voice desperate.

Diego grabs me by the arm and motions I should look inside and he will look outside.

'Mira! Mira!' he says, his tone urgent. I nod, I know I need to look, my eyeballs hurt from trying to take in the panorama and pinpoint my runaway little boy.

I make my way back into the complex, calling and shifting the palms to see if Mr Bob is hiding in the undergrowth. Peering in drains and plant pots, underneath leaves and debris, I soon realise how easy it is for him to hide from me. I shake my head as I search through a pile of rubbish. *This isn't a game Mr Bob, and this is really bad timing.*

Diego pushes open the gate and closes it using brute force and props it shut with an empty plant pot. He says to me (I think) that somebody outside saw Mr Bob in the courtyard and so we should focus our search here. Hands on hips, he surveys the area with an engineer's eye.

'Mira!' he barks, just as a little fluffy tortoiseshell bum leaps into a tiny gap between the buildings. Diego springs into life trying to reach into the space, his arm extended fully into the opening, his hand reaching, clawing. I peer through the slit and can see the lollop of Mr Bob heading for the shoreline at the front of the building.

'We should go to the front,' I say, in a heightened whisper, indicating ahead.

Trying to run quietly and quickly so as not to scare Mr Bob is hard. I'm desperate to make sure he doesn't escape and get into any danger, but at the same time I'm anxious not to frighten him and he go into hiding so I can't find him.

Entering onto the front terrace I see Tamika is still sat

where we left her, tanning her limbs. The discarded wine bottles balanced precariously on the table, shows she hasn't stopped drinking since we spoke to her last. She looks up as we hurry in, but says nothing. I can't decide if it's because her eyes are too drunk to focus or she can't be bothered with more conversation. Spotting movement under her chair, I see Mr Bob is shading himself from the blazing sunlight under her shadow.

'Sorry, Tamika, can I ask you not to move for a minute?'

'What?' She looks up at me and shifts her chair.

'Could you just remain still and where you are *without* moving, just for a few seconds please.' I extend my arms and flatten my palms, imploring her to do as I've asked.

She curls her lips and sighs; she's not used to being told what to do, never mind *doing* what she's been told to do. She squirms in her chair annoyed with the situation, but unsure of the consequences if she does move.

Calmly, I make my way to where Mr Bob is shading himself. Kneeling down I peer at his unblinking eyes, he's purposefully not making eye contact with me. I know he can hear me, but I can tell from his stance, he's not listening. He jerks his head to the side, throwing a glance over his shoulder.

I ignore his tuts and impassive glare and barrel on, there's no time for strops. 'Come here now little one,' I say in a coochi-coo voice, stretching out my arms so I can make a grab for him.

Suddenly, there's a bang and clatter of metal and I jump back in fright. The chair where Tamika was sitting and Mr Bob had been hiding crashes to the floor, knocking the table and empty bottles of wine onto the tiled terrace. Splinters of glass fracture sword-like across the floor, liquid seeps and flows in little puddles from the scattered bottles.

'What the fuck are you doing, coming on at me like that?' roars Tamika, folding her arms quickly across her scantily clad breasts.

'For God's sake,' I pant, 'I asked you *not* to move for just a few seconds... look what you've done now!'

Mr Bob scampers across the tiles and my heart weeps at his bare, tiny, baby-pink paws on the shards of sharp glass. At least the terrace is walled, that means he can't escape anymore – as long as I keep a careful watch. Tamika stares at me and I realise I may've crossed a line in terms of how you speak to guests. With my eyes firmly on Mr Bob's scuttling torso, I turn to her, dragging as much diplomacy as I can muster from the depths of my being and say, 'I was trying to get Mr Bob, he escaped and was under your chair.'

She turns to me, her eyes bleary with alcohol, 'Who's Mr Bob?'

'My guinea pig!' I manage to squeak, before jumping into a sprint as I see his furry little body scooting under a tiny gap in a boarded-out boxed-off area of the terrace.

I can't see her reaction, but I can feel her scornful eye roll at five metres. Some people are born with only enough care for themselves. I wish I could care less; it would really help me in life. Looking over my shoulder I can see she's settled herself in another lounger and has picked up her mobile. Unfazed, unbothered – why should she give a shit about anybody other than herself?

Meanwhile, Diego is trying to prise a panel off the boxed off area with his finger nails. 'Rapido! Agua caliente...' he says, his face puffed with exertion.

I start to claw at the wood cladding, my fingertips crease

white under the pressure. Diego shakes his head and mutters again; he raises his arm about to smash the thin wood covering the hot water boiler. I strike out to stop him. 'No, if you smash it, you may hurt him! Haven't you got a screwdriver?' I gesture the action twisting my wrist next to the rusty screw-heads.

He flicks his eyebrows upwards and says his tools are in his bag. I look over to where Diego has parked his car, calculating if I can get there and back quick enough. I want to run, but I'm scared if I take my eyes off Mr Bob I'll lose him. I stoop lower trying to peer through the gaps of the boarding panels.

'Jorge, toma mi bolso!' Diego shouts.

I look around to see Jorge is walking towards us, or was walking towards us. He's now double-backed on himself and is grabbing Diego's bag from the car and is struggling with the weight of it. Diego relieves him of his burden and Jorge turns to me for an update. I tell him how Mr Bob escaped from the carrier and is currently hiding in the boxed out area housing the hot water tank. My voice is edgy as I watch Diego loosening the parallel screws and removing the panels. With a gap large enough for me to fit my head, I kneel down, scraping my skin on the tiles and reach in. Underneath the water heater all I can see is a load of pipework.

'It's no good, he must be right at the back, can you take some more panels off?' Jorge translates my request and Diego continues removing the panels. At last with half of the front removed, the three of us bend down and peer into the darkness.

'Where is he?' asks Jorge.

'There! There he is,' I exclaim, 'he's right in the corner.' I extend my arm fully and reach out my fingers. 'C'mon Mr

Bob, let's stop playing now, come back to me.' I stretch further trying to grab him, but he bolts and I find myself clutching a jar of some sort. I drag it out into the light and hand it to Jorge. Mr Bob scurries towards me and clambers onto my ankle wanting me to pick him up. I reach down relieved to feel his furry little body back in my hands. 'What an adventure you've been having little man!' I gaze into his shiny ruby-black eyes, he holds my gaze and then blinks.

'This is strange,' Jorge says, looking at the jar I handed to him. 'This jar it has the cinnamon from the breakfast. It went missing. My wife, she told me I lost it. But now you find it here?'

I take the jar from Jorge's hand and inspect the browny-orange powder inside. I sprinkle some on my finger and taste it – it's definitely cinnamon. I lean in so my lips are almost touching Jorge's ear and whisper, 'Patrick was allergic to cinnamon.'

Jorge recoils back as though I've spat on him. His eyes are wild and bright. He bends his head to me and in a heavy, excited whisper says, 'That is why Mr Bob ran away, this is the evidence!' He clutches the jar as if it's a trophy. 'We were right, Tarah. Now we must identify who is responsible. I will call Felipe, he's a friend of mine in the police. We must get everybody here to find who killed Patrick.'

27

LUCAS'S PLANS

'Yooo Hoooo! Tarah!'

I scan the street looking for who's calling. I draw a blank so carry on walking.

'Yooo Hoooo! Over here!'

I spin round, searching the scene. I feel like I'm standing in a giant one-way mirror – the other person can see me, but I can't see them.

A car horn beeps, tooting me to attention. A slender, tanned arm stretches out from the tinted windows of a white Toyota pickup parked two cars down. It's beckoning me. Hesitantly, I walk towards the commanding limb.

Kaitlyn's faintly sozzled overly-made up features come into view. 'Tarah! Tarah! How lovely to see you after all this time!' I smile in recognition. Kaitlyn wasn't the sort of face you'd forget, but I'd only seen her a couple of times about town since she'd kindly given me her cast-offs to fit out my apartment.

'Hi Kaitlyn, I'm so sorry I didn't realise who was calling.'

I step towards the open window and grab her extended hand in greeting.

'Of course not, silly, you couldn't see me in *these* windows. They're tinted so you *can't* see me, very good for hiding!' She giggles mischievously, her slurring tone clearly influenced by too much alcohol.

'How are things?' I say. I don't really want to talk, but I don't want to be rude, so I listen and pretend to look interested while she babbles on and on about this and that. I nod and coo and fulfil my social niceties without really paying attention, until she says: 'What a mess with this death over at your place, not good for business is it?'

I stare at her in alarm. 'How do you know about that?'

She grins a drunken smile and makes her glossy, pink lips protrude and pucker like a fish sucking for air. 'Whatever do you mean? The whole island knows about it!'

'How does *everybody* know about it?' I can feel the surprise lilting my tone. I don't understand how she or anybody else would know about Patrick's death – we didn't tell anyone.

She shrugs, her lips taking on the petulant scowl of a toddler about to throw a tantrum. 'How should I know? You know what it's like here, everybody knows everybody's business!' She reaches for a vibrant pink-coloured plastic bottle in the centre console and swigs noisily from the lime shaded neck. I'm pretty sure it's alcohol she's chugging right in front of me. There's something about the way she's rolling her eyes as she gulps, and the faint, sweet tang of warm white wine is a giveaway. I wait while she pats her lips dry and refocuses her gaze on me. 'Anyway, I dunno about you, but what I find odd is the way Lucas is hanging about your place. What's he up to with all those tourists and his presentation?'

'What presentation?'

'The one he's giving to the tourists!' She smacks her lips together impatiently.

'I dunno, I haven't seen him,' I say.

'How can you *not* have seen him?' She pulls up her sunglasses and rolls her wet, drunk eyes at me. 'What you doing? He's right outside your place!'

'Well, I *am* working you know, I'm not in the habit of hanging around spying on people.' I can feel my hackles rising. I'm annoyed she knows more about what's happening right outside my own front door than me, but most of the time my head is either stuck in front of a screen or in the apartments sorting out the various things that seem to never-endingly go wrong with the properties.

'You should be! If it were me, I'd damn well wanna know what that Mr King Chops is doing with them tourists. He's a dodgy bit of work he is.' She sits back, the leather of the seat squeaks under her sweat and the sunshine.

'So what was it you saw?' I ask, leaning into the car, eager for her to spill.

She twists towards me. 'Plans. He was showing people plans. Don't ask me what of, but I reckon they were houses. I'll tell you this for nothing, I wouldn't touch anything of his if it came up and offered me a free drink! Damn dodgy that man is.'

My brain rolls over this new information. When Diego showed me the land, he said about houses also being built on the water park site, so Kaitlyn's story makes sense. What doesn't make sense is for Lucas, the head honcho, to be selling them himself rather than an agent. Agents always deal with the sales on the island, nobody ever sees or gets to know the developer. So why would a busy, VIP developer (so I'm led to believe) be doing the dirty work of sales? Hasn't he got more important things to be doing... like developing the site?

'What do you think he's up to then?' I ask.

'Honey, if I knew that I wouldn't be asking you – I was hoping you'd know the goss.' She eyes me questioningly and for a moment I feel like I'm under interrogation. What is it she thinks I know that I don't?

I decide it's time to part ways. Her hawk-like gaze is making me feel awkward and I don't know if she can be trusted. I begin the wrap-up of the conversation (errands to run) and agree we need to see each other more (although I know that will never happen). She's keen to talk further but I continue to close down any openings she tries to find. I'm about to leave when she looks over to where Diego's parked waiting for me, and gives me a grin so dirty and slutty I feel I need a shower. I shake my head at her insinuation, but she raises her preened eyebrows and waves me off with a flap of her manicured hand. I can tell the mime she's simulating.

My mind is all of a mess as I make my way to the car. I don't understand how Kaitlyn would know about Patrick, and what's she talking about with Lucas selling to tourists outside our place? Is this something to do with the bad review online? My brain feels jammed trying to think too many thoughts – I need to isolate and analyse.

Passing a group of tourists sat outside a restaurant, I smile at their merriment. They're crowded around the smallest patio table rammed full of tapas, jugs of beer, sangria and glasses. The wide grins on their sun-flushed faces strike me as the epitome of joy.

I'm just about to walk by when the tall, thin moustachioed man of the group stands up, edging across my path. Holding his glass outstretched, he merrily greets me, 'Salut, cheers! Let's bloody forget England and all move to Fuerteventura!' He roars with laughter.

I love the effect this place has on people. When tourists first arrive they're all wound up like little springs ready to pop at any moment, and then within a few days, they've uncoiled, come back from the wall and learned to relax their shoulders from their usual hunch. I know the weather helps, sunshine is a great healer, but I also believe Fuerteventura has a special spiritual core made up of a carefree peace that radiates bliss. It's a lazy loveliness, like the contentedness and warmth you feel after a big slap-up meal. There's no need to rush, there's no need to care, things will happen and work out in their own sweet time.

Here, on what is essentially a spit of volcanic rock in the middle of the Atlantic Ocean, you feel so safe. Bad people don't come to Fuerteventura. Bad things don't happen on Fuerteventura. This is a place full of love and happiness and peace and good things. And that's why I feel so wrong about this whole situation with Patrick. Because if it's true, it means this place and my life is a lie. And I don't want to be living a lie.

That thought turns over again. And again. Cheated. Robbed. Tricked. For the past two days it feels like everything I've come to believe in has been taken from me. I don't feel as I felt. This island, my fantasy life, feels like it's slipping from my fingers and a hole is opening up inside of me. I'm full, yet empty. My head a chaotic mass of thoughts and feelings. I struggle to breathe. I have to think about it. It's like I'm missing the framework for how to live my life now. Everything I thought to be real, seems fake, and I don't know who or what to believe.

I used to feel so safe here. I would look out at the mountains, who've stood for millennia gazing and watching, shielding the island from harm. I'd walk by the beach listening to the roar and crash of the waves and feel comforted by the power, the separation it gave me from the rest of the world. I didn't worry about the people. Only good people came here. That's what I told myself. How naïve.

I go over the conversation I had with Jorge in the hospital. It was awkward and we were both tense, but I understand now, he was annoyed at me for thinking in some way we were to blame. His anger wasn't directed at me, but at the situation. I was the one who'd blown it out of proportion. What he was bothered about was the preservation of our idyllic way of life. If we allow this death to go unquestioned, it undermines the safety and sanctity of our island and all of the people on it. Now, I get the importance of what's at stake. This isn't just about me, or Jorge, or the holidaymakers. Solving who killed Patrick is about everyone and our existence here on our lazy, contented, sleeping dinosaur of a perfect isle. I don't know how I'm going to do it, but I have to prove what happened to Patrick. The future of our beautiful, happy, home depends on it.

28

THE GATHERING ON THE TERRACE

Tamika unfurls herself from the lounger and gives a feline stretch. You can tell she knows she has a watching audience, even if she's not looking, and pretending we don't exist. She pushes out her chest and the sheer material of her tiny white bikini stretches to an almost transparent cling film. Diego's face pops in amazement and I find myself wanting to cover his eyes like a small child who's about to see something they shouldn't. Leisurely, she spreads her legs wide across the lounger and needlessly bends down to show off her deep, full cleavage. I can't help it, but inside I'm a jumble of rage and admiration: how do people get away with this sort of behaviour?

'Oh, I can't reach my top, can you pass it to me?' she says, staring straight at Diego, her false lashes batting nine to the dozen.

'He doesn't speak English,' I retort.

'He can speak the language of body and I know for sure he's appreciating mine.' She turns and licks her plump lips, no hint of shame.

'You can put that body of yours away. We've got serious things to discuss so I suggest you get dressed and look half decent, if that's at all possible.' I'm aware how prim and school-teacherly I sound and want to gag myself. When did I become so fussy and up myself? Why am I letting this girl get under my skin? Am I jealous?

Tamika looks up at me, her eyes large and dewy, like the cutest puppy you've ever seen on YouTube. She curves her voluptuous lips into an innocent, sweet smile and says. 'What's happening now? Are things hotting up?'

I physically want to punch her. Right now I'd like to rearrange her stupid gorgeous looks into a Picasso painting and then piss on her. I look away. Perhaps my reaction is over the top? Jorge glances at me, he doesn't want to get between two warring cats, but I can sense he's warning me to keep it together.

I don't want to engage in any of this. I want time and space to think. I want to focus and try and work out who killed Patrick. Mr Bob's escape was planned – he knew the stolen cinnamon jar had been hidden on the terrace. Had he even seen who'd tried to conceal it? A cold rash creeps up my neck. So many people knew Patrick was allergic to cinnamon, but who would actually want to kill him and why?

A passer-by pauses by our boundary wall and looks in. He's not alone, there's at least four or five people who are walking deliberately slowly and watching intently. I turn my head wondering what they're looking at. At the other end of the terrace, Tamika is unnecessarily limbering up in some fantastical extreme yoga poses and drawing a crowd of admiring glances. I shake my head and wonder what I'm going to do with a girl who has no shame and a belly full of cheap Spanish wine.

'Watch her,' I say to Diego, 'make sure she stays here.'

He looks at me quizzically and then to Tamika.

'Mira,' I say, pointing to Tamika, 'la chica non permission to leave, stay here.' I point at the gate and gesture how the bolt should be locked. 'Aqui, la chica stay here.'

He nods.

I take a deep breath wondering how I've managed so far with so little Spanish and tell myself I need to sign up for an intensive course. This is crazy how I only know a few words after all this time. It's not good enough – I don't want to be like the rest of the ex-pats resting on their English-speaking laurels.

I turn my back on the Tamika scene. I need some space to try and gather my thoughts and work out what I'm going to do. Jorge and his police friend Felipe are currently rounding everyone up for what it seems is going to be a showdown on the terrace. And I'm stressed. No, scrub that, I'm beyond stressed. I'm beyond anxious. I'm beyond any emotion I've ever felt right now. I don't know how I'm going to pull this off or even how I'm going to try and put this all together, but I remind myself of the TV crime shows I've seen and tell myself everything will be OK. All of them fly by the seat of their pants until the very end, and so I'm going to fly too.

Loitering inside the stairwell of the entry to the block I'm aware how strange I look. Every now and again I find myself flicking imaginary dust flakes off the tiled skirting just to bring myself to earth. I want to find a something, I want to see or remember or think a something to put all of this together. I know that's what every good detective would do right now. Apart from the obvious fact I am not a detective: I am a holiday lettings manager.

I was thinking to let myself into the office, but I want to keep my eyes open to what's happening outside. I'm not really sure how this is going to play out and so I need to keep my wits about me.

My ears prick at the creak of the gate opening. I peer outside and see Mick has now come back onto the terrace and is talking with Tamika. I can't hear what they're saying, but my God she's cavorting around him like she's doing a flipping lap dance. He, on the other hand, looks ruddy in the face and his eyes are like pinballs. Another afternoon drinking too much in the sun, I predict. Diego is standing like a brick at the far end, trying not to be noticed. He's been tasked with the unenviable job of unofficial security guard, and he knows it. He knows he's in deeper than he ever thought he was, and to be fair to him, he's carrying on with gusto. There's not many plumbers I know who when they find out they're part of a shit storm, hang about and say 'fetch me my tool bag!'

I stop and think about that some more. What am I doing? I haven't even got a tool bag. What on earth do I think I'm going to do? I'm a holiday lettings manager – I'm not trained in interrogation. Who am I to think I can pull this off? This isn't what I signed up for or thought I'd be doing when I came here. When I came here, I came for excitement, but also security. I wanted to know I would be OK. Life would be OK. But right now, this isn't OK, this certainly isn't OK.

I close my eyes and try and find a place of peace. I need to centre myself. I need to remind myself why I'm here, why I'm doing this. I think back to how life used to be in the UK – a constant treadmill. A constant conveyor belt of shit, shit I couldn't even afford to pay for when it got to the end of the month. Always too much month and not enough money, that was my life. But now, things here are different. I'm no richer, not on a material level – I've got hand-me-downs and boot sale bargains and my apartment comes as part of the job. But I have so much more than I ever thought was possible. Here I have a reason to get up, a reason to live. I wake up and I *want* to go to work. Never did I have that back in England. Never did I get excited about the prospect of a day in the office. But here, here I cannot wait. Here my office *feels* like my home.

I press my tongue hard against the back of my front teeth. I want to try and find the answer, I want to try and make things OK again, but I don't know if I'm capable. I don't know if I'm clever enough to work this out. I'm not a natural sleuth, the only detective 'experience' I have is from watching them on TV. Actually, that should be past tense, as I haven't seen any murder mysteries since moving here. Now, my life doesn't revolve around what's on TV, it's about being out and about. Life here is lived outside. Every day I see the sea, I walk on the beach, at the weekends maybe I stand-up paddle or go surfing. Life is active, it's outside, it's doing things and it's here to be lived. Here, life feels like it's lived in the moment. There's no tomorrow, today is what matters. Having fun and enjoying life is about now, today, now, not later, not in the future.

The front gate clangs again and I see Kris sheepishly stumble in. He certainly doesn't look like he's a 'Karaoke King' at this moment in time. I don't know what he's been told as to why he's been brought here, but I can see a guy dressed in a navy blue outfit who's standing by the gate, kind of like a lookout. I peer out of the gap between the entry doors trying to see what's happening. It definitely looks like there's a guy 'on guard' now. He's not dressed like a police officer, but he acts like one in the way he holds himself – all authoritative and 'don't mess with me' attitude.

Kris is looking very subdued; he's slunk to the corner of the terrace and folded his arms. Mick is looking more animated; he's swinging his arms around like a seven-year-old boy and looking pretty foolish. He's making such a fuss of Tamika; anybody would think he's never seen or touched a woman before in his life. God, he's embarrassing himself. He keeps preening and playing with her hair like she's some kind of doll. I don't think he's even noticed anybody else is around, he's just totally all eyes on her. Lust, love, longing? It's hard to tell, but he looks like a tiger on heat the way he's pawing at her.

Tamika's loving Mick's attentions and she's definitely playing up to his display of masculine affection. She may only be after him for his money, but she appears to know her role well. She kowtows to him in such a way no self-respecting female ever would. I mean, God, the way he's touching her now, if that were me, I'd be slapping his hands and saying 'Geroff me, I'm not a piece of meat!' But then, I guess, it's me having to pay my own bills and make my own way, so I have more of a say in what happens in my life. Or to my body. Oooh am I being completely bitchy? I have to admit her gorgeousness does grate on me, especially the way she knows how to use it, completely. Leverage, I think that's what it's called; she uses her looks as leverage to get what she wants.

How strange, she seems to have suddenly gone rather cool on Mick. I squint my eyes tighter to see more. I don't want to open the door even a crack, I don't want them to see me and try and engage in conversation right now, but I'm desperate to know what's happening. My eyes swivel to where Tamika's looking, there's a new entrant through the gate: It's Lucas. Lucas has arrived and he's looking furious. He looks like someone's just totalled his Maserati and given him the bill. He nods a small greeting to Mick and Tamika, but doesn't go and stand directly next to them, he seems to be keeping his distance. Mick's not having it, he's moving towards him, his face looks friendly enough, maybe he's trying to make small talk? Lucas is nodding at Mick, but he's not opening his lips; it seems like he's acknowledging his presence, but doesn't want to engage. Lucas is moving away, imperceptibly, but definitely, I can see it. Well, that seems a bit odd given how buddy-buddy they've been over the past few days. What's going on there then?

Ah! Tamika's going in for the kill, she won't take no for an answer. Oh! What's she doing? She seems to have walked somewhere else on the terrace now. I scooch my eyes around to see where she's gone. Damn, this door edge is butting on my eyelashes. I relocate her; she's holding out a wine glass to Lucas. My God, that girl is a servant and a half to men. I'm surprised she doesn't start pouring it over her breasts and getting him to lick it off. He's shaking his head; he's turning her down! I can't see her face, but he's waving his palm at her and has got his mouth set so his usually thick lips, are really thin. He looks like he's stonewalling her. He must be really angry. She tries again. She's toying with her hair, coiling strands around her fingertips and gently sucking them while staring directly at him. He doesn't flinch. What the hell is she doing? She's standing up on her tiptoes; she's wobbling a bit, now a lot. It looks like she's trying to dance with him! She's swaying and slithering and trying to paw him. Lucas isn't having it; he turns away to look at the sea.

Diego hasn't moved from his corner of the terrace. I watch him in wonder. It's incredible the way a guy can blend into the background the way he does. I'm not sure how he does it, because I wouldn't say he *doesn't* have presence, but at the same time, I wouldn't say he *does* have presence. He's one of those people who are 'just there', if you get my drift. He doesn't make a fuss or faff; he has a dependable, solid quality to him. Companionable. I think that's the best word to describe him. He doesn't give off any bad vibes or have any zingy auras to him, but he's a nice guy. And I think 'nice guys' are totally underrated, there should be more men in the world who're aiming to be 'nice.'

A sound from the side path makes me jump. I thought we'd blocked the gate off? Who would be coming down this side of the building? I run to the rear of the entrance hall, a window is located halfway up and if I climb a couple of steps, I should be able to make out the courtyard at the rear. I try and focus as best I can, but the glazing is too heavily frosted to see anything more than my reflection in the powdery white glass. I hesitate as the footsteps come nearer, closer to the entrance hall. I can hear the low murmur of people talking. I press my ear against the glass trying to listen, and then recoil – they may be able to see my silhouette from the other side. I lean into the wall and try and make out who it is, but the frisky scrunch of the volcanic gravel scratches out the voices.

I dash back to my viewing post by the entry doors just in time to see Jorge and Pauline coming through the gate to the front terrace. Pauline's eyes are very red and watery, like the insides of two overly ripe tomatoes. Jorge is looking very serious and sombre. If it weren't for his lurid green and black striped aertex making him look like a giant, sick wasp,

I'd be thinking he had a face fit for a funeral. His arm is bent in the cast at a very awkward angle. I can see him getting quickly annoyed with this injury. I'm sure his wife will also very quickly get annoyed with Jorge and this injury, as it'll mean she'll have to do even more running around for him! Not that he doesn't pull his weight, but he's a traditional man who expects things to be done in a traditional manner – a very black and white, inside-outside approach. It means the woman looks after the house and children (and all the things happening inside), and the man provides (read: pays) for everything and deals with life outside the house (work, the garden and all things such as this). It's not uncommon here. I'm not sure if local women take any great exception to their lives like this, most appear to be happy with their lot. Life ticks along, like the expected ebb and flow of the tide. Sleep, eat, breathe, lather, rinse, repeat.

Just as I'm wondering how Jorge got here without his car, I see a police officer coming through the gate, who obviously knows him very well. He's smiling and patting Jorge on the back and looking all chummy. This has got to be his police friend, Felipe, who he said about. The effect of the officer on the gathered crowd is quite something. If before there was an awkward standoff, it's now bordering on becoming a stroppy melee. People are outright eyeing each other up, drawing their visual swords and calculating who to attack.

If I wasn't going to have to go out and be the ring leader, I'd be laughing at this crazy scene. But as I have to be a part of this, I'm not. I'm shitting it. My stomach curls and I feel like my insides are about to explode into my pants. My intestines are twisting and cramping like they're trying to perform a Trucker's Hitch knot. I bend over trying to ease some of the pain from my gut, but it feels like the inside of my stomach is being torn away and shredded.

Breathe.

Breathe.

I need to remember to breathe.

Focus. Deep breath.

I try and push air deep into my stomach, into my gut, to try and separate my tangled insides from devouring themselves. Maybe it's lack of oxygen? Maybe I've been shallow breathing and left my diaphragm short on air. I feel a little light-headed, dizzy, peculiar. I want to sit down, but there's no seats in the hallway. I sway, almost drunkenly, to a stair. I need to sit. I need to breathe. I put my head in my hands and then rest my cheek on my forearm, balancing on my knees. I know I'm crunched up, but I feel safer like this. The closer I am to the foetal position, the more I can forget what is happening. I want to pass out. I want to blank out. Faint. I don't want a part of this anymore. I can't do this. I close my eyes.

'SSSSSSSSSSSSSSSSSSSSSSSSSSSSSSSSSSSSSS'

'SSSSSSSSSSSSSSSSSSSSSSSSSSSSSSSSSSSSSS'

Mr Bob is hissing at me. His furry face is peeled back and he's baring his tiny, sharp teeth. I extend my finger ready to rub his nose, but he backs away. He looks at me squarely and gnashes his teeth like an old-fashioned typewriter. It sounds like a mini AK47 inside his mouth.

I open the carrier door to stroke him, but he flattens himself against the wall and continues to hiss. I reach in again to try and rub his favourite spot just behind his ears, but he jerks his head back and throws me a look of disdain. He turns his back on me and fluffs out his fur, emitting a low growl of annoyance. He's angry with me, I know it. He does this when he's in a mood with me. I stare at his fluffy backside until he turns to face me. He gives me a full-frontal dirty look. I laugh at him and then myself. How on earth have I managed to bring up such a temperamental teenage-strop of a guinea pig?

A wailing baby's cry breaks the stand-off. Mr Bob eyeballs me curiously and nudges his nose for me to go and investigate. I squeeze my eye against the tight framework of the door. I can see a woman in her mid-twenties with the look of a young Penelope Cruz. She has lustrous, long, dark brown hair, huge cocoa-cups for eyes, immaculately arched brows, and glowing olive skin. She's cooing and cradling the pudgy bundle in her arms while chatting to Felipe, the police officer. She laughs at something he says and flashes her stunning, perfectly-aligned, naturally white teeth, bedazzling the gathered group on the terrace. She seems blind to the spell she's cast. She swishes her hair casually, unaware of the hungry eyes eating her up. The policeman is now turning to another to join in the conversation, I twiddle myself round to try and see: it's Alejandro. I take a step back from the thin line of sight and draw breath – this must be his wife and child. But why has he brought them here?

29

THE TRUTH ABOUT PATRICK

The sunlight explodes my retinas as I step out from the shaded entrance way and onto the terrace. Everybody turns to look at me.

I am there.

I am back there.

I am back at the start of the story.

I will find out who killed Patrick and bring his killer to justice.

'I'm sorry to do this to you mate, but I don't think the timing's right for me anymore.' Patrick shifted uncomfortably on the tall bar stool. He hated these type of seats with his legs dangling like cheese-strings and his arse cheeks squidged precariously on the too small pad.

'What do you mean the timing's not right? We spoke about this only a couple of months back and you were all over it then, you couldn't get enough of it.' Kris's face was hard, angry, questioning.

'That was *then*, but this is *now*. Mate, I'm ever so sorry, but I haven't got enough time to try and do all of this.'

'I don't understand what changed?' Kris' voice was close to a whine. 'It was *you* who even convinced me to make more of a go of this... it was *your* bleeding idea I try and make a name for myself! It was *you* who said I could make a proper business out of it!' He took a large gulp of beer from his traditional glass-bevelled tankard and eyed Patrick closely.

'As I said, I'm sorry mate, there's nothing more I can do.'

'*Sorry*, don't pay the bleeding bills! What am I going to do about the bank? I've already bought the new equipment, had it branded – all like what we said. But these payments are crippling me, I've even had to move out of my own place. I couldn't make ends meet.'

'Listen, I don't want you out on your ear, why don't I bung you some money for the mess I've caused?'

'I don't need your charity!' Kris thumped the heavy glass onto the bar top and leapt off the stool. 'I don't *need* anybody to try and make it in this industry. You're forgetting all the greats I played with. I can still be someone you know. It's not just you and your fancy pants business partners who're the only players in town. I'm a player, I'm a feckin' big player, just you watch!'

'Listen mate, I'm sorry, I didn't mean to cause any offence, I'm trying to help you out.' Patrick stroked his glass thoughtfully, picked up a stained beer mat and tapped it lightly on the bar. 'If it was just down to me I'd be taking it easy. I feel too old now to be doing these sort of things, it's a young man's game all this. This is the sorta thing you gotta be feeling tip-top and raring to go for, but I'm not – I'm tired. I'm so bleeding tired even my bones are yawning. All the time I'm working. I'm running from this site to that site, running, fetching, this and that. I don't even know where the time goes, but it surely goes – away and away, day after day, week after week, month after month, and then another year passes and you look back and you've run around like a blue-arsed tit the whole time. Then what? I'm doing all this and for what? I've got a nice house, a nice car, a nice wife, a nice life. I mean, yeah, you could have more, there's *always* more, but what about *now*? I'm not getting any younger, every day another part of me aches. Tell me Kris, when do *I* get to sit back and enjoy the fruits of my labour? In the frigging graveyard?'

'Another drink?'

Patrick looked at his watch. He was due to be meeting Mick and Lucas soon, he didn't really have time for one more, but he was fed up. He'd had enough of his life being dictated by his watch and what time he had to be somewhere. Every day he had somewhere he had to be, somebody he was meant to be seeing, something he was meant to be doing. He felt tired of it all, the constant nag of things to do and the drag of everything. Everything was a drag and a nag. Where was this nice life he thought he had? Only a moment ago he'd declared to Kris he had a nice life, but why didn't he feel it? Why didn't he believe it? Why wasn't he living it?

Kris placed another full beer in front of Patrick taking his silence as agreement. He picked up a cloth and began wiping the bar.

'You know, I know, don't you?' Patrick eyed Kris waiting for his reaction.

Kris paused mid-wipe. 'Know about what?'

'Pauline.'

'What your missus gets up to is nothing to do with me.' Kris fingered an imaginary speck of dirt and set to rubbing it clean to avoid eye contact.

'Everybody knows! The whole bloody island knows. In a place like this, everybody knows everybody's business, especially when she's so bloody flagrant about it.' Patrick looked up and stared at the spirits on display. 'She's made me a laughing stock these last few years with that young boy, thinking she can go sneaking about like some teenager, it's embarrassing.'

'What a husband and wife do in their relationship is down to them, some people make things work in funny ways,' replied Kris.

'You mean you think it's OK for her to be messing about with a pizza boy?'

'I never said that.'

'She thinks I don't know. She thinks I'm fucking blind; like I can't see what she's doing right in front of my own bloody eyes!'

Kris nodded. Patrick obviously needed to let off steam. Kris was used to people sharing their deepest, darkest and dirtiest secrets. He saw it as part of his privileged position as a serving member of the bar. People talk when they drink. But still, he knew his role was to listen. It wasn't his place to go shooting off about what people should and shouldn't do. He knew what was said at the bar, stayed at the bar. But it was awkward, he'd lined up Patrick to be his future business partner, and maybe there was still an in.

Patrick continued. 'I've never said anything to her, but I've *known*. I've known all along from the very start when it first happened. Anyway, I dunno, but I reckon he's dumped her now. She weren't very happy. You know, the first night we arrived here, she came up with some cock and bull bout going to see some shop or something she's been dying to go to since last time. Then when she come back later on, she couldn't even remember what it was she was meant to have been doing! I mean, get your story straight love.'

'What? She went to see him on the first night you arrived?'

'Too right, she's obsessed! He's her holiday romance. But, I gather he's moved on. He's probably found some other bit of skirt more his age and right here on the island.'

'Aren't you bothered?' Kris found himself asking a more intrusive question than he intended.

'Course I am! What bloke wouldn't be? But you know, I can't blame her, it's not *all* her fault.'

'I'm not following.'

Patrick started to shred the beer mat into tiny pieces, flicking whispers of card onto the cleanly wiped bar. He kept his eyes focused on the shredded pieces. 'I've been having trouble in *that* department.'

'*That department*?' Kris pulled a fresh pint of beer and placed it in front of Patrick. He sat back heavily on his stool and leaned his forearms towards Patrick; he needed to show empathy, but not be in his face. This was intimate blokes' talk, a not-so-usual occurrence.

Patrick picked up a tiny paper shaving and rolled it between his thumb and forefinger. He did this multiple times until he had a small collection of miniscule balls which he juggled in the palm of his hand. Abruptly, he started flicking the sweat-moulded bits of paper, scattering them across the shiny wooden bar top. He cleared his throat, took a swig of beer, cleared his throat, flicked some more paper fragments and kept his eyes down.

'Thing is, when I was a lad we used to heap the bricks up and lift 'em no stress. There were no health and safety like today. I was built like a brick shit-house back then, you shoulda seen me – all muscles, no fat, all energy. Ha!' He cast his eyes to Kris, reminiscing the days of old, a small smile formed on his lips. 'The stamina I used to have! I could go all night and all day – unstoppable I was! They used to call me 'the machine'. It was good. Good times. But then, well, then one day I slipped and fell. I'd been on the ladder carrying a pallet-load of bricks. You know back then you didn't need the gym, you used to get fit just going to work! I could eat what I wanted, when I wanted. Me mam, she used to say I had hollow legs the amount I ate and drank, but it never touched me – everything went straight through coz of all the physical stuff I was doing.'

'So what happened?' asked Kris.

'I was halfway up the ladder – it was an extension we were building over Bromley way for an old couple who'd been saving up – it'd been their dream to have a big kitchen diner. Anyway, halfway up and the heavens suddenly open and this ton of rain tips out of the sky, like a jet of water it were, just soaking and barrelling me, pounding me. I could feel the pallet shift and I leant this way and that, coz I could feel I was losing it. It all happened within seconds, the blink of an eye. I remember looking down and seeing Mick, he was right below me. I wanted to call out, tell him to move coz I was gonna drop my load, but I couldn't get the words out. I clung, believe me I fucking clung for dear life with this swinging pallet of bricks. I knew if I dropped it I'd kill him outright and so I tried to keep hold, but the rain it was torrential, just hitting me in the face. It was so hard and I tried to balance myself, like move my foot to try and get a better grip, and I don't know how it happened because one minute I thought I was centring myself and keeping these bricks in check, and the next my hand slips on the wetness. And that was it, I felt my foot go, and I knew I had to try and keep the bricks close to me – I didn't want them to fall on Mick. So down I go, right down to the bottom and these bricks are just raining down on me. I'm yelling – I don't know what – something like 'get outta the way', I should think. I don't really remember, it's so long ago now. But those bricks, fuck me, I've never felt pain like it, they were just pummelling me. I still have the odd nightmare about it now.'

'Jesus Christ, you're lucky to be alive!'

'I know, dead bloody lucky. To be honest, I don't really think I should still be here, but most of them missed my head – apart from a couple, here cop a feel of this.' Patrick brushed a parting in the side of his hair and reached out for Kris' hand to feel the half egg shape unnaturally poking from his head.

'Ooh that's not good, does it hurt?'

'Not really, though every now and again when I get really stressed, it like throbs. It's weird, after all this time, it's like it's a part of my head now, a misshapen part I'll give you that, but still, while I got hair I can cover it, eh!' Patrick chuckled and flattened his hair back to conceal the lump.

'And were you OK after, did you have any other injuries?'

'Well, I was alive, which I was grateful for! I'd bruised a few ribs, bumped me head, got the shock of my life. But really, the more serious damage was down below where quite a few of the bricks had fallen.'

'You mean down below, *below*.' Kris cocked his head to indicate his nether regions.

Patrick nodded and picked up his beer to take a large

gulp. 'In them days you didn't say nowt; you didn't go to the doctors unless you were proper dying, and even then you'd think about it first. I said to the lads on site I was fine, it was wind. I remember they looked at me funny, and Mick tried to convince me to go to the hospital, but I told him I was fine. You couldn't have anybody think you were weak. I was the guv'nor. I wanted to set an example to the boys. Stuff happens on site, but you carry on, you don't let it get to you. I couldn't have them see me limping off. What would that look like, what example does that show?'

'But you were injured!' Kris stared at Patrick in disbelief.

'Yeah, but you get on, that's what you do. Building sites aren't a place for pussies. I dusted myself off, took the cuppa I was offered and trowelled up. No time for pity when you got lads waiting on you.'

'And?'

'So I never made a big deal of it and life went on. The extension got finished and the folks were happy, then we moved onto the next project.'

'OK.' Kris lit another fag and supped from his glass.

'And then one night, me and Pauline, well, we were getting a bit, shall we say, *amorous*. She slid her hand down there, and the pain, fuck me, it felt like she was trying to wrench me goolies off! I told her I'd had a long day, to leave it, I wasn't in the mood. She got a bit sniffy coz she'd been all up for it and thought it was like a slur on her ability to get me ready, but I told her it wasn't her, it was me.'

'Right, and then what happened?'

Patrick frowned, the corners of his face creasing so as almost to touch his chin. 'Well, not much really, it carried on like that... you know.'

'For how long?'

'Well, since then really. It's been years.' Patrick twisted his lips together and fixed his gaze on his feet. 'I know it's embarrassing, it's not something I've ever talked about before now. It's hard, coz every so often I have to perform my husbandly duties, but it hurts so bad I even struggle to maintain it, you know, it takes a lot of effort.'

'And Pauline's never said anything?'

'You've met Pauline; she's said plenty! Course she has! She had the hump several times over thinking I'd gone off her, was seeing someone else – all that bloody palaver. God, she went on something chronic. But I'd talk her down, you know, buy her some nice earrings, a dress, whatever. I'd apologise, tell her I'm tired, stressed, anything really for her to get off my case. But no – if you're asking did I tell her – the answer is no. I wasn't going to admit I had a problem down there, I'm not going to fess up that I'm not *all* the man she thought she'd married.'

'Didn't you go to the doctor's?'

'I thought about it, but what could they do? I knew when I fell I'd done some damage down there. The pain was excruciating; I couldn't piss straight for months after. But really, there's nothing a doctor can do is there? You can't reconstruct a cock after a ton of bricks has fallen on it!'

'You mean it's damaged?' Kris struggled to contain the look of horror that was threatening to erupt.

'Look, I don't wanna get into all the juicy details, but no it doesn't really look quite the same as it did, and it certainly don't feel the same. I guess, it's like this lump on my head, it's just become a part of me now, and I've accepted that. You get a few knocks and bumps over the years, especially in my line of work. We don't look like how we did when we come out of the womb.'

'Mate, that was years ago, medical science has moved on so much!' Kris was exuberant, thumping the bar to get his point across. 'C'mon, think about it for God's sake. Now they can make men into women, and women into men! It's mind-blowing what they're capable of! You really gotta go and see someone. You can't go on like this, it ain't right and it's *unnecessary* in this day and age.'

Patrick pulled in his lips to form a thin line and clasped his fingers tightly. 'I know what you're saying and it has crossed my mind. I've read in the news about the things they do, but it feels stupid to admit now, after all these years.'

'Yeah, but it's better late than never, isn't it? Plus, you may still have the chance to do something about it.' Kris leaned into Patrick, he wanted to poke him, push him, march him down the doctor's office himself, but he knew there were boundaries and he had to respect them.

'Maybe, maybe you're right.' Patrick picked at his confetti beer mat remains and started pouring the remnants from palm to palm. 'I've wanted to tell Pauline a few times now, like just to get it out into the open and not be this dirty secret. But then, when I go to say it, or maybe try and get the subject round so I can do it, the words don't come out. They just get stuck, like here,' Patrick jabbed his throat leaving a blush of crimson. 'And then I find myself changing the subject. I mean, who am I? What sort of man am I to not be able to satisfy his wife and then not be able to tell her the reason why? I can't believe I've got into this mess. And now, I'm sat here with you, telling you. What's that all about?'

'Now you've told me, you could tell her, it'll get easier every time you speak about it, I bet.' Kris felt himself fired up, he was eager to exert a positive influence.

Patrick looked wistfully at Kris. How, after all these

years, had a wrinkly old lush managed to unlock his never-before-spoken-about-secret? 'Maybe. You've got a point. It's just after all this time, it gets *harder*, it's like *too much* time has passed to be able to admit this.'

'It's not going to be easy, that's for sure, but I think you owe it to yourself and to Pauline.'

Patrick supped the last of his drink. 'Maybe. She is a good wife and she's had to put up with a lot. I'm not condoning her playing about, well maybe I am, but I know it was just him and he's a holiday thing away from home. I know she has needs, the way most people do, it's just...'

'Stop making excuses man!' Kris slapped his hand hard on the bar. 'Fact is, now's the best time to tell her. You say she's quit with the other fella here – well, get it out in the open now. Stop beating about the bush or another God knows how many years will pass. Do it, just do it!'

Patrick leapt off the stool and beamed a mighty smile he hadn't felt for years. He shook Kris' hand and bid him farewell. He was stoked and ready to tell Pauline. Kris was right, this had been going on for way too long. And that wasn't all – he'd been bulldozed by Mick for way too long also. Patrick had had enough. He was sick of always being the nice guy, the one who always said yes, who did what others wanted, who always put everybody else's wants before his own. Well, enough. He was sick of playing second fiddle in his own life. He didn't want the risk of the water park. He wanted rest and relaxation and to enjoy everything he'd worked so bloody hard for. Enough was enough, it was time to start living now!

30

OPPORTUNITY OF A LIFETIME

'It's the opportunity of a lifetime, surely you can see that Patrick?' asked Lucas, his thick, shapely eyebrows raising into a tight triangular peak.

'Yeah, I *can* see that, and if I were a few years younger, I'd be well up for it. But now at my age, I don't think it's a good time for me to be taking on a project of this size.' Patrick folded his arms, aware of Lucas' interrogatory gaze.

'How old are you Patrick?'

'Me, I, er, I'm 48.'

'That's no age! A man of 48 is in his *prime*. This is the *perfect* age to be taking on a project like this. Now, you're at the *peak* of your life. You have the money, you have the experience, you have the knowledge, you have *everything* you need. You are ready for the future, for the challenge, for the riches that await. There is *every* reason why you should do this now.'

'But, that's the thing...'

'What's the thing?'

'I want to be sure I *have* a future. I'm not feeling as young as what you say, very kindly that is too, but you see, I'm not like you. I've had a hard life, I've been grafting for years, look here.' Patrick spread open his gnarled hands resplendent with callouses and old scars. His skin was dry and craggy like an abandoned quarry. The palms, usually pink, plump and soft were grey, hard and brittle. His wrists and forearms, despite being freshly scrubbed, were mottled and matted with specks of deeply ingrained plaster and paint.

'Ah! But this is the English weather for you. Here in Fuerteventura you would not have this problem. The sun here makes you more *vital*, it gives you more *life*, more *energy*.' Lucas fist-pumped the air like he was at a rock concert. 'Also, you would use aloe vera, it is nature's secret and the best product for keeping you looking young.' Lucas got up as if to leave. 'We can buy some now, I will show you the difference it will make. You will be like a young man again; you will not have to be embarrassed for your age ever again.'

Patrick chuckled and motioned for Lucas to sit. He wasn't used to a man talking about skincare and products, but he didn't mind. He felt more awkward at the sites when the lads went on about all the tits and skirts and who they'd like to do. He smiled amiably at Lucas, not for one minute did he think his workers would be talking about beauty products – site workers were the same the world over. His gaze fell to Lucas' manicured hands, the nails were buffed and polished to perfection, the light pink nailbed rosy against the whiter than white tip. His hands don't look like they've ever done a hard day's work in their life, he mused to himself. They're more like the hands of a prince, or someone who has servants to look after his every need. I bet he doesn't even have to pull himself off, Patrick thought to himself.

'What do you say?' Lucas' voice broke him from his reverie.

'I say this aloe vera sounds like a miracle product!' replied Patrick.

Lucas laughed, a full smile spread across his face before he pulled it back to a more controlled pleasant game face. 'And the development? What do you think about the development?' He leant forward teasingly. 'We could even include an aloe vera crop so you could have your own personal supply. You'll look twenty years younger by the time we're finished!'

Patrick chewed his lip. Lucas was incredibly charming and incredibly persuasive. But still, he knew whatever the sweet talker said, it didn't change the facts of the situation. 'Look, I think the development sounds great, the numbers stack and it sounds really interesting. You know I love Fuerteventura and I can see the appeal of having a water park, but it's still a big risk... There's a lot of money involved and it's going to be *years* before we start to see any of that back. It's a long game, a *really* long game, and it's a much longer game than I feel ready to commit to.'

'You are right; it is a much longer game. Money doesn't happen overnight when we're talking such huge sums. However, have you considered how many *small* projects, how many *small* clients you will have to run after to get this sort of money? You will never succeed from all of the *small* projects you do – even in a whole lifetime it is not possible. This is why this opportunity is so big, it is the *chance of a lifetime*!'

'I know, I hear you, but I just don't feel comfortable with this level of risk and the time frame. I don't want to still be building in my twilight years. In fact, I've been thinking more and more about retiring, you know, taking things a bit slow.'

'Slow?' Lucas flinched as if Patrick had dropped a slice of chorizo in his lap. 'Who wants to live life *slow*? Life is for living Patrick! *Risk* is what keeps us alive. It is what makes the blood pump faster, it is good for the heart, and the money – well, the money is good for everything! I'm sure Pauline would agree; just think of the life you could provide for her.'

'We have a very good life, thank you.' Patrick smarted, offended by the thinly-veiled put-down. 'I agree this project would make us a lot of money, but it would take up a lot of time as well. And I don't want to spend the time I have left doing this.'

'I see; you have lost your mojo. You need to find your fighting spirit again Patrick if you're going to win in this life.'

Patrick said nothing. He didn't like the way he was being goaded. The way he was being made to feel so small, so insignificant, so rubbish about his life choices. He didn't like the insight Lucas seemed to have and he couldn't work out if the spruced-up charmer was right. He picked at his fingernails, digging out ingrained dirt. Was there any truth in what Lucas was saying? He didn't know and he didn't want to know. He wanted to block it. He didn't want to hear of his lost mojo or anything else. He wanted to sit quietly and brood, about nothing. He wanted to not think of anything. He was sick of running about and always trying to juggle the books. What did any of it mean? What was the point? He wanted time, just time, to do things that he wanted to do, not for clients, not for Pauline, just himself. Maybe he could take up fishing?

'What will Mick say when you tell him you're not doing this development anymore?'

'He's in a different place to me. We're different people, we don't *all* want the same things, you know. He wants the fame and fortune that goes with this development. He's already naming slides after him, he wants the legacy, he wants to be known. But that's him, and this is me.'

'You *are* partners, right?'

'Right, but we're not joined at the hip. We're business partners. Mick wants the money, the big deals, the lifestyle, he's driven more by success.'

'And you? What do *you* want Patrick?'

'Me?' Patrick stared back at Lucas' piercing gaze. 'I told you before, I'm too old for this game now, I don't want the hassle, the fights or the arguments. I want a quiet life.'

'And you're prepared to tell Mick this? To tell him you're not willing to go through with this multi-million-pound deal, this *once in a lifetime opportunity*, because you want to put your feet up?'

'I am,' said Patrick, with a certainty he hadn't felt in years. He knew now what he wanted, and he was going to start living his life the way he wanted it.

Lucas leaned into Patrick, a cheeky smile on his lips as if about to share a naughty joke. 'Even if I told you, as I have already said to Mick, that I've started pre-selling the units. That wouldn't perhaps coax you round, get you to reconsider your position?'

Patrick's firm stance crumbled. 'What units?'

'There's a bigger picture here, a much bigger picture!' Lucas revelled in his surprise revelation and lasciviously licked his lips. 'I don't intend on us *just* building a water park, oh no, we will *also* build a complex of houses and apartments we can sell to the tourists who holiday here. It is the dream of so many people to own a slice of paradise in the sun and we can give it to them. The houses don't need to be big, but they will have big terraces so they can enjoy the weather. We can charge premium prices for the privilege. It is a win-win.'

'And you've already started selling?'

Lucas unzipped his leather-bound folder and flapped several signed sheets of paper in front of him. 'These are what is known in the business as 'pre-sales'. Surely, you have done this before with your business? How long have you been developing property for? This is standard procedure here.'

'I understand about selling 'off-plan'; it's a cash flow thing, it pays for the build and people get a good discount for buying early. But, we don't even have plans or permission yet, do we?'

'Ah! Give it time, they will come, I *know* people.'

Patrick tried to push down a surge of intrigue, and failed. 'What have you sold so far? Have you got any monies in?'

Lucas ruffled the sheets of paper and tapped on his phone calculator. 'From the deposits so far, obviously we will get more later as the development progresses, but we have 720,000 euros. This number will become larger as I still have more leads to follow up on. But demand is high, really high.'

'And where is this money now?'

'In my bank account.'

Patrick kept a close watch on his reactions. He was alarmed to learn Lucas had taken deposits from people, but he didn't want to let on. Instead he said, 'Can I have a look at one of those contracts?'

Lucas passed some printed sheets to Patrick. 'It's all in Spanish, but maybe you understand enough to read it?'

Patrick took the sheets. He didn't read Spanish, all he

could see were lines of foreign words, interspersed with some figures. 'So the people signing these contracts, they understand enough Spanish to know what they're signing?'

'If you're asking me are these contracts legal? Then the answer is yes. I went to the notary and he has signed them. I am not a novice at this game.' Lucas ran his prince-like fingers up and down the sheet of paper as if assessing a crossword. 'We even have a clause where if the buyer changes their mind, we can go after them in their country of origin. If they choose not to pay, we can take any assets they have in their home country to ensure they meet their obligations here. These contracts are watertight.'

A slight tingle developed in Patrick's oval shaped lump on the side of his head. Out of his depth and in too deep. He didn't like how he felt. He flicked again through the contracts signed by unwitting holidaymakers. None of them would've understood what they were signing. Too much sun had addled their brains. People don't think; they dream and dare and don't even consider the repercussions for when things go wrong. He felt uneasy. The site didn't have permission. Up until a few minutes ago he hadn't even known about the proposal to sell houses and now this? His misshapen lump throbbed. He definitely didn't want to be a part of this, but how deep were they? And could he even get out now?

31

THE CONFESSION

'No Pauline today?' Alejandro's face was warm and welcoming as he ushered Patrick to a freshly-wiped table overlooking the street.

'Ah, you know how these women are, see a fancy dress or new pair of shoes and they're off! Like magpies feathering their wardrobes! I said to her: 'Have you ever walked past a shop and *not* bought something? Seems to me, if you aren't spending, you aren't breathing!"

'And you're still here to tell the tale? That is a small miracle!' Alejandro jovially clapped Patrick's back in male solidarity.

'Well, I got *the* look and I hightailed it before she could respond. But these women, flaming hell, they just seem to spend, spend, spend! And if they're *not* spending, they're thinking about what they *will* be spending when they *are* spending!' Patrick chuckled happily at his lot. Pauline always wanted to look 'presentable' – a task which seemed to consume most of her waking day. She would spend hours putting together outfits, planning accessories and purchasing unknown quantities of stuff which he knew she shoved to the back of the wardrobe. But, whatever he thought about her retail addiction, it kept her happy, and that was the main thing: to keep Pauline happy.

'What can I get you today?' Alejandro asked, his face breaking into a gentle smile.

'I thought I'd stop by for a cappuccino while I had a few moments to myself. You make the best one on the island!'

'That's very kind of you to say, thank you. Give me a few minutes and I will be back with you.'

Patrick watched as Alejandro bustled about the open-plan kitchen area at the back of the restaurant. He poured the coffee beans into the grinder and switched it on with a flick. The machine reverberated, chugging noisily, filling the once quiet restaurant with a loud din of throaty chomps as it ate through the beans. A slight haze of coffee aroma wafted. Alejandro selected a clean cup and pre-warmed it with hot water, swirling the contents to heat every last inch of ceramic. He poured the water away and directed the cup underneath the funnel, ready for the black hot liquid to shoot itself into the base of the cup. He checked the contents and then placed it on the side. Taking a canister of milk, he placed it in the steel nozzle on the side of the machine, frothing and aerating the dairy to a cloudlike fluff, before spooning it tenderly onto the steaming black liquid.

'No cinnamon for me,' Patrick called.

'Yes, I remember,' Alejandro replied.

He selected a small biscuit from a sealed glass barrel on the bar and placed it on the side of the saucer. Noticing a small drip on the side of the cup, he wiped away the unsightly brown dribble, before ceremoniously carrying the frothy contents to Patrick, carefully settling the cup on the table.

'Thank you, that's great,' Patrick beamed, licking his lips in anticipation.

Alejandro nodded genially and departed back to his open-plan kitchen area where he busied himself moving around and cleaning various bits of paraphernalia.

'Not so busy today?' Patrick called.

'Ah! It's early yet. We open at this time to make the food preparations. It is easier to be ready for when customers come, if you try and do all at once it becomes difficult. The kitchen is very small with few staff.'

Patrick nodded and took a sip of his coffee, the froth sticking to his upper lip. He licked his lips and took another sip. It was definitely the best cappuccino on the island, if not *the* best cappuccino he'd ever had. He loved the bitter fullness of the blend with the milky topping whisked to perfection, never too milky, never too coffee-y. He took another sip.

'I saw some places in town, they advertise they add Baileys to their coffee...' called Patrick to the empty space where Alejandro had been stood.

Alejandro poked his head back out of the counter, his hands holding a dishcloth. 'Yes, this has become very popular, especially in a latte or after a meal. You should try it one time - unless you want me to make you one now?'

Patrick looked at his watch. 'I think maybe it's a bit late for me to be having another coffee, but I'll take you up on that another time, sounds like a perfect combination! Thanks.'

'No problem at all.'

Patrick sat back and took another sip. He took a small bite from the biscuit and toyed with dipping it into his drink.

He thought better of it, he didn't want to leave crumbs in the liquid, that would be sacrilege. He popped the remainder of the biscuit in his mouth and chomped it in one. He scrunched the napkin tight, wiping his mouth of the coffee stains and crumbs.

'You normally sit with us when I come in with Pauline?' Patrick asked, his tone light but enquiring.

'Ah! I'm so sorry Patrick, forgive me. I was trying to prepare too many things; I will be there in two minutes.'

Patrick pushed out the plastic chair ready for Alejandro to sit down. He would do it now. He wanted to clear the air. This holiday was about getting his life in order. He'd realised now he didn't want to live a lie anymore. Later, he would tell Pauline. He took a deep breath. He felt good. Nervous, but good. This was the first time, in a very long time, that he felt he was taking control. He was being the man. He was taking a stand. He wasn't going to remain on the side-lines; he was going to be a centre-forward and score goals.

Alejandro flicked his dishcloth on the side and joined Patrick, easing himself into the white plastic chair. He smiled casually at his companionable customer.

Patrick took another sip and wiped his mouth again before he began. He kept his eyes focused on the cup. 'There's no easy way to say this, so I'm just going to come right out and say it, so it's out in the open.'

Alejandro cocked his head slightly, waiting for Patrick to meet his gaze.

Patrick fiddled with a loose fray of plastic on the table edge before looking up. 'I know about you and Pauline.' His words were clear and constant. 'I don't want you to go all defensive and try and make up excuses or worse, pretend it didn't happen and lie to me. I'm not stupid, and as one man to another, I'd prefer it if you could treat me with a bit of respect that we're having this conversation because I want you to know, *I know*.'

Alejandro broke off from Patrick's stare and gazed at the table top. He traced his fingertips along the ribbed edges. He hadn't been ready for this. Stupidly. He didn't look at Patrick, but he could feel the heat of his eyeballs on him. He took a small, yet audible breath in. 'I'm sorry, I don't know what to say. I never meant for it to happen. But if you know, then I think you must also know, it's over.' He flicked a glance at Patrick.

Patrick dug his fingernails into the paper covering of the tablecloth, tracing grooves into the surface. 'I guessed as much. What was the reason?'

'I met my wife.' Alejandro stammered and had the decency to look embarrassed. 'When I met her, I wanted to do things right and so I could not carry on.' He spread his olive-skinned fingers wide on the table. 'I knew, from the start, it was wrong, but I...' he paused, before continuing, clasping and unclasping his fingers, 'but I, have no excuse. I'm sorry. I'm very sorry for any hurt and pain I have caused. I was... I have no excuse.' Alejandro dropped his hands to his lap.

Patrick swirled the teaspoon in the remnants of his coffee cup. He hadn't expected the confession to come quite so easily. Granted, he'd set it up and told Alejandro not to lie, but still, he'd expected some sort of resistance, some sort of pushback. He hadn't been ready for the philanderer to be quite so honest, or upfront, so quickly. He leant forward peering at his rival. 'Can I ask you why?'

A deep claret flush coloured Alejandro's neck, spreading seamlessly to his sculpted cheeks. 'I am a very bad person. I cannot tell you why or how. The thought, the right and wrong, it did not enter my brain. It was an action, a thing that happened. It was like an animal instinct, something I *had* to do. I'm sorry, it sounds bad and it is.'

'Did you enjoy sex with her?'

Alejandro pushed back his chair and stared wide-mouthed at Patrick.

'I can only presume you did; I mean; you've been having holiday sex with my wife for years now. Is she the only one? Or one of many tourists you show the *highlights* of the island?' Despite the content of his question, his tone was normal, his expression normal, as if he were asking the results of the football.

Alejandro put his face in his palms. 'I'm sorry Patrick. I don't have a good explanation; I am a bad person. All I can say is I am very sorry and if there is any way I can make it up to you, tell me.'

'Tell me what's she like in bed?'

Alejandro scrunched his face at the directness of Patrick's line of questioning. He knew he'd done a bad thing and at some point was likely to be caught, but never had he considered a conversation such as this. He stared at the middle-aged man who was confronting him. 'Why would you want me to tell you something like that?'

'I dunno. Maybe I want to know what it's like for you?' Patrick paused. Why was he saying this and did he really want to know the answer? He picked at a flake of plaster stuck on his knuckle. Maybe the masochistic part of him wanted to know, but the rest of him didn't want to, not really. What he really wanted to get off his chest was the reason why. He wanted to assert himself, take back his masculinity in whatever shape and form he could. 'The thing is,' he said, his voice confident, '*I know* why Pauline was with you – it's because of me.'

Alejandro's face clouded with confusion. 'You, it's because of you? Why? Are you homosexual?'

Patrick stifled a laugh and Alejandro watched him nervously. 'No, it's not anything like that. I had an accident when I was younger, it means it's difficult... very painful for me, to... you know.'

'I'm sorry, I had no idea.'

'Why would you? Even she doesn't know why we don't do it! She's accused me of affairs and not being attracted to her – never homosexuality though!' Patrick smiled at his former opponent; his faux pas had lightened the tension.

'Pauline doesn't know?'

Patrick shook his head. 'I know I should've told her. I know that now, but not then. It was pressure. I didn't want to have to deal with it. I thought maybe one day it would sort itself out, but I guess, broken things don't fix themselves!' He took a deep breath and watched a passing car turn left at the roundabout. 'That was one of the reasons why I didn't say anything about you and her carrying on. I knew what was happening and even though I didn't like it, I said to myself at least she was doing it here away from home – not on our doorstep. If it had been back home, I would've felt very different. Here it was contained, for a set period. She has needs, I know that, and you could meet them. You were like a sticking plaster for that department.'

Alejandro picked at his nails. He'd never thought about what it must've been like to have been in Patrick's shoes. A wave of shame at his selfish actions tweaked at his temple. He needed to learn from this lesson in life, he needed to think more about how it feels to be the other person. 'How do you feel now?' he asked.

A blissful smile crossed Patrick's face. 'I've realised I need to come clean. I need to tell her about my problem and go to the doctor and get this sorted. I've been crazy to live for so many years putting up with this and the consequences of me not doing anything about it. So now I feel ready to make a change. This holiday has made me a changed man.'

Alejandro reached out, he wanted to hug Patrick, but felt it was a step too far, so instead half-rubbed and half-slapped him on the back. 'I am happy and sad to hear this. I am happy because you look filled with fire, like a man who will take on the world and win, but I am sad for the things that have happened and what I have done to make this situation bad.'

'We are where we are lad. We can't change what has been, we can only change what will come.'

Alejandro marvelled at the depth of Patrick's philosophy. Having had such a big, deep conversation he felt they were in need of a drink. He got up and poured them both a large shot glass of honey rum. They drank it back in one go, the sweet nectar coating and burning their throat.

Patrick watched a red car turning right at the roundabout. 'That reminds me,' he said. 'Lucas is putting pressure on me to do this water park. He's got some idea in his head we can also build houses there to sell to tourists. You know the area better than me. What do you think?'

'Ah! They're building everywhere to sell to tourists – I cannot recognise this island sometimes for there are so many developments. The people they love the sun and so they like to buy.' He poured them another full glass of honey rum. 'The water park is also a good business, but I think, will have more risk. I do not know how many times the people would come. Maybe they will come once, but then again? I'm not sure. Always you will compete with the beach which is free.'

'Yeah, those are good points, thanks. What's it like to get planning here for developments?'

Alejandro twerked his eyebrows and let out a sigh of cynicism. 'It is a very slow and expensive process, and you must *know* people if you are to take the permission. They are very strict here. The land is zoned and maybe you will be in the right area and you should to take the permission, but you must have the right people and the money. Still it will take *years*. My cousin, he has a house over in Lahares; he wanted to change the building because it was falling down. He knew who to ask and had the money saved, but *seven years* it took him to take the permission! This is the way of the island, they do not do things quickly, especially in matters like this. If I was to tell you my honest thoughts on this project, it will be many, many years before you dig the first hole. Maybe it will be quicker to dig your grave!'

'But Lucas would have the right connections, know the *right* people to make it happen quicker?'

Alejandro snorted a spurt of air through his nose. 'Lucas? I do not think so. He does not have a good name on this island. He likes to think he is like a movie star and a very successful man, but everyone else they think he is an arsehole.'

Patrick shook his head at this new information. He didn't know what to say and so he looked at Alejandro waiting for him to continue.

'I'm sorry if I say things that offend you, but you asked me and I want to be honest with you. People see the fancy clothes and his fast cars and think he must be rich and important, but he is a shark, and an arsehole. I would not want to do business with him, not that you have to listen to me, but you asked.'

'No, it's good,' Patrick shook his head again, 'I prefer to hear your opinion, you're local and so know more things than me...' He left the sentence hanging.

Alejandro looked about to make sure nobody was within earshot, poured them another glass of honey rum and edged his seat closer. 'There was a rumour last year, I do not know how true it is, but it was said he left Gran Canaria in a lot of debt and owing a lot of money to people. People said he only came back to the island to try and get away. But then I hear now he has started doing this business with you, so maybe things are different, I don't know?'

Patrick chewed his bottom lip. 'It's interesting to hear this side of the story, because I heard he came back here to repeat his business success in Gran Canaria!'

'Ah! There are always so many sides to the same story, it all depends what ending you want. Who knows the truth? We live in different worlds – same island – but different worlds. His business is nothing to do with my business. He lives in a big house; I don't know how he got it, but you do not get the things he has with no trouble. For me, I prefer to live a more simple life with no troubles. I like to be able to sleep at night. People forget for money you must have trouble, but life doesn't have to be so hard, that is what I say.'

Patrick nodded his head and mused. 'It must be a way of thinking here because I've been thinking pretty much the same recently. Maybe it's the air?'

'We have a saying here; I don't know if it makes sense in English, but we say the shrimp that falls asleep is carried by the current. It's like don't let the world pass you by, don't fall asleep at the wheel, don't be carried off by the waves. I see so many people they are always chasing for the gold and they get a fat purse, but they lost their life. I don't want this; I prefer to have a small house and my life. Maybe my way is not for everybody, but I believe it is better to enjoy now, take your time and your life now, because tomorrow – who knows?'

32

NO MEANS NO

'Are you fucking kidding me?' Mick's face was red and angry. He stared at Patrick, his eyeballs greasy with sweat.

'I'm sorry mate. I said to you before this was out of my comfort zone, and while I've been here I've been doing some more research and giving it more thought, and this project isn't for me.'

'So just like that, you're gonna fuck me over and screw up my chance of the big time?'

'I'm *not* screwing you up and I'm *not* doing you over. I don't want to do the water park development – something I told you from the *very* start. It's not a level of risk I feel comfortable with, but I'm not stopping you from doing it – be my guest.'

'I don't get you. I don't get why you've dragged me here on this trip if it wasn't to meet Lucas and get this deal signed and sealed?'

'I didn't *drag* you anywhere. I was coming here on holiday, like I *always* do at this time of the year. It was *you* who thought it would be a good idea to combine the two.'

'Yeah, coz you've been coming here for years and you were the one telling me what a great idea it would be.'

'I didn't say anything about it! I told you I loved it here and how much I enjoy coming here, it was *you* who said about the water park idea. I agree, maybe I would've said 'yes it would be a good idea', but that was when I thought I was going to be a *punter*, not bloody building the thing and risking my neck...'

'You're not risking your neck! Stop talking like such a woman. Fact is, you're passing up the opportunity of winning big – of *us* winning big. This island is *perfect* for a water park: year-round sun, plenty of tourists, a known developer who wants to work with us and has already started selling houses, getting money in. You're being offered it on a plate with gravy and trimmings, and still it's *not* good enough. What more could you ask for?'

Patrick bit his lip. He didn't want to fall out with Mick. They'd been business partners for many years, but he'd never seen him so wired before. He felt uncomfortable with the pressure and unsure how to handle the guy he'd known for so long. He took a deep breath and purposefully lowered his tone, talking slowly to try and dial back the tension. 'I understand this could be a really good opportunity, but it's not one for me, I did tell you that mate. I'm more than happy for you to go ahead without me, I really don't mind. But it's not something I can do now, I'm not in the right mental state.'

'Mental state? You *are* fucking mental!'

Patrick's resolve collapsed. 'You're calling me mental? When have you ever stopped to think about how *mental* this whole scheme sounds? Think about it – just for one minute. Why has this never been done before if everything about this water park is so *pissing* perfect? And while you're thinking about that, can you also tell me why Lucas, this big *hot-shot* developer, is even talking to the likes of us? If he's so bloody amazing and successful, then why's he talking to a couple of random small-time builders from England? Because I know if I was him, and I was *half* as successful as what he tries to make out, I wouldn't be talking with us. We know *jack* about building a water park or a development of that scale. What's his *real* game, eh?'

'You just can't see it can you?' Mick's face twisted in bitterness. 'Your *negativity* has clouded your mind. He can see we've got *potential.* He's clever, he's got brains. He can see up ahead, he's got vision, not just thinking to the end of the month and bills to pay. That's the *real* difference. He knows he needs to get in with the tourist market, that's where we come in – we *are* tourists. We *think* like tourists, but we got the experience and expertise to then *execute* on it and do something about it. We can build this with the tourists in mind.'

'Have you even worked out how much we need to raise for this project? I mean like *proper sums* – not back of a fag packet – because this is proper, real money. This ain't a flipper Mick, this ain't a quick 'fix up and flog on' like you're used to. Don't kid yourself you know what you're doing, because you don't. You're out of your depth and you haven't got a clue what you're talking about.'

'What and *you* do? You think you know it all don't you? Just coz you do a few figures in the books every year, that don't make you the smarty-pants of this company. You know I've got ideas too, an all–'

'Yeah, above your station.' The words Patrick had been thinking were out in the open before his brain engaged.

'Well, at least I *got* a station I'm aiming for, unlike you!

All you wanna do is sit around doing nothing, just waiting to die you are. I wanna get on, I wanna make something of my life, I don't wanna be held back anymore. I've got the chance to do something big and I intend to grab it with both bloody hands.' Mick banged his fist on the table.

'And I get that. I'm not stopping you.'

'But you won't be my partner?'

'No.'

The puff in Mick's cheeks deflated a little. 'But we've been partners for almost thirty years. This is the sort of opportunity which could make us.'

'Or break us.'

'C'mon mate, try and see it from my point of view. This is such a great opportunity. We could be remembered forever for doing this and make a ton of dosh.'

'I don't know how many different ways I can say no. I'm sorry Mick, I just don't want in on this, but I'm not stopping you.' Patrick looked at his business partner with sadness, he didn't want to be pushed into a corner like this and cause a rift, but he didn't know how else to get his point across.

'Is it because you don't trust me no more? Coz I cocked up that VAT return?'

'It's got nothing to do with that. We've been partners for years. If I didn't trust you now, it would be a bit bloody late!'

Mick folded his arms defensively. He wanted to come back with something clever to make Patrick look stupid and wrong, but he couldn't come up with anything. He chewed the skin around his fingernail and spat it on the floor. He dug the heel of his foot hard into his shoe and jutted his jaw forward, his teeth tight. 'You're gonna regret this decision you know. Tammy's already got so many people interested in the site, people are gagging for it.'

'I'm sure.' Patrick hid his smirk. He'd been on Tamika's site. Property porn was how he saw it, although she presented it differently – said it was an inside view of how successful property developers did deals. He knew there was a big guru-led market out there. People were always on the hunt for how they could make passive income and property was an easy way for the man on the street to feel he had an in. But Patrick didn't fall for it, he knew the numbers were skewed and the problems papered over. Life in property was a stressful hellhole. The people watching her site were gullible dreamers who got off on her low-cut tops and short skirts way more than the properties she was showcasing. But he'd never shared any of that with her or Mick; he knew when to keep his mouth shut.

'I know you're not really up with the internet,' said Mick, his tone more normal now, 'but her site attracts a lot of professional property investors. That's how we got the introduction to Lucas, remember?'

Patrick stalled. He'd momentarily forgotten how they'd got in with Lucas, but now that he remembered, it all seemed to make sense. He knew there was something that had never felt right about the situation and now he could feel his cells connecting to show him the problem. He looked at Mick, his face eager and willing. He was so keen, so caught up in the dream. Logic had been left behind and in its place was a whole load of razzamatazz. Mick wasn't thinking straight; Patrick could see that. Mick had been blinded by the idea of a big life, a big dream. He saw himself as a big man, a man not to be messed with, but Patrick knew if something was too good to be true, then it was. It may have been negative, but it was a rule that had served him well all his life. He said nothing of any of this though, he just nodded in reply to Mick.

'Whatever you think, Tammy's done a lot for us making this introduction. I'm really grateful, she's rescued me from a nobody life. If she hadn't sent all the videos of our work to Lucas, we wouldn't be where we are now. She really put a good word in for us, helped us so much. She's excited about this project, can see how big it will be.'

'Sure.' Patrick didn't want to engage or inflame the conversation, but his mind was working overtime. Coincidences. There were too many of them. Mick had always banged on about how lucky it was he'd met Tamika and then how lucky it was she found Lucas. It was also seen as luck how Lucas just happened to have this great development opportunity. But Patrick knew luck didn't work quite so logically or linearly. Scam. His brain screamed scam. But how could he say anything?

'Maybe it would be a good idea for us all to sit down and go through the costings like you've suggested?' Mick's tone was placid, appealing. He wanted to reach out and make this work.

'Like last time?' Patrick raised his eyebrows wryly. 'I seem to recall when we tried to do some costings before, Tamika called me, what was it now? – 'a neghead'. Said I went on too much about all the negatives – like trying to figure out access and supply issues – because apparently in *her world*, these things miraculously solve themselves! I also seem to remember she went a bit crazy and stomped out. Wasn't that what happened?'

Mick reddened a little at the memory. 'Oh, you know how these women are! They don't like to hear too many negative things; think you're putting barriers in their way. It's all that feminism stuff, made them think they're being hard done by.'

'I'm not being sexist, I'm being realistic. If you can't have an adult conversation about costings at the beginning, there's not much hope for it working out with a happy ending.'

'P'raps I could talk to her? Lay some ground rules? I know you're all OK with me doing this without you, but it feels like I've lost my wingman.'

'I'm sorry mate, let's not go over this again. This isn't for me. Can we just leave it be?'

33

GONE IS THE GOOD LIFE

'Listen Tamika, I don't wanna cause bad feeling between us, but you gotta understand, I don't want to do this deal anymore. It's nothing against you, so don't take it personally. It's just not right for me at this time in my life.'

Patrick stuffed his hands into his short pockets. He didn't like confrontation, and especially not with a woman. The meeting with Lucas and Mick had ended badly and he was trying to get back to his apartment. Coming across Tamika on the terrace wasn't part of his plan, but he was keen to try and clear the air so they could all move on. If he could get Tamika on side, or at least get her to see things from his point of view, maybe she could alleviate some of the stress.

Tamika shook her hair like a mare on heat and turned her face away. 'Whatever. You wouldn't know how to make money if it came up and slapped you in the face! Anyway, Mick's clued up, he'll see through your bad attitude and make it work with Lucas.'

Patrick nodded. 'I hope he does.'

'You just need to keep your fat boots out of it. I dunno

why you brought up all the stuff about the services and time frames today. Like that really matters right now at *this* stage.'

'You mean at the planning stage?' Patrick held back from saying anything more.

'Don't take that attitude with me!' Tamika tossed her head, smacked her lips and shot him a look so dirty he felt the need to wipe his face.

He winced; she was on the attack and he'd barely said anything. This was not going at all as he'd hoped and he was unsure how to deal with such a mad bitch. If she didn't think they should work out if a project was going to stack and make money from the start, at what point *did* she think they should do the sums? The girl was clearly off the scale when it came to mad ideas, and as a man of simple logic, he had no idea how to try and reconcile the two viewpoints.

'I'm sorry,' he said, shrugging his shoulders in defeat. 'I didn't mean to offend you in any way. I was just trying to understand your thinking on this. I mean, when do you think a project should be costed?'

She said nothing and so he continued. 'I hold my hands up. I've never developed a water park or a project of this scale before, and so maybe I'm not doing it right. I'm going from my previous humble experience where I costed and planned a job before we started, to know if it will work and we want to definitely commit.' He paused. 'But perhaps I'm not seeing the bigger picture, and you've got a different way of doing things?'

Tamika lit a cigarette and blew little plumes of smoke purposefully wafting them in Patrick's direction. He didn't react, didn't even do his usual po-faced put-on cough. She could see Mick was spying on them from their balcony, but she didn't acknowledge his rubbernecking. She knew she'd already rubbed him up the wrong way in the earlier meeting. He'd told her she shouldn't speak to Patrick like that and accused her of being disrespectful. Said it made him look bad, especially in front of Lucas. But that had been the whole point; Patrick the fucking dunce needed to be shown for the twat he was in front of Lucas. His negative clueless thinking was jeopardizing the whole deal; he was literally shitting on their lottery ticket.

Tamika blew puffs of smoke out into the sea breeze. She was seething, but knew she had to keep it together if she was going to get her own way. She'd worked so hard to convert Lucas from a viewer of her channel to a potential business partner, and at this moment she was on the cusp of this mega deal happening – or not. Men like Lucas didn't often get involved with men like Mick and Patrick. Lucas was a prime time developer while Mick and Patrick were effectively nobodies, but she'd sold them well, presented them as the perfect partners. A partnership where she was due to take a healthy cut. Mick had been easy to convince, he'd quickly seen how golden a ticket she'd handed him, but Patrick had always been the problem, him and his fucking 'realistic' pessimistic bullshit. He was the one who stood in the way of her mega-success, and she really wanted him to step aside.

Her phone pinged and she looked at the screen.

C'mon babes, don't argue anymore x

She rolled her eyes at the text from Mick and looked up at him peeping at her from behind the curtains. What did he take her for? She wasn't a little girl; she knew what she was doing. She turned to face Patrick; she could sense he was on the verge of leaving.

'Patrick, I think it's about time we got some things out in the open so we can have an adult conversation and move on.

I know you don't like me and you don't approve of my relationship with Mick, but you shouldn't allow those opinions to affect how you assess a business deal. The two things are very separate, and I'd prefer it if we could keep things on a professional level and not pollute this deal with your line of thinking.'

Patrick's face turned rosy red with anger, his skin shimmied and shone with pent-up words he'd wanted to say for a very long time, but hadn't dared. 'You? You're accusing *me* of being unprofessional? Have you really lost the plot? I don't know what goes on in that head of yours, but I'll tell you right now and in no uncertain terms, my decision *not* to do this project has got *nothing* to do with what I think about you and Mick. What he gets up to and who he does it with is up to him, it's nothing to do with me.'

'You say that Patrick, and I know you want to *believe* that's what you think, but I can tell, call it a woman's intuition.' Tamika gave him a small knowing smile and nodded her head to show she understood the subtext. 'Perhaps it's Pauline? Maybe she's the one who doesn't like it? Has she been worming in your ear telling you how I'm a baddie?'

'What *are* you talking about?' Patrick felt his underlying rage surge and he struggled to contain his anger. 'Pauline's got nothing to do with this! She doesn't get involved in my business affairs and she wouldn't dream of saying anything. This business is between me and Mick, it's nothing to do with her or anybody else for that matter!'

'That's what all men say about their wives, but behind closed doors, we all know who's *really* running the shop.'

'You leave my wife out of this, she's got nothing to do with it!' Patrick jabbed his finger at her. 'And you'd better watch what you say young lady.'

'Or else? What you gonna do? Slap me about a bit? Is that how you keep women in line?'

Patrick's face fell in astonishment; he couldn't get over how quickly her mood had changed. 'I don't think it's wise for us to carry on this conversation while you're in this condition.'

'I didn't mean to call you up on something that's obviously too close to home, I'll take it back. We need to talk as we have to get this sorted.'

Patrick took a step away. 'There's nothing to sort, I've told you where I'm at and that's the end of it.' He turned to leave.

'So what *is* the problem then?' Tamika's tone was cutting, venomous. 'Is it jealousy? Yeah, that must be it. Just because you've realized you're not cut out for better things you're trying to stop Mick getting his chance at the big time.' She eyeballed Patrick. 'I reckon that's it, you're plain fucking jealous! You don't want him to be better than you, so you're trying to keep him back at your level. You don't like him acting all young again – all that energy, life, sex, freedom. It's a real bugbear to you ain't it?'

'You're high as a kite!'

'I get it now; I've got your number. You don't want me to be a part of the business and so you're trying to scare Mick into thinking he's making the wrong decision.'

'I've told you before what Mick does is up to him and that's it.'

'Yeah, but that's not the end of the story is it? Not now I'm going to be his wife.'

Patrick swayed a little. Mick had said nothing about proposing to Tamika. He pressed his lips together tightly, he daren't let his thoughts escape. What was happening? Was the whole world going mad and he was the only sane person left on the planet?

'He hasn't told you, has he?' Tamika held back an obvious smirk. 'Well, I'm happy to share the details with you, as he hasn't. We're getting married at the end of next month in Mauritius. It'll be a beach wedding at a five-star complex. I saw it on Instagram and fell in love.' She paused and waited for Patrick to return her stare. 'And so given this changed situation, I'd appreciate it if you didn't keep telling Mick how he should see his kids and maintain communication with his ex. Nobody needs a busybody in their life, and seeing as we won't have time or even be around, it's better if it all just stops now. I'm sure you'll agree.'

Patrick cocked his head, he wasn't sure he'd understood what she was saying or asking him to do.

Tamika bristled with contempt at his slow incomprehension. 'We're going to be living *here* in Fuerteventura Patrick, we're not coming back to England. I've got a fan base to cater for, and Mick's going to be far too busy overseeing the build of the water park to hold your hand on shitty little projects back there. He don't need your crappy kitchen fit-outs, he's got bigger and better things to focus on.'

'OK,' Patrick shrugged. 'I'll talk with him about how he can exit the company then.'

Tamika dragged her fingertip over her lips as though deep in contemplation. 'I don't mean for us to fall out about these things, but I think it would be a lot cleaner and easier if we did it that *you* left the company. I mean, you've been saying how you want an easier life, early retirement even? I'm sure that sounds really good doesn't it? You'd have plenty of time to do all the things you *don't* get to do now.'

He stared at her, his mouth wide open ready to tell her

where to stick her patronising jumped up ideas, and closed it. He was never going to win. You couldn't argue with idiots, he knew that. But what he didn't know was what had got into Mick. How, after all these years had he left him in the lurch like this? All the years they'd worked so hard, planned so much – and for what? For this tart to waltz in and take half the company he'd spent the best years of his life building? The rage built and burned in his stomach, but he let it stew there. He wasn't going to let her have the satisfaction of seeing she was getting to him. No, two can play that game. He nodded calmly, his tone metered and measured, not an ounce of anger in it. 'It's something we could look into, I'm sure. I'll talk with Mick and see where we go from there.'

She smiled at him, the most beatific smile, that showed how very beautiful the girl could be.

He nodded again and took his leave. With every step he felt like a piece of him was dropping off, wilting and dying. Where had the good life gone he'd been promised?

He shoved his hands deep inside his pockets, picking the fluff and dust out of the crevices of the corner lining. He didn't need this aggro. He didn't need any of it any more. He'd had enough of every bugger pushing him and telling him what he should be doing with his life. Everybody seemed to be a fucking expert on what he should do. Enough. He'd had enough. He wanted a say in his life now – it was *his* life and he was the one living it. If he didn't want to spend the rest of his days cocking up a water park that was his bloody prerogative.

Patrick stalled and surveyed the expanse of blue overhead. The sky was so big and so blue, how could he be feeling so down at heart when he was here in paradise? He inhaled hard, exhaled harder and felt the sea breeze, it's salty specks catching on the inside of his cheeks. He let the wind whip and whistle through his thinning hair without bother. He didn't try and pat it down. He would go with the flow. He was done fighting. Life was too short for him to waste any more time on building dreams that would probably never come true.

34

SO MANY WASTED YEARS

'Hey love, did you have a nice time?' Patrick smiled as Pauline shuffled into the apartment, her arms straining under the bulk of her bags. Patrick was sat on the balcony, his shirt half undone, the top button of his shorts open to allow his belly to flop over, a ring of white skin and hair blooming over his waistband. A half empty beer bottle was in his hands.

Pauline glanced at her husband, a sprinkle of mischief and guilt on her face. 'I bought a few things, just some bits and bobs I needed, you know how it is.' She trailed off as she tried to hide the myriad of bags behind her legs. Even she knew she didn't need any of the things she'd bought, but there was a big difference between need and want. She gave up trying to conceal her hoard and grinned sheepishly. She knew, and he knew, she was caught red-handed, but they both knew he wasn't going to say a thing. It was a charade they played well. He would pretend to tell her off and she would pretend she was being told off. Pathetic or pragmatic, she didn't really care – it worked for them and that was all that mattered. Keen to deflect attention from her stash, she changed the subject. 'I thought you were going out with Mick and Lucas?'

'Yeah, I was, I did. I've been and come back.' Patrick took a swig of beer and watched his wife trying to smuggle her latest buys from view.

'Everything all right love? You're normally out all hours drinking and planning – 'a drink for every brick' I thought was the motto?'

'I don't like it love.' Patrick put down his beer bottle and waited for her to stop pratting about with her shopping and look at him directly.

Sensing his stare, she looked up. 'What don't you like?'

'I don't like the project. It's high risk, gonna take years to come to fruition and I don't like the people who I'd be working with. Oh, and maybe I've caught this off you, but I got a bad feeling about it, something doesn't quite add up.'

'But I thought you said this was the 'big one', the one that was going to change all our lives. Didn't Mick say this was THE million-pound project you'd be waiting for all your life?'

'Well, Mick says a lot of things, but you can't always believe what he says.' Pauline stifled a look of surprise. She knew their business relationship had been under some tension lately, but she'd never heard Patrick say a bad word about Mick, he never said a bad word about anybody. Too bloody nice, was what she would always list as Pat's main fault.

'Do you think it may be possible you're getting cold feet because of the size of the project? Maybe it's bigger than what you're used to and so it feels like a bit *too* big? Maybe it's nerves?' She said it, but didn't believe it. She knew Patrick had never suffered nerves in his life, he either wanted to do something or he didn't. When he decided a course of action he got his head down and got on, until it was done. Nerves, worries, uncertainty, they didn't really touch him, he was level-headed and logic driven.

'I don't trust Lucas and I don't like his plan. There's something not right about it, I don't know exactly what, but I'm telling you Pauline, it's something we gotta avoid. We're not to get dragged into it because it's going to be trouble with a capital 'T'.'

Pauline sat down in the chair opposite her husband. She was perplexed by his sudden change of mind and grim mood. He wasn't usually a changeable sort and his bleak outlook unnerved her. 'Has something happened love? Do you need to talk to me? Is there something I should know?'

Patrick fiddled with the label of the beer bottle, digging his nails in to rip thin shards of paper which he flicked onto the table. 'I can't explain it love, but something doesn't feel right. You know I've always said to you about something being too good to be true and all, and I don't trust it. There's something, I can't put my finger on it, but... I don't get a good vibe from Lucas either. I know I've got to allow him some room for being arrogant coz of his success, but from what I've heard, I'm not sure he's all that, and I can't help but feel we're somehow being led up the garden path.'

'Have you spoken to Mick?'

'Yeah, that went down a treat *not*! He was well pissed with me, told me I was making the world's biggest mistake and all that malarkey. He laid it on right thick, but I told him no in no uncertain terms, and I reckon I'm right. I've been sitting here mulling it over and I don't feel bothered, I don't feel I'm making a mistake. I reckon if I was making a mistake – or thinking maybe if I *was* making one – I'd feel it. I'd be questioning if I did the right thing, but I'm not, so I know it's the right thing to have done.'

Pauline eyed her husband. He never normally consulted her on anything to do with the business and she was unsure what stance to take. Did he want advice or an ear to listen? She got up and poured herself a glass of wine to buy some thinking time. Her head felt cloudy like she was coming down with a head cold. She popped a couple of paracetamol with a mouthful of white wine and cursed herself for not getting a glass of water. Patrick watched her, waiting for her response. 'You know love,' she began, unsure where she was going, 'I don't get involved with you and the business and after all these years I don't think I should start now. For all this time I've trusted you to know and do what's best and that's worked fine for us, so that makes me think what you do is up to you. I will stand by you whatever you decide. The only thing is maybe you should sleep on it. Perhaps you're feeling like you want to be in a holiday mood, and having to do this business stuff now doesn't suit how you're feeling. So if you want my advice, which I think maybe you're asking me for, I'd say sleep on it, if you feel the same way in the morning then go with that.'

He leant over and patted his wife's hand. 'That's good advice, thank you love. My mind's made up and I've said my piece to them, so I don't think it'll change overnight, but I'll go with your idea and see how I feel in the morning.'

Pauline smiled and sipped at her wine. She enjoyed being useful. Noticing Patrick was about to open another beer, she said: 'Are you almost ready for games night? We'll be meeting soon on the terrace. Have you had a shower?'

'Yeah, but in this heat it only lasts a few minutes.' He wiped his brow of perspiration. 'I'll have another splash about before we go down – it's not like it'll take us long to get there!' He laughed as he looked over the balcony to the front terrace where the night was being held. 'I wonder what sort of games we'll be playing?'

'They seem to have quite a selection from what I saw when I went past. That Tarah seems a nice girl. I think she's got a nice life out here.'

'What with looking after all them bleeding tourists? I reckon it would be stress on a stick if you ask me!'

'Well, we don't have to be looking after tourists or running a complex like what she's doing, but maybe it's something we could start thinking about. I mean,' she paused, 'I don't want to sound out of line, but it's not like you're getting any younger and you'll not be able to go up and down those ladders and lay bricks in your 70s!'

Patrick eyed Pauline closely. He wanted to tell her. He wanted to tell her now. But somehow, the occasion didn't seem to fit, it seemed too ordinary, too humdrum. After all these years of not saying anything, he wanted the moment to be more special, more melodramatic, more something.

'You've suddenly gone very quiet.' She peered at him, trying to work out what he was thinking.

'You want another one?' he asked, indicating her empty glass.

'I probably shouldn't, I can feel I've got a cold coming on.' She reached over for a tissue and patted her nose. 'Plus, we don't want to be late and miss the start of the games!'

'We're on holiday love, we can be as late as we want! And I don't know when having a cold has ever stopped you having a wine before? Why don't we have a glass of this lovely rioja I picked up earlier and then we can head down. What d'ya say?'

Pauline crumpled her used tissue into the ashtray and nodded. She knew she really shouldn't, but at times her husband needed her to be less sensible, and she could have just one small glass after all. Patrick bustled in the kitchen area looking for a corkscrew ('in the top left hand drawer'), clean glasses ('in the wall cabinet on the right next to the cooker hood') and made so much noise and needed so much assistance, Pauline wondered why she hadn't fetched it herself. Despite the fact he'd needed constant management to pour two glasses of wine, he returned to the table looking jubilant.

He raised his glass. 'To us,' he said, his eyes more moist than usual. He wanted to tell her he was sorry for how much time he spent at work, and how he felt he was spending his life running in circles and never getting anywhere. But instead he nodded and commented on the quality of the wine, to which she agreed.

Sensing he wanted to tell her things, she reached across and held his hand. He stroked his rough fingers on her smooth freckled skin. It felt beastly to caress her tenderness with his thick, tough touch. He wanted her though, no matter how mismatched and ungainly he felt, he wanted her with all of his being. He rubbed the middle of his fingers, the softest part of his palm, on her exposed wrist. He wanted to feel close to her, cherish her; she was his wife and he loved her so very much. He took a large mouthful of wine, a gulp that almost drained the glass. A dark burgundy smear smudged across his lips.

'You know love, I've realised I'm not going to go on forever.' Pauline said nothing, she waited for his next words and stroke of her hand. 'I dunno if all this talk of the water park made me understand how old I've got now, how I'm not so young any more. But anyway, whether it was that or something else I dunno, the end result is the same; life is running past and I don't want to be a shrimp caught up in the waves. I want to actually enjoy some time before I've got none left.' She sat statue-like listening, she wanted to say plenty, but she knew it wasn't her time. 'You know I love you, like *really* love you, don't you?' Her eyes watered a little, but she didn't dare break the moment and dab them. His emotion was so raw, so real, she found it a bit frightening. What had brought on this heavy emotion? Her husband never did big feelings or touchy stuff, he showed her he loved her in his own way. She didn't need long speeches or big displays of affection, she loved him and knew he loved her. What more can any wife ask from her husband?

He gently let go of her wrist and headed back to the kitchen to fetch the rest of the rioja and poured them both another glass. She watched as he lightly sipped from the rim; he'd over poured the wine way too much. A dribble of crimson tracked its way down the outside, dripped onto the stem and pooled at the base, staining the table. She said nothing. They both said nothing. Silence. They both stared out to sea watching the waves cresting and foaming. A catamaran sailed by, her jib flailing in a quick gust of wind. Idle chatter from passers-by floated up to their top floor balcony. Companionable. Congenial. Comfortable. They both took another sip of wine as if choreographed. A small knowing smile flashed between them: in sync, in love, in deep.

'I went for a cappuccino at Best Pizzeria today,' said Patrick, his tone neutral, his face still staring at the sea.

Pauline shifted slightly, a shiver of unease tingling her spine. Her hands trembled imperceptibly as she lifted the glass to her lips. 'That's a long way to go for a coffee love. How come you didn't have one down in the harbour?'

'Alejandro does the best cappuccino and I fancied the walk.'

'Was he there?'

'Yeah, we had a good catch-up. I was talking to him about the water park, about Lucas. Thought I'd pick his brains for the local knowledge, I mean he lives here so he knows more than me.'

'Is that why you don't want to do the project now? Did he say something to put you off?'

'Not really, I think he confirmed what I already knew.'

Pauline drained her wine glass. She waited for him to say something more, but when something more didn't arrive, she got up and opened another bottle of wine and poured them both another glass. She settled back into her seat and hugged the full contents to her breast. She wanted to gulp it all down, but the imperceptible hand tremor had progressed to a more noticeable shake.

'I don't blame you, you know,' said Patrick.

Pauline kept her eyes down.

'I do love you so much, but, sometimes, no, most often-times, I'm not able to express it... physically.' He kept his eyes on the horizon. 'I probably should've told you before, but I didn't. You see, when I had that accident all them years ago, the bricks fell on my bits. It's never been the same. When I try and you know, it hurts. It's not that I don't want to, more that I can't – well not without a lot of pain. I hoped it would sort itself out, but it never did.' He turned to face her full on. 'I never stopped wanting you, but I couldn't, it was too much.'

She reached out her hand and placed it gently on his knee.

'I don't want to go into details, but I want to ask for your support. I understand why you did what you did, and maybe you could extend that same understanding to me? When we get back home I want to see a doctor.'

She sniffed, then coughed, sniffed again and then collapsed into years of tears she'd been fending off. Grief, guilt, regret, shame sobbed through her body. For so long she'd believed she was the problem, had felt inadequate in her wiles. In the beginning she'd tried so hard to entice him, but the rejection and failure had scarred her. Their sex life was an open wound she no longer wanted to pick at. Love, she decided, was a rainbow; theirs was a different colour. He wrapped his wide arms around her, holding her tight. Her fingers wet with tears clasped into his. He buried his face in her neck like a young child. Together they cried. So many wasted years.

Who can say how many tears can replace so many years of hurt? The hole, the emptiness, the void, the vacuum, the hollow feeling. Together they poured their anguish, their sorrow, their faces red and sticky with mourning that need never have been.

He stroked her hair and shushed her. Told her how everything would be OK now, she didn't have to worry, he was there, he was there for her. He told her again and again of his love for her, how she meant everything to him and she sobbed in response. She crushed his arms to her breast and told him she loved him too. For so long she'd felt lacking, lonely in her body, longing to be embraced by him. He told her things would be different. How they would move on. Whispered to her his plans of an early retirement, of long days in bed. He promised her the earth, the moon, the sun and the stars and every universe ever known to man. She promised him her fidelity, devotion, care and support in everything. Together they conspired a new life, a new tomorrow. They talked excitedly about renewing their marriage vows; they wanted everyone to know of their unshakeable, unbreakable love.

35

GAMES NIGHT REVISITED

The sun is hot on my face as I glance at the gathered people. I take a quick swig of breath. Just 48 hours ago I was here, standing on this same terrace, looking at these same faces ready to host games night. Not everyone's here who was here then, but almost. I didn't bring back Mark and Sindy, guests with us who didn't know Patrick and who only stayed for the first round, nor Miriam, who's still in hospital. There's also a couple of extras – Kris and Lucas weren't at games night, and Alejandro had only stopped by, but still, I think they have potential. Potential connections and potential reasons.

Standing here now I can see Patrick as if he's stood right in front of me, real flesh and blood. He's smiling at me, asking what games I've got lined up and if he'll know any of them. He nudges me and asks if I've got any cheat sheets to be sure he'll win. I remember thinking he somehow seemed lighter, freer, less bothered, less wrinkled even. Him and Pauline seemed *very* together. They didn't look like a middle-aged married couple, more like a couple of young teenagers out on a first date. They were so cosy and cute together, holding each other's hands, diving into each other's eyes. I'd smiled at their public display of affection. Thought how sweet after all these years. And wondered if ever I would one day meet somebody who I could be like that with. I remember catching a glance between them and feeling like an intruder on their intimacy. There was something so deep and so shared in their eyes, it was as though they'd bared the secrets of their hearts to one another.

I can see them now, so in love with a freshness and vibrancy you'd usually find in spring flowers and newly cleaned pools. I can see myself offering them some cava I'd just taken from the fridge. Pauline's face lights up when I mention bubbles and while she tells me she really shouldn't drink any more and she thinks she's got a cold, she's downed the glass in one. She holds out her empty glass again ready for a refill, while Patrick nudges her playfully and tells her to leave some bubbles for him. They're fizzing with energy. I remember thinking what high spirits they were in, bouncy and lively like a couple of young puppies.

Mick was pawing at Tamika, needy and lustful, hands trying to go too many places; his face was ruddy and bruised with alcohol. She'd looked terrifyingly gorgeous, sullen as hell, and as sexy as sexy gets. Her attitude reminded me of a cat, the way they wheedle and wind their way between your legs and then when you bend to make a fuss of them, they stalk off, aloof-as-you-like without a backwards glance. I hated her, but wanted to be like her, and I couldn't fathom how those two emotions even went together. Her attitude was so lousy, so low, so repellent, but at the same time so appealing. It was like it was so wrong you wanted it to be right. I mean, how many people can really pull off the 'I-truly-don't-give-a-fuck-what-you-think' style. It's so inimitable that it compels you to want to copy. I remember thinking it wouldn't work with me; I don't have the worshipful face or body and so I imagined her covered in bleach, scarred and ugly. That made me feel cleansed, but not by my own thoughts.

Mark and Sindy were the new arrivals, new to the island and new to Jorge's Place. They didn't want to play games as they were hungry and had been on their way out. Miriam had nabbed them as they'd tried to stroll off down the promenade. 'Come along now my dears, you don't know what you're missing until you've tried it,' she'd said to them, easing them into a table and chair set she always favoured for herself. 'I'll help you along and explain the rules.' She'd smiled a gleeful grin at them, glad to have new faces and fresh blood. Miriam loved games night, saw it as the highlight of her stay. No matter what, she always found herself a space and a way to cosy up and latch on to any unsuspecting guest to 'help out'.

'We'll stay for one round then,' Mark had said, patting his belly to remind her they were hungry and had been en route to eat.

'Yes, of course, my dears,' Miriam had simpered. 'This course is like your aperitif, to get you in the mood for food!' Her lips had parted wide, revealing waxy pink lipstick smudged on her front teeth. I'd made a mental note to say something to her in private, when I got the chance, but I don't think I ever did. I recall she took control very quickly and Mark and Sindy were a willing and obedient audience, rather like a couple of stuffed teddies, or plastic dolls at a child's pretend tea party. I remember thinking how nice of them to humour her and knew she'd be revelling in the details when she told me the next day. I watched as she settled them down, selected Trivial Pursuit, opened the board and gaily explained the rules, wagging her perfectly manicured finger at their nodding heads. I'm sure they were well aware of the rules, everybody knows the rules to Trivial Pursuit, but they were polite enough to say nothing and pretended her instructions were the most fascinating things their ears had ever heard.

And then I remember hearing some chairs scraping on the other side of the terrace and seeing Pauline, Patrick, Mick and Tamika had come together as a foursome settled at the far end table. The group had looked awkward, like a forced marriage between two couples who'd had a falling out. I can see myself pondering on taking over a bottle of wine as some sort of peace offering, but then Mick, overly cheery with the over consumption of alcohol, clumsily dropped the game he'd declared they should all play. Drunk and out of control, I decided I really couldn't be encouraging that sort of behaviour, so held off on the more wine option.

I watched them from afar, not wanting to get involved, but feeling like I was already involved. Mick was on his knees scrabbling around picking up little plastic red and green houses and trying to catch the dollar notes that were scattering and flying across the floor. Pauline was taking the contents from his hands and stuffing them back into the box. When he'd collected all the bits she'd closed the lid, firmly.

'C'mon now you lot, Monopoly is the *obvious* choice for us all.' Mick had swayed and leant heavily on the table, the plastic legs creaking unhappily as he bore his weight hard on one side. Their faces had looked doubtful about whether it could take the pressure and their fingers had crept towards their glasses, ready to steady them in case of a fall. 'Jeez, c'mon, it'll be good – Patrick can show us what a shit hot developer he is!' Mick had laughed loudly. It had rung about the terrace and vibrated way too much.

Undeterred, he'd grabbed the box and tipped the contents onto the table. His hands had been blundering and gawky and he'd tried to do everything too quickly and ripped a tear in the middle fold of the board. The others had looked away, pretended they hadn't seen as he'd tried to stick the paper back over the torn fold. 'I'm going to be the racing car as that's my favourite,' Mick had declared. 'Tamika, you can be the top hat because you'd look good in a hat, and you're a classy chick! Pauline you can be the dog, and Patrick...' Mick had fumbled amongst the innards of the box and held up two metal markers, 'you can be the boot or the wheelbarrow'. He'd held up each piece for closer inspection, his eyes squinting as if looking for a hallmark, and had pronounced Patrick could be the boot.

Mick had then pressed the playing pieces onto the 'Go' square and lumbered clumsily across the table for the dollar notes. They were too far out of reach and as he'd tried to grab a handful, the board had split further. Pauline had paused mid-wipe of her nose and offered to be banker on account of the fact she hadn't had as much to drink, and was perhaps better placed to count. Mick had accepted her offer with a shrug and sat back while she collated the notes and distributed them to each player, starting first with Patrick to her left and serving herself last.

'Right, all of us should throw the dice and see who gets the highest number. They'll be the first person to start,' Mick had said loudly, keen to take back authority. He'd then seized the two red cubes and shaken them like a top cocktail maker, spraying them across the table so they both ended up on the floor tiles. He shoved his head under the table and said, 'five and three, that gives me an eight for the rest of you to beat.' Snatching the dice up from the floor, he'd passed them to Tamika. She held her hands aloft, as if holding a winning trophy, and with a delicate but firm flick of her wrists, gave them a shake. 'Two and three, bad luck,' Mick had said as he checked the dice. It was Pauline who plucked the dice next. She gave them a quick shuffle and clattered them onto the table. Mick had been impressed with her throw, she'd rolled a ten and was now in the lead, unless Patrick could do better. Patrick had grabbed the dice and vigorously shaken them in his cupped hands. 'Ah, four and three, bad luck mate,' Mick had said. 'Pauline's beat us all. Go on then old gal, show us what you're made of!'

I remember watching them, feeling uncomfortable, but intrigued. Monopoly was never a wise choice for any of the guests to play, and I'd already seen it end in a number of arguments and threats of divorce. How this would pan out was not looking good, but I didn't know if there was a way I could step in. How could I try and change the course of this inevitable car crash?

'This is a question from arts and literature. Now are you listening?' Miriam's dulcet tones interrupted my thoughts. 'Who painted the Mona Lisa? Was it a) Vincent van Gogh, b) Leonardo da Vinci or c) Michelangelo? This may be a bit tricky so take your time, my dear.'

Mark clutched his chin in thought. 'Hmm, that *is* a deliberately tricky one. I know it's not going to be van Gogh as I think that was before his time, and Michelangelo, well, I can't think. Wasn't he the one who did the ceiling, or was that da Vinci?' He paused. 'I'm going to say da Vinci.'

'Is that your final answer?' Miriam asked, enjoying her role as question master.

'Yes, I think so,' Mark replied, trying to look certain in his choice.

'You are correct! Now Sindy, it's your turn. Let me see what colour question I need to ask.' Miriam started to fumble with some cards. Sindy sensing her opportunity to escape, grabbed it.

'Miriam, this is a good game and we *are* enjoying it, but it does take an awfully long time and we were on our way to eat. Do you mind if we go and get some food and we can rejoin you later? We could carry on then?'

Miriam looked at Sindy as though she'd stolen her false teeth, 'But my dear, we've only just started, we've several rounds to go. Why don't you have some pizza, that will be along shortly.'

Sindy shifted uncomfortably. 'I'm really sorry, but I'm on a new diet which means I can't eat wheat and so that wouldn't do. I hope you understand.' Sindy exchanged a look with Mark and started to get up. 'I'm ever so sorry, but we'll come back after we've eaten.'

Miriam looked at the pair crestfallen, said she understood and wiped the corner of her eye with her floral handkerchief. Mark and Sindy looked at each other awkwardly, then scraped their chairs back, apologised again and waved goodbye, before unlatching the gate and striding off down the promenade towards town without a backwards glance. Miriam put the contents of the game carefully back into the box and helped herself to a pack of cards.

'I don't need anybody to play Solitaire with,' she muttered to herself as she laid out the cards.

A trickle of laughter seeped over from the foursome playing Monopoly, Patrick looked at me and called out. 'Did you hear that Tarah?'

I shook my head.

'Tamika won second prize in a beauty contest. We've all gotta give her a tenner. But Mick reckons I've fixed the game and she should've come first so now we've all got to give her a twenty!'

'Now, now, play nicely children,' I called back, reminding myself of my mum.

I scanned the promenade and saw Jorge and Alejandro walking towards the terrace, their arms stretched wide with boxes full of pizza. Good timing, I thought to myself. Food at this point will be much better for the players than another glass of plonk.

'Start putting your playing bits to one side gang, food's on the way,' I called.

They groaned at me, annoyed to have their playing interrupted, but delighted to avail themselves of free food brought straight to their table.

'Just you remember where my counter was, I'll be watching you,' said Pauline to Mick, a humour to her tone suggesting any previous animosity was forgotten.

Alejandro smiled at the waiting crowd. He placed two pizza boxes in front of the foursome and two on the table where Miriam was sat. She looked up at him aghast. 'My dear, I know they think pensioners don't eat well, and I appreciate you trying to fatten me up, but I can't eat all of that!' I winked at Miriam and told her Jorge and I would be joining her, so she shouldn't worry too much about not fitting into her tiny bikini because I was very hungry and capable of eating plenty.

'And after pizza, tonight we have special treat!' Jorge proudly held out a stainless steel dish covered in foil. 'My wife, she made a favourite island dessert, crema catalana.'

The group buzzed with delight at the prospect of a homemade dessert to follow their free pizza and free-flowing drinks. Pauline carefully carried the Monopoly board and its pieces to a neighbouring table, while Mick flung open the boxes and started helping himself to a slice. Having ensured everybody had napkins and everything they needed, I settled myself at the table with Jorge and Miriam.

Jorge turned to me, his eyes sweeping over the foursome. 'How is the games tonight?'

'Surprisingly OK,' I replied, chewing a crisped salami slice. 'I thought there were going to be some issues, but they appear to have ironed them out and now they're all smiles and laughter. I think there's still a bit of tension, but the wine seems to be sorting that out – for now!' I crossed my fingers and smiled.

'Good, good,' Jorge nodded. 'The games are good for the people to sort their problems.'

'So many things we say in jest, we *really* do mean,' interrupted Miriam, giving us both a knowing look.

I pulled a second slice of pizza from the box, the melted cheese stretched and yawned, its elasticated tentacles pinging splashes of tomato juice onto my arms.

'You're such a mucky pup, you need a bib,' laughed Miriam eyeing the dollops of red splattered onto my top. I took the offered napkin and rubbed the offending marks, doing little more than smudging the juice further into the fibres.

'Tarah, would you like me to get some serving bowls for the dessert?' Tamika was stood next to me, she glanced at my top. 'Ice is good for getting rid of those stains.' I smiled at her, surprised by her helpfulness. She held out her hands to take the bowl of home-made dessert.

'That's very kind,' I replied, 'but you're a guest. I can sort it in a minute, everybody's still eating anyway.'

'It's no bother, you're always running around after us. Why don't you sit back and have a little break?'

'Well, that's very kind, thank you. Do you know where the kitchen is?'

'Sure, I'll find my way, don't worry. Enjoy your pizza while it's still hot.'

Tamika sashayed to the building, her hands delicately balancing the bowl as if it were hot. Jorge turned and raised his eyebrows. I returned his eyebrow raise with a twitch and shrugged. The temptation of another hot slice of pizza was too much – I dived in and took a piece. Chewing on the thick layer of mozzarella I surveyed my surroundings. I loved the terrace and the town at this time of night. Early evenings were always full of such promise. Anticipation tingled and tangled with freshly applied after sun, some cheeky bronzer and new lipstick bought especially for holiday. Wafts of perfume and aftershave carried on the breeze as tourists strolled by eager for sundown drinks and deliciously-exotic-but-not-too-exotic evening meals. The air was full of expectation, a low buzz of excitement: good times to come. Jorge stood to inspect the pizza, his eyes travelling over the toppings. He curled his lip, picked at the pepperoni and said he'd be asking for chorizo next time. He ate a slice, cursed, and then went back for more. He ate five slices.

A deep sense of contentment filled me. There was an amiable hum on the terrace, interspersed with pinpricks of passing laughter. Slow, happy, appreciative. That was the mood. Sit back and enjoy. The competitive spirit had been fed, tempers were spent and bellies were full.

Tamika appeared next to me clutching some bowls, her

face was flushed red. 'Er, Tarah, I've made a bit of a mess with the dessert. I didn't know it had a hard top so I ended up mushing it a bit.' I looked down at the light yellow splodges she'd manhandled into the bowls, it looked like foamy béchamel custard. 'No problem,' I said reigning in a smirk, 'I'm sure it tastes delicious, thank you for that.' Tamika handed round the bowls, her usual arrogant stature slightly dented.

'What did you say this was again?' Called Mick.

'Crema catalana,' replied Jorge, licking his spoon and seemingly unfazed by the mess in a bowl he'd been handed.

I scooped up some of the eggy dessert and found myself pleasantly surprised. Despite its appearance, it was very tasty, although I wasn't sure Jorge's wife would've appreciated Tamika's more creative take on its presentation.

Pauline started gathering up the bowls and empty pizza boxes. I was grateful for her help, but ushered her back to her chair. I'd had enough of guests helping me for one night. Collecting up the crockery and cutlery I scraped the food remains in the waste bin, filled the dishwasher and set it to run. Since the cockroach incident, I'd become paranoid about leaving any scraps anywhere and ensured rubbish was put out immediately. I tied the bag tightly ready to dispose of it in the community waste bins just outside in the street. Letting myself out of the side gate, I picked up a bag of empty bottles and clinked with every step. Here comes the marching wine band, I chuckled to myself. Dumping the bags into the giant bins I made my way back to the terrace.

I'd only been gone a few minutes, but when I returned to the terrace it felt like there was a shift. The easy going idleness no longer felt so comfortable, there was a prickle of tension, a stab of something unsaid having being said.

'Everything OK?' I asked Jorge.

'All is good, they eat and drink plenty and now they ready for bed,' he replied.

'That was lovely my dear, thank you. I'm off to bed now to read my book,' said Miriam, patting me on my hand.

'Aren't you meant to be finishing your game with Mark and Sindy?'

'Oh, I think they'll eat and then have a drink and won't come back until much later. It's all right, don't you worry, my book's plenty of company for me.'

I waved goodnight to Miriam feeling a little deflated for her, I knew how much she loved playing with new guests and getting all the latest gossip. She may've been one of our oldest guests, but she was probably the youngest at heart. A loud crash attracted my attention and I cringed as Mick lurched unsteadily from his seat to grab the Monopoly board to resume play.

'C'mon then, let's get this game won!' shouted Mick, flinging the contents onto the table.

'I think I'll sit this round out,' said Patrick, 'I'm not feeling so good.' He wiped his forehead with his hand.

'You can't sit out a round in Monopoly, that's pointless! You may as well quit now if you don't feel up to it. Is that what you wanna do?'

'Yeah, yeah, I'm gonna have to. I'm feeling a bit off, maybe Pauline's passed her bug to me and–' Patrick's sentence evaporated into a violent coughing fit. He scraped his chair away from the table and hung his head low, his chest and back heaving with the effort of the dry retches. He looked up, his eyes bright and tinged red with the effort. Pearls of spittle hung from his bottom lip. He wiped his mouth with the back of his hand.

Tamika shifted her chair. 'Keep your germs to yourself!' She covered her nose and mouth with a patterned scarf and rolled her eyes.

Pauline handed him a glass of water and rubbed the top of his back. 'Drink some water love. No more alcohol, I think you've had quite enough.' He took the water and tipped the contents down his throat before the next cough erupted. 'Why don't you call it an early night? Let's go up and you can take some paracetamol. After a good night's sleep, I'm sure you'll be right as rain.'

Patrick turned his head and coughed violently in agreement. He waved goodnight, and still coughing, made his way across the terrace. I called out goodnight to him and said I hoped he'd be feeling better in the morning.

But his next morning never came. That was the last time I saw Patrick alive.

36

THE END GAME

As I walk onto the terrace I look a lot more confident than I feel: *Fake it till you make it, fake it till you make it.* The words echo round in my head and I gesture for the gathered faces to sit down at the empty tables. I place Mr Bob in his carrier on the side. His nose twitches and his eyes widen as he takes in the occupants of the terrace.

Pauline sits first, followed by Mick and Tamika, Kris, then Alejandro and his wife and child. Jorge, having settled Pauline, steps back by the gate, lining up with Diego. They nod at me as if to say 'We've got your back.' Lucas remains standing, refuses to sit with the others, until Felipe, Jorge's policeman friend and not a fan of such defiance, fires Lucas a warning look and taps his baton intently on his thigh. Lucas curls his lip in contempt; he's not a fan of being told what to do.

'What's the meaning of this? Why are we here?' Lucas strides forward, his finger pointing at me.

'If you'd like to take a seat, we can begin,' I reply.

His face flushes with anger. 'Why would I take a seat? I

have no intention of staying, say what you've got to say and we can all get on!'

I tremble a little, taken aback by his quick temper and accusing finger stabbing at me, but I refuse to be intimidated. 'Fine.' I take a big step forward so I'm in the middle of the terrace, able to make eye contact with everybody. 'As you all know,' I start, building up volume, 'a guest of ours, Patrick, died here two days ago.'

'What's that got to do with us? He had a heart attack,' says Lucas, his arms swotting away my words as though they're annoying mosquitoes.

I continue. 'The initial reports found Patrick died from a heart attack, but I have reason to believe,' I pause and look across at Jorge, '*we* have reason to believe, his death could've been prevented.'

Pauline gasps, her hands clutching to her mouth. 'What are you saying? You mean he *didn't* have a heart attack?'

I nod and shake my head simultaneously. 'I'm sorry, it's complicated. We think he *did* have a heart attack, but we don't believe it was a *natural* death.'

A wheeze of disbelief exhales across the terrace. Mr Bob scuffs bits of straw onto the floor and scurries about impatiently. Chair legs scrape as people fidget uncomfortably, threads of clothing are pulled and picked at. Lips are bitten, hair preened, fingers clasped and unclasped. Nobody wants to look at each other, but everybody wants to look at each other. Sidelong surreptitious glances. Who's to blame? Stare at the floor. *Was it you?*

'This is obviously a bit of an awkward situation,' I stammer and have to pinch my fingers to hold it together, 'and what I'm about to say, you won't like. But all of you here, *could* be said to have a motivation for Patrick's death.'

The hush descends into a roar. Voices shout and clang. Lucas stomps his feet and Mick yells I'm a liar. Pauline sways in her seat as though high on Valium.

I ignore them all and ask for quiet. They carry on jeering and heckling until Filipe bangs his baton against the railings. The metallic swipe stuns them into silence. Mouths open and eyes even wider stare at me. Suspicious. Mistrustful. Disbelieving. Their gaze says it all.

'I know what I'm saying is controversial, and we didn't believe this either in the beginning. But, and I know it sounds crazy, it was Mr Bob who alerted us to the fact this was no normal death.'

The assembled crowd gasp and rotate in unison to stare at Mr Bob. Hearing his name and aware of the stares, Mr Bob presses his face against the bars. He peers out at the crowd, fluffs his fur, takes one step back, then two forward, pokes his pale pink nose through a gap and lets out one long massive high-pitched wheek.

'You are joking right? You know how crazy you sound?' I swivel to look at Kris, he visibly shrinks under my stare.

'Kris, I know you and Patrick had your differences, and you were disappointed he wasn't going to be investing in your karaoke business,' I pause, 'which was made all the worse given you paid the investment upfront and left yourself in a financial mess, but–'

'But, we sorted that, I told you all this,' Kris interrupts.

'I know, I was about to say that, if you'd let me finish.' I give him a warning glance before continuing. 'I agree with you; Patrick was worth more to you *alive* than dead. If he were still here now you could at least try and talk him round. As it is, you've no chance.'

Kris shakes his head and tuts. 'You don't have to make me sound so heartless!'

'I'm sorry Kris, but I'm dealing with facts and the fact is, while Patrick went back on his promise to you and caused you a whole heap of trouble, I know you didn't kill him. There was nothing for you to gain from this. Everything *you* needed meant you needed him alive. So I know it's not you.'

Kris folds his arms crossly. 'Too blooming right I didn't kill Patrick. Why would I do a thing like that?' He looks about, his face pinched with hurt. He wants everyone to know he's out of the frame. It wasn't him, and it was a downright cheek to have suspected him in the first place.

The gathered crowd pivot their eyes to my next target. Alejandro stands up, alert to my impending questions. 'Obviously, you having an affair with the victim's wife, did make you a prime suspect.' Alejandro begs to speak, but I press my fingers against my lips to indicate he's to stay quiet. 'That was, until we learned, you were no longer together.'

A flash of embarrassment crosses his face at the shared news, before a shy smile appears and he squeezes his beautiful wife's shoulder. 'When I met Christina, it was like 'boom'. She was the one, the love of my life. Then, for me, I knew it was over. It wasn't easy because me and Pauline... we had long history, but we were bad, we shouldn't have, but...' He trails off and Pauline nods. She stares fixedly at the table. The air is thick with judgement.

'Of course,' I continue, 'most people thought Pauline was to blame. I mean, as the wife, she was the one who stood to gain the most from Patrick's death.' A murmur of agreement ripples across the terrace. 'But then,' I strengthen my voice, '*most* people wouldn't know Pauline only stood to gain the marital home she lives in. She doesn't *actually* get any of his business assets. That's a whole different matter, isn't it Mick?'

'What?' Mick leaps from his chair, knocking over the bottle of beer he'd been drinking. 'I didn't kill Patrick! I *needed* Patrick! I needed him to be alive to sign off on everything to do with the business. It makes no sense for me to have killed him! You're talking rot! I'll have you!' He jabs his finger at me, his face seething with rage. 'I'll bloody have you for slander and libel and...'

Felipe steps forward, his arms outstretched ready to catch hold of Mick. Tamika pounces, her feet swift and light. 'Calm down baby. We'll sort her, don't you worry. And don't you listen to the crap she's saying. You're so much *more* of a man than Patrick would ever have been! You'll run the business better without him; we don't need his sort.'

Mick brushes her away. 'I know you mean well honey, but Patrick was a good guy. I couldn't have done any of it without him. He was the one who held it all together, who made sure we made it.' His face sags and his eyes well with tears. 'Without him, well, I don't know where I'd be. I thought the world of him, he was like a brother.'

Tamika strokes his arm and twizzles her long hair under his chin, canoodling into him as though they're slow dancing a love song. 'Don't underestimate yourself baby, you're amazing. You'll be better off without him, you'll see. We don't need him and his type.'

Lucas stamps his feet; the heels of his expensive leather shoes reverberate on the tiles as if he's about to start a flamenco. His usually even-toned olive skin is bruised with anger. 'You're a crazy English girl! You got us all here for what? For you to think you are like a Columbo?'

I bite my tongue. The rush of Tamika's emotion for Mick

had set him off. But this wasn't the time to share how I knew he was obsessed with Tamika, how I'd seen he'd been stalking her online for months. How it was bloody obvious (to me, at least) the way he was trying to wheedle his way into her affections and get her away from Mick. Instead I say, 'You don't need to be Columbo to work out you're flogging dud apartments.'

He tosses his glossy hair and bares his brilliantly white teeth. 'How dare you! You don't know the first thing about my business or how I develop.'

I keep my cool. I'm not impressed by his posh suits and expensive shirts. He may've had the most deliciously hydrated skin and the shapeliest eyebrows ever known to man – and a car collection to die for – but his fancy ways had no sway with me. 'I may not know about your business or how you develop, but I know the area you're claiming you can build on is *not* zoned for development because it's a protected natural park.'

'The law of this island says building on that land is prohibited,' Alejandro says.

Lucas waves his arms dismissively. 'You both have no idea what you're talking about, I know what I'm doing.'

'Yes, of course you do. You've done this before haven't you?' I say, my tone dripping with sarcasm. 'I mean, selling properties to unsuspecting tourists when you don't even *own* the land, that's your business *thing* isn't it? Otherwise known as fraud, I would think.' I shoot him down with a look. I can't believe I didn't think before now to check him out online. The Canary Islands forums were full of threads from tourists who'd been ripped off by Lucas. Alejandro had been right, he'd done this before – not only in Gran Canaria, but also Tenerife. Selling off-plan properties that would never be built was his stock-in-trade, and who would ever question such a smartly dressed developer with a different company name each time. It meant joining the dots took longer, and by then the tourists had already left, and he had their deposit money, in his bank.

Mick lurches forward his fists bunched. 'You wanker, you absolute fucking wanker! I put my trust in you, my faith in you and you fucking lied! You've had me on!' Felipe jolts into action putting his body as a barrier between the two men. Diego and Jorge rush over to hold down his thrashing arms. 'I'll fucking 'ave you I will, you fucking con!' Lucas takes a step back, edging for the gate, but Felipe moves quickly, blocking any thoughts he had of a sharp exit.

Tamika totters slightly, her five-inch patent silver heels angling precariously. 'You mean none of this was real? There ain't going to be a water park, or a hotel, or a development of thousands of houses or...?' Her perfectly symmetrical features twist in confusion. 'But, I, I, thought we were gonna be rich. I thought this was the big ticket, I told all my fans this was it...' Her golden cheeks flush pink and she swallows hard. 'But this ain't what I signed up for. I'm here to do a deal, to make money, this wasn't part of the plan.'

Mick's fury evaporates at the sight of her teetering. He presses his lumbering frame against her quivering limbs, comforting her as if she were a child. 'It'll be all right; we'll be all right. We've done nothing wrong. We didn't sell any of those places and we've had none of the cash. It's nothing to do with us. The police will see that. We'll be ok, don't you worry.'

She looks up at him, her eyes two deep pools of unshed tears. 'But I, but I...'

'Was banking on the fame and fortune this development

would bring.' I finish the sentence for her. 'What will your fans think of you now?'

She turns to stare at me, her face blank.

'You were an easy target for Lucas. He knew how much you craved a big development, how important it was for you in your role as an *influencer*.' I air quote the last word over-expansively. I know I'm mocking her and twisting the knife, but I don't care. 'You needed this project to validate your position, your *authority*. You had advertising deals lined up, promotional posts that were willing to pay big, but all of them were reliant on this water park happening. And so when it looked like maybe it wasn't, you had a problem.' I pause and look about, ensuring everybody's listening. 'When Patrick pointed out the realities of the project and started questioning how this would work, he got in your way. That wasn't good for you and it wasn't good for business was it?'

She shakes her long blonde hair. The strands cascade and frame her face, making her look even younger. 'You don't know what you're talking about, you don't know nuffin' bout me and it's *their* business, it's nothing to do with me.'

'But you made it *your* business, didn't you?' I say. 'You had plans on how big this was going to be and your role in it. Patrick was in the way; he wasn't part of your future. And how frustrating that he convinced Mick to carry on supporting his ex-wife and children with money from the business. You didn't like that did you? Thought everything should be about you.'

'Patrick didn't want to be a part of the business anymore; he was past it. He didn't have the balls to see how things could be.' Her cherubic face curls into a sneer.

'No, he didn't see how things could be in *your* world view. He thought Mick should do the right thing and honour his previous life, his family commitments, but that made you feel threatened, didn't it? And you want to be in total control, don't you?' I stare her down as if looking through the barrel of a gun. 'You knew Patrick was allergic to cinnamon, you put it in his dessert on games night. You mashed up that crema catalana and made up some bullshit to hide the fact you'd put it in there. It was you who killed Patrick.'

Mr Bob who'd been silent until now, thrashes about in his cage littering the terrace with a confetti of shredded straw. His teeth chatter like a café full of kids. And then with a voracity I've never heard before, lets out a high-pitched squeal. The huddled faces look from Mr Bob to me to Tamika in disbelief.

'You're fucking deranged, woman!' Tamika spits, her face contorting with rage. 'They need to have you sectioned coz you're truly mental!' She twists on her heels ready to leave.

'Maybe, but we can prove it.' I hesitate, willing and waiting for everyone to catch up. 'You see, unluckily for you, our dishwasher didn't run that night, and so the bowls never got washed. I've still got the bowl and spoon Patrick ate from. The police can test it – along with the shaker you hid under the hot water boiler.'

Tamika sways a little and grasps onto the wall. Her too tall stiletto heels bend and snap. Her big bright future in 'What Tamika Saw Today' was over.

EPILOGUE

I've often wondered how Mr Bob knew Patrick's death wasn't natural. For ages I figured it must be an animal instinct survival thing. I mean, most animals are highly dependent on their ability to perceive any environmental stimulus or changes if they're going to make it (bees can even detect the earth's magnetic field!), and so it made sense.

For me, I decided Mr Bob was more attuned to the world. As a prey animal he's had to develop his sense organs to keep him out of danger, if he's to survive. And from everything I read, it all added up. Humans are lazy and less connected to the world, whereas animals work at a far higher intensity and sensitivity. And it may sound strange, but I was willing to go with that explanation and accept it.

But then recently, my mum sent me a book. It was an old book about guinea pigs in Andean culture. It said how guinea pigs were used in religious ceremonies and for traditional healing rituals by folk doctors. They were seen like a supernatural medium. Guinea pigs were rubbed on the bodies of sick people to diagnose what was wrong with them. And maybe it sounds crazy and a load of superstitious bull, but when I read those words and looked across at Mr Bob I swear he winked.

Now I know his truth: he's channelling his Andean ancestors, he *can* definitely sniff out trouble!

I really hope you enjoyed *Who Killed Patrick?* and it would make me so happy if you could leave a review on **Amazon** to share the love!

FREE BOOK: *The Little Book of Insanely Silly but Curiously Fascinating Facts about Guinea Pigs* is available free when you sign up to my newsletter on my website at **www.sylwaters.com**.

READ AN EXCERPT FROM ETERNAL FOREVER

Prologue

Sunday: Spain

They didn't see the man approach. "Perdón, dónde está... ?"

Tito looked up into the face of a handsome young Spaniard, chestnut hair, long and loose, like an adolescent Antonio Banderas.

"Sorry, mate, I don't speak Spanish, so I can't help you." Tito smiled apologetically and went to move on, clutching Jessie's hand closer to him.

"I'll help you." The young Spaniard's smile switched to a hard snarl. His hands clenched Tito's collar, gripping his sweaty skin, bunching his flesh between his fingertips. Tito turned, but it was too late.

The blade punctured his chest. He could feel the hard metal hot inside of him, blood spurting and spouting all around; tightness in his chest, an urge to vomit. He grappled with the handle, tried to wrench it from his flesh. Wet fabric clung to him, his hands slippery, sliding, unable to grip. Pain scorching. His head full, banging, heavy, dull. Shallow breaths, forced air, trying to pump his lungs. Eyes wild, hunting the street, screaming: "Jessie! Jessie! Jessie!"

Then an empty cobbled street and the blood-covered torso of what had been an extremely handsome young man.

One: Introducing Eternal Forever

>Of course eternal life can be yours. Who wouldn't want to live forever?

I scanned the email again. It was signed off by Mack. Who has a name like Mack? I can't help thinking of Mack trucks. Maybe it's short for something, like Mackenzie? Would it be rude to ask him? Maybe I'll just google it.

It means 'son of'. It's got Gaelic roots and despite being a popular name 100 years ago, it's now pretty unique. Apparently people with the name Mack are sturdy, courageous, masculine and value freedom above all. Born to win, Mack is a man of conquest, but also considerate and efficient.

Do I think a man like Mack is the right man to look after me when I'm dead?

Jessie pondered the question. Tito, her manager, had told her it was all about the rep – image was everything. Everything. She shrugged dismissively – what did she care? She'd be dead by the time this mattered, if it even did. She electronically signed the contract and hit the send button.

Monday: England

Mack Majors gave his coffee another swirl with the

spoon, his thoughts were elsewhere. He was a good-looking specimen who carried the latest fashions well on his 6ft 1", slender, toned frame. At 29 he looked younger than his years, but acted immeasurably older, most of the time. Responsibility and the hardship of life had come early to Mack. Not that he would freely admit how fucked up he was at his mother's death on account of his father's drunken blood-soaked fists and feet. But he was. Emotional baggage? He had a whole container load on order from China, but he kept it in check, the way he did most anything that mattered in his life. Feelings were for laters, for other people; action was the key to making progress, to getting on in life. That's what he told himself. He might not have been able to save his mother, but if he could help preserve the lives of others now, then maybe, just maybe, he could make up for the past...

He clenched his chiselled jaw and the tension flicked across his defined cheekbones. He loved his job as a digital legacy director, but some days he couldn't help wondering about the clients who contacted him, and what he was actually promising.

Life. Eternal. Forever. The gift of immortality. That was his offering. It made him feel good and the salary more than helped pay the bills. He smoothed his hand down his skinny jeans. No suits in his place – they might be dealing in death – but the median age of his co-workers was no more than 25. Death was dealt with by the young, they got it. They understood it. Death wasn't 'The End' – it was an in-between stage before the next status update, tweet and posthumous email, from your digital legacy manager.

You don't have to be alive to be online.

McJimini Pop sauntered into the office humming the

theme tune to Ghostbusters, his glossed, pinky lips pursed in musical reverie, his blonde, coiffed hair quavering in harmony. Mack looked up from his laptop and watched him. He glanced at the clock on the other side of the sprawling, open-plan office, rolled his eyes and fought not to confront his employee for the umpteenth time. He cast his eyes around the offices of Eternal Forever, a former factory building which had been converted to start-up cool. Exposed brick walls met gun-metal grey girders standing proud and exposed on the warm, pine floorboards, their previous industrial use now a symbol of on-trend office design. The double-height ceiling and huge windows filled the place with a sense of openness, of space, of possibilities. Mack scanned the sea of bobbing heads, their eyes fixed intently on their screens.

The transformation was hard to believe. Two months ago it hadn't been like this. Hell, just six months ago him, Fran and Duncan (the original trio) had been crammed into Fran's kitchen, the three of them all with their laptops and phones, typing, scrabbling, coding, trying to get the company off the ground. Their idea of digital life after death had caught the market's imagination and flung them into the wave of speculative start-up fodder. The interest had been incredible. The investments had been something else. And the speed with which they'd had to recruit meant they'd now quadrupled their headcount – hence the move to bigger quarters.

McJimini Pop, or J Pop, as Mack preferred to call him, had been a result of the desperate recruitment drive. Mack had known the kid didn't want the job, that he had been forced to attend the interview by a job centre jobsworth, but despite being a dicksplash at the interview, Mack had given him a chance. The kid knew a lot more than he let on and Mack needed a social media guru, so even if the boy did have a stink attitude, once you got past that, the results were worth it.

J Pop uncorked his headphones, expertly twiddling them into his pocket and opened his laptop. Another day, another dollar. He tried to coax himself into giving a shit, but it was yet another day of his life wasted doing crap he didn't want to do. And for what? His blonde quiff shook in annoyance and his lip involuntarily curled. The whole job thing was a waste of time. He didn't want to be doing this stuff, he had bigger stuff, better stuff to be doing – he was going to be a reality TV star. He'd sorted his life plan; he'd worked out how he was going to make the grade – until that stupid bitch at the benefits office interfered. Threatened to cut off his money if he didn't go for the interview. Just WTF was she thinking, getting him involved in this company that dealt in dead people's online profiles? He didn't give a toss about dead people. He didn't give a damn about living people, not unless they were celebs. Or in the Big Brother House. Or on Love Island. He bared his teeth like a dog threatened with having its food bowl taken and looked about disparagingly, his eyes meeting Mack's.

"Morning, Kiddo!" Mack smiled over-enthusiastically and ruffled J Pop's hair. The boy's persistent lateness was a major drag, but he was a whizz online, so Mack cut him a surprisingly unhealthy amount of slack.

"Leave off the hair and stop already with the dumb names." J Pop snarled, pulling away. He glowered at Mack before averting his eyes to his screen. Jeez, why was the guy always on at him? He glanced around the office queasily. God, he shouldn't have stayed up so late for last night's eviction from Celebrity Big Brother. The two bottles of sparkly he'd downed while roaring at the telly had squidged in his tummy, and turned decidedly acidic after the few hours' sleep he'd managed to cram in, before the alarm had interrupted his alcohol-induced slumber. If he'd been a contestant on Big Brother he'd still be sleeping now, the ever-watchful camera eyes hungrily feeding on his half-exposed toned physique. He'd already practised how he would artfully wrap the bed covers around him, showing enough, but not all, of what he had to offer. He might not have made it yet, but he'd studied enough reality TV shows to know you shouldn't give the viewing public all they wanted right away. He needed to make them lust after him, before they'd love him.

Mack smiled amiably. "Get a caffeine hit, improve your mood and then we'll talk about the hot celeb news which involves you... " He left the mention of the news dangling in the air like a gold-encrusted carrot. Mack, although not trained in people management, knew exactly what made them tick. He feigned interest in the papers on J Pop's desk, flicking through them and allowing some sheets to fall on the floor. He knew he was being annoying and he enjoyed it. He knew the boy would bite – he could tell he was bursting – it was just a matter of time.

J Pop tutted and stabbed his fingers on the desk. He wasn't going to play Mack's games. He wasn't going to get psyched up because he'd mentioned celebrity stuff. He had other stuff to do, more important stuff, stuff that involved him, just him. He was going to be a hotshot celeb himself, he didn't need to hear what Mack had to say. He looked at the fallen sheets on the floor and pretended to busy himself with the papers on his desk, the papers that Mack was now also pretending to read. He looked at Mack, motioning for him to move his arm off his bundle of documents, but he didn't say a word. Mack moved his arm slightly so J Pop could reach for the bottom-most sheet.

J Pop scowled and busied himself deep in the text to avoid Mack's gaze. He really wanted to hate him. The guy was so committed to the company and dicked out about "possibilities" and making stuff right for people, it drove him to distraction. He didn't get why Mack cared so much, how he could even muster such big emotion. It wasn't like this stuff even mattered when their clients were dead. Dead as a dried up, burnt up, crisped out piece of ash. What he cared about was his living, his life. He wanted to big it up, max it out, live it large. He craved attention, to be somebody who was known.

Having a name, being a name was what got you into the meat market of ad promos and makeup kits – that's where the big moolah was. Advertising, sponsorship, that's what it was all about really. And he had ideas, plans, ambitions. Making a name for himself as a job bimbo was not part of the plan. But despite his best efforts to get the sack, Mack continued to think he was a hero. It beggared belief. Even the fake news item he'd seeded last week, with a spoof undertaker claiming people wanted to be buried with their phones to check their status updates, had won him praise rather than his P45. It was insane, the more ridiculous the idea, the more likely it was to be a winner.

"I can see you're busy... " Mack left the words hanging and stood up.

J Pop flinched, looked away and back at Mack who was making a move to his desk. He didn't want to ask. He didn't want to care. He didn't want to be curious. And he especially didn't want to have to stoop so low as to ask Mack for more details. But his interest was piqued, well and truly mountain peaked. And in the battle between his hatred of having to kowtow, and his curiosity which fizzed and over-flowed, it was the latter which won out. What was this celeb news and how did it involve him? He cleared his throat and quickly gestured to Mack to stay close by.

"So this celeb you said about," J Pop asked lightly, "anyone I know?"

Mack paused, looked back and beamed broadly, "You heard of Jessie Adams?"

Despite not wanting to show any form of eagerness, J Pop screeched excitedly. "THE Jessie Adams? Like hot star of the moment with the bad-ass manager, loadsa tattoos?" His face fell off a cliff.

"The one and only," Mack said smugly. "Her hit I Want U Now is currently number one in fifteen countries, I believe."

J Pop eyeballed Mack intently, his juices razzing. "How did you get this gig?"

Mack puffed himself up proudly and toyed with the idea of spinning the boy a yarn to teach him a lesson, decided it was too early days and cut straight to the truth. "Her manager Tito got in touch. He loved the undertaker gag, thought any company that could rip into themselves like that was worth a punt and made the intro to Jessie."

"You mean it was my joke that got us Jessie as a client?"

"Well, you and a bit of my charm. We make a good team."

J Pop glowed. Despite himself and his despair at having to spend eight hours a day in an office when he should've been living the life, work was turning out to be – dare he think it – fun. He beamed back at Mack, his pride swilling and swelling so much, it made his fingertips throb. Deftly and with instantaneous timing, he loaded his screen with images of their newest client. He bent forward, poring over a close-up photo of Jessie Adams. He sat back, his perfectly outlined eyebrows creasing to ampersand mode. "Only thing is, it's a bit weird innit?"

"What is?" Mack asked.

"Like, she's only 23 or something, seems a bit young to be thinking about death, especially with her being a pop star and all."

"That's exactly why her manager signed her up."

"I don't follow?" J Pop looked at Mack waiting for him to explain.

"If she's already a fully paid-up member of Eternal Forever – and OK, I know we don't have many – but anyway, as she's now paid-up and fully on-board then her afterlife is guaranteed. With us managing her profile she's always going to be alive online." He smacked his lips before summing up. "Sensible decision, if you ask me."

"OK," J Pop replied, still unsure he'd fully followed the explanation, "so what's my role given she's alive?"

"I've been thinking about this – and here's the good news – I've decided to give you like a promotion." He paused and waited for J Pop to acknowledge the significance of his words. J Pop stopped faffing with his keyboard and stared at Mack direct. Mack continued, "Not only are you a Social Media Manager, but you're also now an Account Manager. And what that means is you're going to be her Account Manager here at Eternal Forever."

"For Jessie Adams, the pop star?" J Pop's reply was quite breathless at the announcement.

"Yep, she'll be your first, then I reckon we'll focus on

getting more fully paid-up people and you can manage more accounts."

J Pop flashed a smile with a small amount of tooth display. He didn't want Mack thinking he was too made up by the news, but under his desk he punched the air. Not even two months into the job and already he had his own celeb to manage in the event of her death. Things could be looking up.

ALSO BY SYL WATERS

Eternal Forever

ABOUT THE AUTHOR

Most people know crazy cat ladies are a 'thing', but I'm a proud crazy guinea pig lady! I love fun in the sun and plenty of cocktails. My happy place is flip flops. I write stories to keep me company – my characters ensure I'm never lonely and always smiling (when I'm not tearing my hair out!)

Sign up for Syl's free author newsletter at **www.sylwaters.com**.

twitter.com/waters_syl

instagram.com/mrbob.guineapig

ACKNOWLEDGMENTS

Writing a book drives you pretty crazy. I'm so lucky D puts up with all my madness and continues to shower me with love and support. Thank you babes x

I'm really grateful to Sarah Brown, Margarita Paschali, Ruth Partlett and Jo Johnson who gave me invaluable feedback and inspired me to keep going.

I'd also like to say thank you to Sharon at The Golden Ball for allowing me to spend time with her cherished guinea pigs. I adore them, but as yet, am not adult enough to look after another living being!

Big thanks are also due to Ashley Santoro for bringing Mr Bob to life with her wonderful designs and to Julie Stock for all her technical wizardry in making stuff happen.

I'd also like to acknowledge each and every person who's ever had to listen to me yak on about my books. Your patience and understanding is gratefully appreciated.

Printed in Great Britain
by Amazon

48576551R00189